LAURIE'S TIME

FAIRFIELD SERIES

MARYANN JORDAN

Cover design by: Graphics by Stacy

Cover photography by: Eric McKinney of 612Photography

Ebook ISBN 978-0-9916522-2-8

Print ISBN 978-0-9916522-3-5

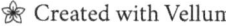 Created with Vellum

ABOUT THE AUTHOR

I am an avid reader of romance novels, often joking that I cut my teeth on historical romances. I have been reading and reviewing for years. In 2013, I finally gave in to the characters in my head, screaming for their story to be told. From these musings, my first novel, Emma's Home, The Fairfield Series, was born.

I was a high school counselor, having worked in education for thirty years. I live in Virginia, having also lived in four states and two foreign countries. I have been married to a wonderfully patient man for forty-three years. When writing, my dog or one of my cats can generally be found in the same room if not on my lap.

Please take the time to leave a review of this book. Feel free to contact me, especially if you enjoyed my book. I love to hear from readers!

Facebook

Join my Facebook group: Maryann Jordan's Protector Fans

Sign up for my emails by visiting my Website!

Website

(AGE FIVE)

Laurie's mother watched her play on the swings in the city park. Laurie's long brown hair would fly out behind her only to sweep back into her face with every movement of the swing. Higher and higher she would go, her giggles catching on the breeze as her mother looked over at her five-year-old daughter. Sarah leaned back, letting the spring sun warm her face, smiling at her Laurie's apparent happiness. She may not have been a planned child, but Sarah loved her fiercely, as a lioness watches over its cub.

"Mommy, Mommy!" Laurie called as she came running over. Sarah gathered her precious child in her arms.

"I love you, baby girl," Sarah whispered in her ear.

"Will you love me forever?" Laurie asked as she looked into her mother's beautiful face.

Kissing Laurie's forehead, hugging her tightly, she replied, "I'll love you forever."

Sarah sat with Laurie napping in her lap. Her mind

took a trip down memory lane thinking about Laurie's father. She had turned sixteen years old, and one of her best friends convinced her to go out one evening when her parents and sister were out of town. While Sarah had never been one to take chances, she felt the need to break out of the constant good girl image that everyone had of her. They went out that evening and managed to slip into a crowded outdoor concert next to a bar across town where no one would know them.

Swaying to the music, Sarah was completely unaware of the effect she had on the men around. A petite brunette, with long shiny waves of hair down her back, she had curves in all the places that make a man sit up and take notice. Her beautiful face, with minimal makeup, made her look almost fairylike, the type of woman that a man would also want to protect. Dressed simply in a light blue sundress that was not designed to be sultry at all, surrounded by other women dressed for sex, she was one of the most beautiful women there. And Brock Sinclair noticed.

Brock, a young soldier between tours in Desert Storm, was in town visiting with some of his Army buddies. They had decided to hit one of the neighborhood bars for a night of drinking and hooking up. Brock, who had a busty redhead sitting on his lap nuzzling his ear, had been drinking steadily ever since they arrived at the outdoor bar. Knowing he was going to get lucky with … well, he didn't know her name, but with the tits on the redhead, he didn't care what her name was. A few more beers, and then he planned on taking the redhead back to the hotel he was staying in and banging her until the sounds of artillery no longer rattled in his dreams.

Sarah and her friend had just arrived, and Brock noticed the natural beauty the moment she walked into the room. Suddenly, the idea of the screwing the fake-boob redhead wasn't as appealing as the vision standing near the bar looking nervous. A strange sense of protectiveness washed over him, and he instinctively knew she was not old enough to be in the bar. Looking around, he realized that he was not the only man noticing the beauty.

"Wouldn't mind tapping that ass tonight," said the buddy next to him.

Growling in answer, Brock stood up, effectively dumping the redhead in his lap. "Here, you need a piece of ass? I'm sure this one will do. She won't care which soldier she fucks."

And true to his prediction, the redhead stood up grumpily at first, then turned to his buddy and began nuzzling his ear.

Brock walked over to his princess...*his princess? Where did that thought come from?* Shaking his slightly inebriated head, he continued over to Sarah.

Sarah felt a presence behind her, and she slowly turned around. Looking up, she stared into the stormy grey eyes of the most handsome man she had ever seen. Tall and slender, he had dark brown hair cut in a short military style and a face that would have filled every one of her teenage dreams.

They had talked for several hours before he took her back to his hotel room. Knowing she shouldn't go, she trusted him and found that she desired him more than anything she had ever wanted. Brock never asked her how old she was, assuming she was, at least, eighteen. As the evening progressed into the wee hours of the morning, they kissed and fondled until they were both so engulfed in lust, they gave in to their desires. He was slow and caring, although he did not realize that she was a virgin until it was too late. They fell asleep in each other's arms, Brock dreaming of his fairy princess and Sarah of her handsome prince.

She woke early to the knocking on the door. Slipping out of the bed, she opened the hotel door after putting on his Army T-shirt. Recognizing one of his buddies at the door, she told him that Brock was still asleep. The friend slid his gaze up and down her body, making her wish she had more clothes on before he told her to hit the road. Confused, she just stood there immobile.

"Look doll-face, we got shit to do today, and Brock don't never like wakin' with one of his hookups hangin' around. So, take off quietly and have a nice life." With that, Brock's friend headed back to the room across the hall.

Sarah, confusion melding into embarrassment, turned and looked at Brock as he lay tangled in the sheets. The realization that she was a one-night stand rushed over her, and she couldn't wait to leave before he woke up and further burst her bubble. Quickly and quietly, she dressed and looked at him longingly one last time before leaving, grabbing the T-shirt before she shut the door. She just wanted to have something to hold as she remembered this night.

Sarah never knew that when Brock woke up, he reached for the beautiful girl sleeping beside him only to find her gone. The evidence of their lovemaking was left on the sheets, so he knew he had not created her in a dream. Brock was furious when his buddy explained that he had gotten rid of the girl and vowed to start looking for her. But the call came through – their leave was being cut short, and it was time to head back to the base.

He never knew that nine months later his princess had given birth to his daughter. He also never knew that twelve years later his princess was killed in a car accident, leaving their daughter an orphan.

***

Laurie (age ten)

"Mommy, tell me the story of my daddy again," Laurie begged on the eve of her birthday. Each year, on the evening before her birthday, Laurie and her mother would sit on her bed, snuggled together as Sarah told Laurie all about her dad, the handsome prince.

Sarah, at sixteen, found herself pregnant from the one night she spent with the handsome soldier. Her parents were shocked but loved her unconditionally and helped her raise Laurie. They lived with her parents and sister, Emma, in a small house. Sarah had finished high school and worked as a secretary since graduating. Her father had wanted to find the man responsible for impregnating his daughter, but they were unsuccessful.

"Mommy, stop daydreaming!" Laurie admonished. "Tell me my daddy story."

Sarah smiled indulgently at her beautiful daughter. She had Sarah's hair but had her father's grey eyes. "Well," she began. "One evening a friend and I went to a place to listen to music and have some fun. While I was there, a man came over to me, and when I looked at him, I just knew he was everything I could have ever wanted."

"What did he look like?" Laurie interrupted.

Sarah laughed. "You hear this story every year. I think you know what's coming!"

Quieting, Laurie settled in for the rest of the tale.

"When I looked up into his eyes, they were the same color as yours are now. And he was tall, strong, and so handsome he took my breath away. His name was Brock, and we talked, danced, and fell in love. But he had to go away and wasn't able to come back to us. But he gave me the most wonderful, beautiful, present in the whole world before he left. You. And so even though he has never been able to be with us, I've something to remember him by always."

Laurie threw her arms around her mother, hugging her closely. "I wish I could have known him, Mommy," she said.

"I know, baby. I know. I wish you could have too." Sarah tucked her daughter in bed, leaned down to kiss her goodnight, and then headed out to the living room. Her sister Emma, who was only sixteen at the time, looked up from her homework.

"Laurie get her birthday story?" she asked, smiling up at her sister.

Sarah nodded and smiled while she sat down on the sofa. Their father had passed away two years ago, so it was just the women of the family left. Sarah's mother looked up from her reading and smiled at her daughters. She and Emma understood Laurie's need to feel as though her father was a real person and Sarah's need to provide her daughter with the truth, albeit a slightly embellished version.

The three women sat into the evening talking and enjoying each other's company as they always had.

In the bedroom down the hall, ten-year-old Laurie lay in bed, dreaming of handsome princes, soldiers in shiny uniforms, and a daddy who would love her.

Laurie (twelve years old)

Laurie stood next to her Aunt Emma, holding her hand by the gravesite of her mother and grandmother. The last few days had passed in a blur of shock, tears, and fear. It was only four days ago that she hugged her mom goodbye as she headed off to school. Emma used to take her to school each day, but since Emma had left for college a couple of months ago, Laurie had to catch the bus. She had only been at school a few hours when the principal came to get her out of class. The other kids snickered at her as though she must be in trouble. When the principal told her that her mom and grandmother had been in a car accident and she needed to go to the hospital, she felt fear. She sat in the hospital with the nurses until her Aunt Emma came to get her. Emma scooped her up in her arms, and Laurie clung to her. The doctor had told her that they weren't coming back. She knew what that meant. They were dead. Just like her grandfather.

Now standing at the gravesites, Laurie looked up at Emma, seeing her holding back her tears. Laurie wanted to cry but felt all cried out. She turned back to look at the two side-by-side coffins.

What happens now? Where do I go? Who will take care of me? I wish my daddy were here. He would take care of me.

Over the next couple of days, Laurie sat listening to Emma talking with a woman who called herself a social worker. She did not know what that was, but the lady seemed nice. Emma had explained that since she was an adult now she would take care of Laurie, but it seemed like the nice lady wanted to keep talking about it, saying that Emma had to prove she could take care of her.

What if they take me away from Emma too? Then where will I go? Who will I be?

Emma ran into their little house waving a letter and grabbed Laurie up in a huge hug. She was laughing for the first time since Mom and Grandma had died.

"We did it, we did it!" Emma yelled, swinging Laurie around in a circle.

"What did we do?" she asked, giggling as she got dizzy.

"I get you! The judge signed the paperwork that says that you and I can keep living together, and I'll be your guardian."

Looking up at her aunt, she felt the heavy weight bearing down on her being lifted just a little. Finally, they had an answer; Laurie and Emma were the only family left, and they would take care of each other.

***

Laurie (eighteen years old)

Sitting on the beach, soaking up the sun, listening to the waves crash on the shore, Laurie and Emma felt as though they were in heaven. Money had always been tight, so they had never taken a vacation. But Laurie had just graduated from high school and was turning eighteen tomorrow, so Emma splurged for two nights in a hotel and two days sunning on the beach. Laurie looked over at some guys on the shore, flexing their muscles as they played volleyball.

"Emma, Emma." Laurie punched her aunt. "Look over there. Those guys are gorgeous."

Emma rolled over and glanced where Laurie was looking. Her niece had good taste, she had to admit. The men were all handsome, tanned, had toned abs, and they occasionally looked at the two beauties lying in the sun. A group of girls walked down the shore, wearing skimpy bikinis, carrying designer beach bags and sunglasses and strolled by the men. They cooed and waved at the men as they went by, completely capturing the attention of the muscled men.

Laurie huffed and flopped back over on her stomach, shutting her eyes. Emma smiled indulgently at Laurie. Her niece was gorgeous in her hand-me-down bikini. Their beach towels were slightly faded, and their flip flops were worn. When Laurie's grandfather died, his insurance money covered his funeral costs and allowed her grandmother, mother, and Emma to keep living in the small house. When her mother and grandmother died, the insurance money ran out. About a year after they died, Emma and Laurie moved to a small, one-bedroom apartment over the restaurant where Emma worked. The restaurant owner's kindly mother would come sit with Laurie in the evenings when Emma worked late. Emma worked hard, taking college classes when she could to become a counselor.

As soon as Laurie turned fifteen, the restaurant owner let her start working there too. Her feet would hurt at the end of her shift, and she would head upstairs to finish her homework. Laurie graduated with honors, received scholarships to the college in town and in another month would be taking classes with Emma.

"I'm sorry I could not have given you more," Emma said softly.

Laurie raised her dollar sunglasses up on her head and looked into her beloved aunt's eyes.

"Oh, Emma. You gave me everything. You gave me a home. You gave me a family." Laurie was genuinely surprised by Emma's statement. "Why are you saying that now?"

"I don't know," Emma answered honestly. "I suppose on the night before you turn eighteen, I'm just a little emotional."

Laurie sat up and turned to face Emma. Taking Emma's hands into her own, she said exactly what was on her heart. "Emma, my life could have been so different. I could have been placed in foster care at the age of twelve and for six years been living in a horrible situation or a great situation. Who knows? But I would never have had a family. I would have never had you."

Emma's eyes teared, as Laurie continued, and she grasped her hands tighter.

"Maybe we didn't have a lot of money, but we had love, laughter, and a lot of memories. Hell, we've even shared the same bedroom since I was two years old! I wouldn't know how to live by myself!"

They laughed at the realization that what she said was right. The two women packed up their belongings and headed back to the hotel.

"And Em? Don't think I don't know what you gave up raising me."

Emma hugged her niece. "Laurie girl, I gave up nothing but got everything instead." Smiling, they headed off to dinner.

The evening before they left to head back home, Emma announced that it was time for presents. She pulled out two wrapped gifts and a cardboard box. Laurie squealed in delight and plopped down on the bed to open her gifts. The first one was a gift card to a trendy clothing store. She was shocked at the amount, but Emma assured her that the restaurant owners had chipped in for the gift. The other one was a new laptop. Laurie stared at it, not knowing what to say.

Emma explained that since they would both be in college the next year, they needed a laptop to go along with the old computer that they used in the restaurant's office. Laurie was thrilled. She knew that Emma had worked a lot of extra hours to purchase such an extravagant gift, and that made it all the more valuable.

Finally, she looked at the cardboard box with a questioning look. Emma confessed that she did not know what was in the box but that it was from Sarah, Laurie's mom.

"Where did it come from?"

"When we packed up the house and moved to the apartment, I found it in the attic. It was sealed up, but the writing on top caught my eye because I recognized Sarah's handwriting."

Laurie leaned over the box and saw the writing.

For Laurie's eyes only, when she is an adult.

She carefully opened the box and she and Emma peered inside. There was an old, musty-smelling T-shirt and a note. That was all that was in the box. Laurie opened the letter and read her mother's writing.

I have no idea where life will take us, so I want to make sure that I save this for you to have. My stories about your father were true; I did fall in love with Brock that night. I always told my parents that I did not know his name because I did not want him to feel trapped. His last name is written on the inside of his shirt. I kept the secret from all, but you deserve to know it now. I'm afraid that I was a fling for him, but for me, I loved your father. I hope I can be there to give this to you on this special birthday, but just in case I'm not, I'm packing it up for you. I love you, always, my Laurie girl, Mom

By the time Laurie finished reading the shocking letter, Emma was already in tears. Both women sat in stunned silence for a few minutes, letting their thoughts drift over the revelations.

Emma knew that Sarah had loved Laurie's father but had no idea that she had buried his name in her heart. She looked up at Laurie, not surprised to see tears in her eyes and her shaking hands still holding the note.

Slowly, Laurie reached into the box and pulled out a faded, grey Army T-shirt. She rubbed her fingers over the Army lettering on the front, smoothing out the material. With her hands still shaking, she turned the shirt around so that she could see the name tag sewn on the back of the T-shirt's neck. There, in block stitching was a name.

Sinclair, Brock T.

My father has a name. I have a name. He doesn't know I exist. He never knew my mother beyond one night. Did he care about her? Would he have cared about me?

Laurie and Emma sat without speaking for several moments, each lost in their own musings. Laurie continued to trace her fingers over the name tag of her father. She looked up at Emma.

"You never knew?" she asked her aunt.

Emma shook her head slowly, still looking down at the note that Laurie had passed to her.

"No," she said softly. "I used to ask Sarah about Brock. She would always look wistful but would never tell me any details. I had no idea that she knew his last name all this time."

"If she knew his name and that he was in the Army, she could have found him. She could have told him about me." Laurie felt tears threatening to fall. "Why didn't she?"

"I don't know, Laurie. But I know Sarah. She must have had a good reason to keep this from him. But she also knew that no matter what, as an adult you'd deserve to decide for yourself what you want to do. There's no way she could have known she wouldn't be here to give you this herself, but it was important enough for her to take precautions to make sure you got it."

Emma and Laurie went to bed, but both slept fitfully that night. The next day dawned, and Emma woke to find Laurie gone, having left a note that she was down on the beach. Following her there, Emma sat next to Laurie on the beach wall. She leaned over and gently shoulder bumped her niece.

"Happy birthday, Laurie," she said.

Laurie looked over at Emma, smiled and threw her arm around her shoulders and gave her a tight squeeze. Knowing that Emma was wondering what she was thinking, she tried to put her thoughts into words.

"Emma, I've thought over and over about what to do. For whatever reason, Mom did not want to find Brock to tell him she was pregnant. I don't know why, but I do know that Mom was a smart lady even if she was only a teenager when she had me. She must have felt that he wouldn't want to know." Looking over into Emma's dark brown eyes, she continued. "I'm happy. Yeah, we've had times of tragedy, but I'm happy. You and I've been together since I was born. We're family, you and I. I've never had a father, so I don't really miss what I never had." She paused for a few minutes, continuing to collect her thoughts. "I've decided to do nothing. Out there somewhere is a man who's probably close to forty years old who's never known about me. He doesn't miss me because he never knew. I don't miss him because I never knew. So why rock the boat now?"

Emma sat with her arms around her niece, nodding. "I'll support you in whatever you want to do. I'll do anything to help you in any way I can," she declared.

Laurie laughed. "Emma, you have been doing that my whole life! You and me, girl – we're family!"

2

(SIX YEARS LATER)

The summer sun blistering on the highway caused waves of heat to rise, creating a vision that made the world seem as though it were a mirage in the distance. As Laurie drove away from the only city she had ever known, she felt as though she were driving towards a mirage.

Fairfield. Is it real? Is it a dream? Am I really leaving? Am I actually leaving Emma? Please God, don't let this be a mistake.

Driving away from her past and towards her future. At least, she hoped it was her future. Tangles of thoughts flew wildly through her mind, much like the air coming through the open window was tangling her long brown hair. She smiled as she thought back to her small goodbye party last night. A couple of college friends, co-workers from the little restaurant she worked at, and, of course, Emma were all there to send her off. College had not been easy, and it had taken her two extra years to get all of her credits for a degree in

Elementary Education. Now, with a job offer at an elementary school in the small town of Fairfield, she was on her way.

Away…. that still seemed strange. Away from everything she had ever known. Away from the little apartment she and Emma had shared for the past eleven years. Away from the restaurant that she had worked in for the past nine years. Away from Emma, her aunt, her pretend sister, her surrogate mom. She wanted to look for a job close by, but when the job offer from Fairfield came in, Emma encouraged her to take it. Emma told her she needed to experience life on her own for a while, saying it was her time. Her time to step out into the world; her time to find herself.

Turning on the radio, Laurie needed the loud music to drown out the voices in her head. Her little yellow VW bug was filled with everything she owned. She packed light but living in a furnished apartment once she got there, she would not need much. Driving past the sign announcing that Fairfield was only twenty miles away, she began to bounce in the seat to the time of the music, feeling lighter than she had all day.

Emma is right. This is my time. Time to meet new people. Time to find out what I can do on my own. Time to find out who I am.

Smiling to herself, Laurie pulled into the outskirts of town. Noting a few shopping centers, she made her way towards the center of the city. Fairfield was a small town where the downtown area had been revitalized, filled with quaint little shops. Finding the small hotel, she pulled into the parking lot.

Through Craigs List, Laurie found a young woman looking for a roommate for her two-bedroom apartment in an older but charming apartment building. The young woman, a nurse at the hospital whose roommate recently married, needed another. They chatted online, then on the phone, developing an instant rapport. The nurse, Carol, would be on duty today, so Laurie decided to spend the night at the hotel and move in the next day.

Walking into the hotel's office to check in, she was greeted with a blast of cold air from the air conditioner. Sitting behind the counter was an older man who looked up and smiled as she walked over. Standing to greet her, she could see that he was spry and wiry with an energy radiating off him as though he were getting ready for a race.

"Helen, we have a new guest!" he shouted into an office behind him.

"I'm not deaf, Roger. You don't have to yell down the house." A pleasant looking woman came out of the office, her face beaming.

Laurie couldn't help but think of Mrs. Santa Claus as she looked at Helen. Plump body, hair pulled back into a bun, she absolutely beamed.

"You must be Laurie Dodd," she said. "I'm Helen, and this here is my husband, Roger. Welcome to Fairfield!"

Surprised by the exuberant greeting, she couldn't help but smile back in return.

"Your new roommate, Carol called earlier to say that you'd be coming in today. We just weren't sure when to expect you." Helen noted Laurie's look of surprise and just laughed. "Oh, it's all right, honey. We take care of our own here in Fairfield."

Roger leaned over the counter and said conspiratorially, "And my Helen will adopt you right here and now!"

Laurie laughed at their banter and felt at home. "Thank you. I'm excited to be here!"

By the time they finished the check-in procedure, Laurie realized that Helen and Roger had wriggled a lot of information from her. They now knew that she would be working at the elementary school and that she was single. As she looked at Helen, she could already see the wheels turning in Helen's mind.

Roger gazed over at his wife also. "Yep," he said. "My Helen is already figuring out who she can fix you up with."

"Oh hush, you old coot. I just know that there are some very handsome, unattached men in this town who need a beauty to look after."

Laurie rushed to explain that she wasn't looking for anyone yet, but Helen just politely shushed her. "Darlin', no matter what anyone says, everyone needs someone to take care of and to care for them."

Laurie laughed and agreed as she took the room card from Roger. Turning to leave the office, Helen spoke again, this time seriously. "You will find it here. You will find who you are meant to be. You will find *your* time."

Laurie stared at her in awe, not knowing how to respond.

Roger, walking around the counter to show Laurie to her room, just patted her arm. "My Helen, she sees things, dear. If she says this is your time, then she's right." Leaving the cool office, they walked to her room, Roger talking the entire way.

Settling in for the evening, Laurie called Emma.

"Hey girl, did you have any problems on the road today? How is Fairfield? Did you get checked in okay?" Emma asked, barely taking a breath.

Laughing, Laurie answered, "No, great, and yes."

"I suppose I was firing questions off too quickly, wasn't I? I just already miss you, that's all."

"I know, Emma, I miss you too. But I had a great trip and met the hotel owners. They're a little odd but really friendly. And I think they are trying to set me up with some guys already!"

"Sounds like the place to be then," Emma agreed. "Just make sure to enjoy yourself. You deserve it."

Hanging up, Laurie enjoyed a long, hot bath before climbing into bed. Realizing she had only been in a hotel one other time years ago with Emma, she thought back to her eighteenth birthday. Finally, chasing memories from the lurking corners of her mind, she slept better that night than she had in a while.

Waking early, she showered and headed down to the hotel's little lobby. Helen told her to come down once she was awake, and they would have breakfast there.

Walking in, she could hear voices coming from the back office.

"Oh, she's darling. You're going to love her; I just know it!"

Laurie recognized Helen's voice.

"Well, I can't wait to meet her, that's why I came right over."

Just then Helen walked out of the office accompanied by a beautiful petite blonde, whose face burst into a huge smile as soon as she saw her. Laurie stared at the woman in front of her. The gorgeous woman was a few inches taller than she but was very tiny with a slim athletic figure. Her hair was loose around her face and its color could only be described as a natural yellow blonde that gave her an angelic halo around her head. Laurie could imagine that if this woman had wings, she would make a perfect angel, flitting around giving off sunshine wherever she went.

"Laurie, perfect timing!" Helen exclaimed. "This here is your new roommate, Carol Fletcher."

Laurie could not help but smile back at the beaming woman and walked over to shake her hand. Carol rushed forward, engulfing her in a huge hug. Surprised, Laurie hugged back. Separating, Carol beamed at her. "I've been dying to meet you. I just know we're going get along perfectly," she said softly.

Helen, smiling as though she had made the match instead of Craigs List, walked over, offering coffee to both women. They chatted amiably for a few minutes over coffee before deciding to head over to the apartment. Laurie, in her yellow bug, followed Carol's little convertible. Driving through town, she looked around. A pink awning was perched over what appeared to be a bakery. Shop owners were opening their stores, and she saw trendy clothing stores, a hardware store, several professional offices, and an old-fashioned diner. Smiling to herself, she was already feeling at home.

I can't wait until Emma sees this! Laurie shook her head. *No, Emma was right. I have to do this by myself now. I have to have time to find me.*

Before she knew it, they were pulling into a parking lot at the side of a large U-shaped brick building. Parking next to Carol, they both jumped out of their cars. Carol rushed over to grasp Laurie's hand.

"I can't wait to show you the place. I hope you like it!" Carol said, appearing nervous, as though she desperately needed Laurie's approval.

"It'll be perfect, I'm sure," Laurie agreed.

Climbing the stairs to the third floor, they walked down the hall and entered a corner apartment. Walking into the apartment behind Carol, Laurie looked around in amazement. The living room was larger than most of the apartment she and Emma had shared for years. The walls were painted a soft taupe, and a slightly darker taupe covered the dining room walls. She could see that the living room and connecting dining room were comfortably furnished with a large burgundy sofa and chairs plus a four-person breakfast table. The floors were wood, softened by a rug in the middle of the room. A large screen television was on the wall opposite the sofa, and the other wall was taken up with a large picture window overlooking the park next door.

Laurie walked over to peer out of the window, looking down at trees, grass, and flower gardens. Lifting her gaze to the distance, she saw mountains rising in the background beyond the town, and she felt tears threatening to fall. Carol, appearing at her side, looked at Laurie's face.

"Oh, you don't like it!" Carol exclaimed.

Laurie turned quickly and hugged her new friend.

"No, no," she assured her. "I love it! I've never lived where there was a view and this...," she swept her hand out toward the vista outside the window, "is amazing!"

Carol returned the hug and pulled Laurie around to show her the rest of the apartment. The large kitchen was off the dining room, and Laurie could see that it was appointed with new stainless appliances. A hall divided the apartment with two large bedrooms at the end. Since the apartment was on the corner, both bedrooms had windows with views. Laurie couldn't believe that the large bedroom was all hers, and she even had her own bathroom. The furniture included a matching bed, dresser, and small desk and chair. The bed was covered with a light mauve comforter, and the pillows were a riot of pinks, mauves, and blues.

Carol was standing in the doorway, carefully watching Laurie's reaction. "You can change anything you don't like," she said quickly. Laurie looked over at Carol and instinctively knew that Carol needed her approval.

How can such a beautiful creature feel insecure?

Walking over to her, she took Carol's hands in hers and assured her that the room was perfect. "In fact, the whole apartment is more than I've ever had and more than I could have expected!"

Carol beamed again, pulling her in for another hug. "Well, let's get you moved in!"

They moved her few possessions from the car into the apartment. Carol then took a nap since she was working the evening shift at the hospital. Laurie quietly set up her room, hanging her clothes in the closet. Smiling as she shook out her clothes and hung them up, she was stunned at the size of the closet.

Guess I'll just have to buy more to fill it up. But first, a new laptop!

Unpacking her books out of the boxes, she pulled the old laptop out of its case and put it and the books on the desk. Money was still tight, and she had another month to go before her first teaching paycheck would be coming in. Having unpacked all of her meager possessions, she walked into the kitchen. Knowing that Carol would be sleeping for a few hours, she thought that it would be nice to fix dinner for her before she had to go to her shift that evening. She decided to drive to the grocery store she had passed on the way to the apartment.

3

Laurie stood in the cashier's line at the store, having picked up a few items for dinner. As she glanced around, she noticed two men standing at the end of an aisle talking. Both were tall, muscular, and gorgeous. As she looked back at them, she could see the profile of the one closest to her. She found herself staring at the most handsome man she had ever seen. Dark hair trimmed neatly. His large frame was bulky, filling out his T-shirt tightly and his jeans....*oh my*...his jeans. His thighs stretched the denim and his ass was...

"Excuse me, can you move forward?" said a voice directly behind her. Laurie jumped and realized that the line had moved while she was still standing in the same place ogling the hunk. She quickly turned and pushed her cart forward, blushing furiously. Embarrassed, she unloaded her items quickly.

Rob McDonald was tired of standing in the grocery store arguing with his buddy over who would pay for the beer. Rubbing his hand over his closely trimmed dark hair, he growled.

"Shit, Jim, I paid last time!" he claimed.

"Yeah well, I didn't know we were making a beer run when we headed out. I ain't got my wallet, man."

Continuing to grumble, Rob turned around, pushing the cart over to the cashier's line. Looking up, he saw a woman at the head of the line paying for her groceries. She was tiny but curvaceous. He couldn't see her face with her hair hanging over the side. As he was leaning forward slightly so he could see her better, her tiny hand swept her hair back away from her face. *Jesus, she's gorgeous.* But her hair was what first caught his attention; thick, glossy, and long. So long that it hung way down her back toward her luscious ass.

Damn. I could see that hair spread out on my pillow. In fact, I could see my hands holding that hair as I pounded into her. I could see me...

"Move on up, asshole." Jim shoved into him, breaking his train of lust.

Quickly adjusting himself so that the hard-on he was sporting couldn't be seen, he turned back around to keep watching the beauty as she pushed her cart outside.

Motioning to the cart, he said, "Here, take this shit. I need to go outside and find something."

"No fuckin' way, man," Jim answered back. "I told you, I ain't got any money."

"Damn!" Rob swore. Standing in line with the slowest cashier in the history of cashiers, he finally made it outside. But just as he knew she would be, the beauty was gone.

That afternoon, Carol woke to the enticing aroma of spicy tomato sauce cooking on the stove.

"Oh my!" she exclaimed. "I could get used to this! Let me shower first, and I'll be right back." In a little bit, she came back into the kitchen dressed in pink scrubs.

The two women sat down to eat dinner before Carol had to leave for the night shift.

"I can't wait for you to meet Tom," Carol said. "We've only been dating a little while, but he is so sweet. And.... I happen to know that he has some gorgeous, *single* friends that we could hook you up with."

"Oh, I'm definitely not looking for anyone now," Laurie answered back. "But I'm looking forward to meeting some new people."

"Well, I think we can arrange that," Carol said, laughing. Cleaning up her dishes, she grabbed her purse and said goodbye. "This is my last evening shift for a while," she said. "I work in the ER at the hospital. I'll be going on days and am really looking forward to that! The money won't be as good, but it sure will make dating easier. Tom hates it when I'm in the ER all night. He's always afraid something will happen to me." Carol looked nervous as she confessed, "I've had some unwanted attention from an unknown person lately, so Tom is super protective."

"Are you okay?" Laurie asked quickly.

"Oh yes. I'm not in danger, just annoyed," Carol answered.

After Carol left, Laurie settled in for her first evening in her new apartment. Picking up her cell phone, she called Emma.

"Hey, girl! How's the new apartment?" Emma answered with exuberance.

"It's amazing!" Laurie replied. "It's huge and the furniture is so lovely. And, oh my God, Emma, you can see the mountains from the windows!"

Emma knew how important a natural view was to Laurie because she felt the same way. Having lived in a tiny apartment without a view for years had made them both long for the sunshine to pour through the windows and for a view of trees instead of another brick building.

"It sounds perfect. How's your roommate?"

"She's also amazing. She's a nurse at the hospital and is working a shift right now. She did say that she was going to start working days since she's dating someone. That will be nice so that I won't have to tiptoe around the apartment when she needs to sleep."

"I'm so happy for you, Laurie. Is there anything you need? Anything you want me to send?"

"Just you!" Laurie said only half joking.

"I know, I wish I could be there too," Emma admitted. "But I need to finish out this year at the school I'm working at and then we'll see. Maybe if Fairfield ends up requiring a high school counselor, I'll apply." There was a pause, then Emma continued. "Just remember, Laurie, that this is your time. Make the most of it!"

"I will, I promise," Laurie answered. Promising to talk soon, Laurie put her cell phone down. She turned on the TV but found nothing that kept her interest. Walking into her bedroom, she picked up her Kindle. Taking it back to the living room and settling down on the sofa, she continued the romance novel she was currently reading. Her mind wandered back to the man she had seen at the grocery store. He looked just like the men in her stories - tall, handsome, built with powerful arms that could surround her, protect her, love her.

Will I ever meet someone like the heroes in these stories? Do they even exist? When she was little, she used to think that one day her dad would come riding into her life, like a fairytale, sweeping her mom off her feet again. But Laurie had long since realized that life was not like her fairytales.

And heroes don't really exist. With that, Laurie clicked off her Kindle and crawled into bed, falling asleep and dreaming of a handsome prince with dark hair riding up to sweep her off her feet.

Rob was at Smokey's, a local bar owned by Wendy and Bill Evans, family friends for as long as he could remember. He was meeting Tom and Jake, his two closest friends from childhood. As he entered the building, he saw Bill behind the bar keeping an eye on his beautiful wife, making sure that none of the newer customers were giving her looks. Bill was an enormous mountain of a man with a scruffy dark beard, still protective of his knockout wife and had been for the twenty years that they had been married. Giving Bill a nod, he headed back to the pool tables to find his friends. Jake and Tom were detectives, partners in the Fairfield Police Department, and the three of them had been friends since growing up on the same street as children.

Rob was aware of the looks from the women in the bar as he made his way to his friends. They had all played high school and college football together, and he knew women liked the way they looked. His Celtic looks with his black hair and blue eyes never failed to impress. Smirking, he realized how easy it was to get a woman in this town. Well, at least, a woman for a quick tumble. But one to spend time with... he hadn't found that yet.

His mind wandered back to the beauty at the grocery store. He sure would have liked to have had a chance to get her number. *She looked sweet. Maybe she would have been worth knowing and not just screwing. Maybe... hell, where are these thoughts coming from?*

"Hey man, you're late. Jake here is kickin' my ass, and I need *your* sorry ass in here so I can look good," Tom called out.

Jake had been staring at him. "What the hell were you thinking of as you were walking over here? You looked like you were thinking of a sweet piece." Jake was an intuitive detective, and Rob felt himself redden under Jake's perusal.

Rob laughed, knowing he couldn't hide something from these two. "Just a gorgeous piece of ass I saw at the store earlier. Didn't get her name or number, though, so I guess I'm out of luck!"

"Carol called earlier and said her new roommate moved in. Said she was super sweet and pretty as well," Tom said. Tom had been dating a gorgeous nurse at the hospital for a couple of months and Rob knew that a new roommate was coming into town.

"Oh no," Rob answered emphatically. "No dating Carol's roommate!" When Jake and Tom looked at him in confusion, he continued. "Look, you and Carol are starting something and you're already pussy-whipped. Carol's a sweetheart and would have stars in her eyes about her roommate and me. Then when I pull one of my typical fuck-and-runs, Carol will hate me, then you'll hate me...damn, that is too complicated."

"Fuck and run?" Jake shook his head. "Man, I'm stuck between Tom, the reformed *friends with benefits* man and you who admittedly defines his sex life as *fuck and run.*"

The friends laughed and ordered another round of beers, continuing the banter as they spent their evening at the pool tables. By the end of the evening, a few heavily painted women in tight clothing had made their way over to the men. Jake, never interested in a local hookup, quickly divested himself of the busty blonde that tried to attach herself to him. Tom, who just a few months ago would have already picked out his flavor of the night, was also having to forcefully push away one of the scantily clad women trying to lean her large tits on his arm.

Rob just laughed at his friends. Grabbing the cute redhead pressing her leg against his crotch, he headed out of the bar. Thoughts of the sweet-looking brunette from the grocery store flitted through his mind, but he pushed them back, deciding that a night of mindless sex would be just what he needed. They walked the short distance to her place; he stuck to his rule about not taking women to his apartment. For one thing, he hated the feeling that someone would assume they meant something to him by seeing where he lived. The other reason was probably more practical – his mom might drop in at any time!

Jolted out of his musing, he allowed her to pull him into her apartment. The smell of cigarette smoke assaulted his senses. A quick glance around gave evidence of the girl's inept housekeeping skills. *Hell, I saw cleaner frat houses when I was in college.*

There were dirty dishes piled in the sink and clothes scattered around the floor. She turned quickly once inside and pressed herself up against him again. Grabbing the front of his T-shirt, she pulled him in for a kiss. She forced her tongue into his mouth, but the taste of her whiskey shots intermingled with stale cigarette had Rob pulling back quickly.

"No kissing," he spoke curtly.

"No problem, handsome," she purred. She led him down the hall to her bedroom, pulling her top off at the same time. She stepped into the bedroom, turned, and began fondling her breasts. Rob suddenly found himself thinking again of a pair of natural looking breasts in a cute top. Before he knew it, the redhead in front of him was naked and had backed up to the bed. Rob looked at the bedroom that was just as nasty as the rest of the apartment, then looked down at the bed. Not focusing on the naked woman squirming in front of him, all he could see were the soiled sheets on the unmade bed. The knowledge that her sheets hadn't been cleaned since the last hookup she had brought here turned his stomach.

Shaking his head, he backed out of the room. He couldn't remember the last time he turned down free pussy, but he literally felt his dick shrink at the thought of being with this girl.

"What the hell?" she yelled, following him out of the bedroom, still naked.

"Sorry, babe. I just can't be your next fuck for the night, and you sure can't be mine," he stated as he headed out of the door.

He walked out, her curses still ringing in his ears. Feeling very sober at the moment, he walked back to his car at Smokey's and headed home. Entering his own apartment, he looked around as though seeing it for the first time. The furniture was clean and comfortable, if not new. The kitchen sink was empty, with the dishes filling the dishwasher. He never thought much about being so neat, but ever since he left college, he had wanted to live as an adult. His mother's constant reminders not to live like a slob when he was growing up must have paid off.

This is a nice place. I could easily invite a girl here for an evening. A beautiful brunette with a great body and a sweet smile. God, if Jake and Tom could see me now, they'd ask if I had grown a vagina in place of my dick!

Knowing he wasn't getting laid tonight, he headed to the shower to take care of things himself.

4

Laurie and Carol spent time the next week exploring Fairfield. They visited several of the boutiques, but Laurie was only window shopping.

"Can't you find anything you like?" Carol asked as they walked out of the shop.

Laurie explained honestly, "Oh, I'm just looking now. Until I get my first paycheck at the end of September, money is a little tight." Laughingly, she continued, "And as much as I love those clothes, I'm a first-grade teacher—tight skirts and high heels just won't work when I need to squat on the floor and chase the kids!"

Carol nodded in understanding but rushed to assure Laurie that if she needed to put off her rent payment for the first month, she would understand.

"Oh goodness, no! I have plenty of money for what I need. Believe me, my Aunt Emma taught me how to budget! But there is just no extra money for a new club dress right now." Laurie said smiling.

Carol noticed how Laurie spoke so easily about money, budgets, and even lack of resources. Laurie seemed so self-confident, something that Carol knew she struggled with constantly. Looping her arm through Laurie's, she steered her down the sidewalk. "Well, I have just the place for us to visit. Bernie's Bakery. They have the best coffee and pastries in the town. Let's indulge – my treat!"

Bernie's Bakery was in the center of the renovated downtown area. The pink awning over the doorway invited customers in, and once in, the smells of the homemade pastries and coffee enticed them to stay. Bernadette MacDonald was the owner of Bernie's Bakery. A dynamo to watch, she would call out coffee orders to the barista, while plating the pastries that were ordered. Known as Bernie to all of her friends, she was familiar with most of the customers in town, evident from the personal greetings that she gave to everyone who came into her shop.

Her son, Rob, was visiting with his mom this morning as he was picking up an order to take back to the firehouse. His dad was the Fire Chief of Fairfield, and Rob worked alongside him. Rob had left Fairfield to play football in college, and upon graduation he came back home as he had always planned to do, to work for the Fairfield Fire Department. He loved his job, his family, and his friends but was beginning to want more. More than just a night at a bar looking for a hookup.

More than just a hook-up. More than just a one-night stand. Thoughts of the long-haired beauty came to mind. *Why can't I get her out of my mind? She is haunting me and damn, that has never happened before now. Maybe I just need to get laid again. And soon.*

"Hey, Rob!" His mother's voice broke into his thoughts. Jerking his head up, he looked into her sparkling eyes. Smiling back, he headed over to the edge of the counter where she was waiting.

"Are you all right, son?" she asked. "You looked lost in thought."

"I'm fine, Mom," he assured her. "Just letting my thoughts run away with me today." Rob had a good relationship with his parents, finding that he could usually tell them anything. But he wasn't ready to talk about his personal life right at the moment, knowing that as soon as he did, his mom would start trying to set him up with all the single women she was constantly scoping out.

Watching him carefully, she pulled him in for another hug. Considering that he towered over her by at least eight inches and about sixty pounds, he still found her hugs comforting.

"Well, make sure when you get back to the station you only let your father have one pastry. His cholesterol was a little high last month," Bernie instructed.

"Sure Mom," Rob agreed, knowing his dad would have at least two pastries, if not three. He walked out of the bakery, his arms full of a large coffee container and bags of his mom's goodies. Leaving the shop, he turned to the left to head to his truck.

Coming immediately from the right, Carol and Laurie walked up to Bernie's Bakery. Glancing over, Laurie noticed the huge dark-haired man walking away from them, his arms loaded with Bernie's bags. She wondered if Fairfield was full of well-built men. Her eyes traveled down his back, landing on the jeans stretching over his ass and thighs. Eyes widening in surprise, Laurie thought that he might be the same man from the grocery store. *Good God, I recognize someone from their ass! What the hell is wrong with me?*

Just as the man was getting ready to turn around to get into his truck, Laurie was pulled into the pastry shop and away from the gorgeous mystery man.

Bernie looked up and saw Carol entering her bakery with another woman that she didn't recognize. The stranger was petite with the most beautiful hair that Bernie had ever seen. It hung long, thick, and wavy down the woman's back. As Carol and her friend approached the counter, Bernie saw that the new girl's face was enchanting. Grey eyes, shining with laughter, smooth ivory complexion, and the barest of makeup enhancing her features. *Oh, please let her be single!*

Laurie was looking around the bakery in awe. The soft pink walls were decorated with pictures of baked goodies that made her want to sit and try them all. The white chairs, paired with white and pink tables were so inviting. And the smells... it made her realize how very hungry she was. She was so entranced by the delightful shop, she did not notice Bernie walking over to them.

"Carol," Bernie greeted warmly. Carol turned and hugged Bernie, then turned back around to introduce Laurie. Before she could even get the introduction out, Bernie had already moved in to hug Laurie.

"Carol, who's your friend?" Bernie asked, looking Laurie up and down approvingly.

Carol laughed, knowing Bernie's propensity to want to make matches for her son, Rob. "This is my new roommate, Laurie. She just moved in and will start teaching first grade at the elementary school next week."

"A teacher?" Bernie asked, glowing with the information. Laurie felt like a bug under a magnifying glass, although she felt sure that she was meeting Bernie's approval. Approval for what she did not know. She turned, looking quizzically at Carol.

Carol, knowing Bernie's desire for her son to settle down with a sweet girl, wanted to answer Laurie's unspoken questions. "Bernie has an unmarried son. Rob is a gorgeous firefighter here in Fairfield, and I think Bernie is wanting to introduce the two of you."

Bernie laughed but noticed Laurie's discomfort. "Oh, my dear, please ignore me. I do want my Rob to settle down, but I would never force anyone on you. But... perhaps an introduction wouldn't be wrong."

Laurie could not help but smile back at the older woman's enthusiasm but had to answer honestly. "Bernie, it's so nice to meet you, but I have to say that I'm not looking for anyone right now. I'm just getting started with a new job, a new apartment, a new life."

Bernie pulled Laurie into another hug, patting her

back lovingly. "That's fine dear. But if you ever want to meet him, you let me know. Who knows? Perhaps it could be the start of something wonderful!"

Letting the girls find a table, Bernie took their orders and headed back to the counter. Seated at the quaint pink-and-white table, Laurie looked over at Carol, who was smiling at her. Carol reached over and patted her hand. "Did she make you feel uncomfortable?"

"Oh no, honestly!" Laurie exclaimed. "I just feel like so many new things are happening in my life, and adding the stress of trying to meet a man right now just seems overwhelming. I got the feeling that Bernie would expect instant love!"

Carol laughed along with her. "Actually, Bernie has a good eye for people, and I know she could tell that you'd make an incredible partner for Rob. But... well, I do have to say that even though I'm aware Rob is a great guy, I would warn you that he has a reputation for being a player."

Laurie's eyebrows rose at this new information. "Oh, then he's definitely not for me! I've never been anyone's one-night stand and don't plan on starting now!" She spoke so vehemently Carol wondered if there was a story behind Laurie's statement. She wanted to ask but knew that might be too intrusive. She felt sure that Laurie would share when she was ready.

The girls finished their coffee and treats, hugged Bernie goodbye, and headed out of the shop.

Bernie was already on the phone to Rob working her magic.

5

The weekend before Laurie began her teaching job, Carol and Tom decided to meet at Smokey's and introduce Laurie to several of their friends. Carol had warned Tom that while Laurie was gorgeous, she was not going to be any of his friends' hookup. He assured her that he would keep an eye on his friends to make sure no one acted inappropriately.

Laurie was excited to go to Smokey's after hearing about their great food and that the locally owned bar was a town hangout. She knew from Helen and Roger that Smokey's was owned by Wendy, their daughter, and Wendy's husband, Bill. Checking with Carol to see what she was wearing, Laurie decided on dark skinny jeans and a soft blue shirt that draped in the front, showing a hint of cleavage. She paired the ensemble with her trademark heels. Always hating being the shortest woman around, she usually wore four-inch heels with all her outfits. Simple but elegant makeup enhanced her naturally beautiful features, and she brushed her long hair, allowing it to fall down her back.

They were meeting Tom at Smokey's since Laurie wanted to have her own transportation. Knowing that Carol would leave with Tom, she wanted to have control over when she could head back home. Hopping into her VW, they headed down the road towards the bar, singing loudly to the radio.

———

Rob, Tom, Jake, and several other friends were already at the bar, having just arrived. Rob's mom had already filled his head with her impressions of Carol's roommate. Hearing she was a beautiful girl made him dread meeting her. While he trusted his mom's assessment of a beautiful girl, he also knew that his mom was looking for wife material. Right now, Rob was looking for more than a hookup, but Carol's roommate would be a disaster. If he didn't like her, it could be awkward. And being Carol's roommate, he would never be able to have her for his usual "fuck and run".

"Guys, remember to be on your best behavior tonight. Don't do anything that'll piss off the new girl. That'll piss off Carol. And if Carol gets pissed off, that'll piss off me!" Tom reminded them.

Jake and Rob looked over in amusement. "Just how pussy-whipped are you, man?" Rob asked.

"Fuck you, Rob," Tom scowled back. "It's just that for once try to be a gentleman, for the girls' sakes."

Jake just laughed. He never went for a hookup in

Fairfield. It was too difficult in his job as a detective to take a chance on always running into a previous one-night stand. At thirty-one, he was ready to settle down, just waiting for the right one to come along. And a sweet twenty-four-year-old girl was not what he was looking for. But Rob? Jake continued to chuckle. A sweet twenty-four-year-old just might knock Rob on his ass.

Rob strolled over to the pool tables in the back to shoot a game while waiting on the women to arrive. Not overly interested in spending time with them, he was in no rush to be introduced. Within a minute, he was joined by one of the local barflies, fake breasts falling out of the top of a barely-there shirt. *What else is new? Same old, same old.*

Laurie and Carol entered Smokey's right on time. Laurie, looking around, was immediately impressed with the beautifully restored bar. The dark wood floor and walls were clean and gleaming. The polished wooden bar lined one side of Smokey's with a large mirror behind it. The mirror was decorated with brass lighting fixtures giving the place an old-time feel. Behind the bar was a mountainous man, who was big and bulky with a thick beard, filling drink orders. Beside him was a blonde beauty, who Laurie recognized from pictures at Helen and Roger's office as their daughter, Wendy. Looking up from behind the bar, Wendy waved to Carol, pointing towards the back indicating where Tom was. Carol pulled on Laurie's arm, leading her towards the back of the bar.

As Laurie and Carol approached the table in the back, she recognized Tom and noticed several handsome men sitting there as well. The men stood as the women walked up, Tom leaning over to give Carol a kiss before moving back to greet Laurie. As introductions were made, Laurie glanced around nervously. She wondered if Bernie's son would be there, but he wasn't at the table. Sitting down, Tom handled ordering for the group.

Laurie noticed one empty chair at their table, just as she heard Carol whispering to Tom, "Where's Rob? I thought he was coming tonight."

Tom whispered back, "He's over at the pool tables, of course."

At this, Carol rolled her eyes, nodding in understanding. Laurie couldn't help but wonder if Bernie knew of her son's reputation as a player. *Surely, she must*, Laurie thought. *This town is not that big.* Her eyes drifted over to the pool tables, and she noticed the gorgeous man that she had seen at the grocery store and outside of the bakery. There was no way she could miss the way his faded jeans stretched tightly over his thighs and ass. He was huge, easily over six feet tall and built like a football player. Wide shoulders tapered down to his waist, thick thighs filled out his jeans, and his dark T-shirt stretched tightly over his pecs and abs. Muscular arms bulged from the sleeves of the T-shirt.

Laurie knew she was staring and wondered who the man was that had been filling her dreams for the past two weeks. Suddenly she realized that his eyes were staring right back at her.

Hearing noises coming from his table, Rob looked over to see the other men rise. He could barely see Carol's blonde hair shining from among the much taller men at the table. *They must be here. Time to head over and make nice.*

Suddenly, as the men were taking their seats again, he caught a glimpse of the girl with Carol. *Goddamn. It's the woman from the grocery store.* Her hair was just as long as he remembered it, and he knew he wanted to see it spread out on his pillow. Her face, with its subtle makeup, gave her a princess look. Her tiny frame was filled out just the way he liked. He had not gotten a good look at the front of her at the grocery store, but her front view was just as fantastic as her ass.

He couldn't believe that the woman he had been dreaming about for almost two weeks was standing at his table. With his friends. His single friends. *Damn!*

Suddenly aware of her grey eyes staring back at him, all of the air seemed to be sucked from the room and for a moment, he wasn't sure he was breathing. Everyone faded away into the background, and it was just the beautiful woman staring back into his eyes. He found himself starting to move towards her, desperate to claim the woman that filled his thoughts.

"Rob," an annoying voice interrupted his thoughts as he felt his arm pulled back. Jerked out of his musings, he realized that the busty girl who had been hanging onto him hoping to get lucky for the night was attempting to drape herself over him again.

Rob quickly turned toward her, brushing her hand off his arm. "Get lost, Amber," he growled. Huffing, she narrowed her eyes at him, seeing where his attention had been.

He turned back to the table only to see a look of disappointment cross the princess' face. He watched as she turned away from him, taking the seat in between Carol and another friend of theirs.

Damn! How do I fix this?

Not knowing what he was going to do, Rob stalked over to the table, determined to meet this girl and change her first impression of him.

Laurie looked up as the handsome man from her dreams walked towards the table. He seemed to have rid himself of the girl that had been hanging onto him, but she watched him warily as he approached.

"Rob, glad you can finally join us," Tom greeted loudly. The others at the table laughed, knowing his reputation for always having a woman on his arm, but Laurie noticed that he scowled angrily at his friends.

"Just playing a little pool," he answered smoothly, "but if I had known the women were joining us now, I would have been over sooner." Walking over, he greeted

Carol warmly then turned his dark gaze towards Laurie. "I'm Rob, and you must be Carol's roommate."

Laurie was not taken in by the smooth transition from a player with the girl in the back to the man trying to make an impression on her. Raising one eyebrow, she replied, "Yes, I'm Laurie. But I assure you that you did not have to leave your date at the pool table just to meet me."

The others at the table chuckled as Tom noticed Rob's tight-jawed expression.

Rob recovered quickly and pulled up a chair next to Laurie and said, "I assure you that there's no one here I'm more interested in being with than you."

Laurie looked into his eyes, and while he seemed sincere, she knew she was very inexperienced when it came to men. She was wary of his intentions.

Carol looked over at Tom quickly with a questioning look in her eyes. He placed his arm around her pulling her in tighter, leaned down and whispered in her ear, "Don't worry, angel. He's a good guy. Maybe this is exactly what he needs." She looked dubious but trusted Tom to know his friends.

Rob, determined to make amends, sat close to Laurie with his arm on the back of her chair, essentially claiming her. Jake looked over with a smirk on his face, knowing Rob had never claimed a woman. They usually threw themselves at him allowing him to take his pick. Jake and Tom shared a look over the women's heads, both recognizing that Rob may have just met his match, in more ways than one.

Laurie was determined to have a good time, but the

presumptuous behavior of Rob was keeping the other men at bay. It was as though there was an unspoken man-rule: if a man is sitting close to a woman with his arm on the back of her chair, then other men know to back off. *What the hell? He may be gorgeous, but he's not the prince of my dreams. Well, he looks like my prince. And he hasn't looked at another woman since we laid eyes on each other.*

She started to relax and enjoy herself. Rob was attentive and seemed genuinely interested in her. The others at the table joked and laughed with the camaraderie of shared experiences and friendships. She learned that Rob, Tom, and Jake had grown up together in Fairfield, left town to go to college and then returned to their hometown. Jake was reserved but with a compassionate personality, and she thought how wonderful he would be with her Aunt Emma.

Tom and Carol seemed well suited. Both blond and beautiful, he had his protective tendencies, and while Carol was a strong woman, there seemed to be a fragility about her.

Whenever the conversation turned toward Laurie, Rob noticed she deflected most of the questions, giving little information. She was so friendly and outgoing, it made him wonder what part of her past made her so cautious. She did divulge that her aunt had raised her after her mother passed away but gave no indication as to her father or other family members. He was amazed that he was so interested, having never cared about a woman's past or present life other than for the night. Her beauty captured his attention, but it was her personality that enchanted him. She seemed independent, self-confident, and intelligent, as well as genuinely happy. Her smile lit her face, and when the smile turned towards him, he swore he could hear his heart beating in his chest.

Once, as he leaned over to hear her better in the noisy bar, he noticed her vanilla scent. With his mom owning a bakery, he was used to the scent of vanilla, but it had never made his pulse race as this subtle flavor emanating off this girl was doing to him. Her shirt was just low enough for him to glimpse the tops of her breasts, keeping his attention but making him uncomfortably aware that what he could see, any man around could see. Feeling unaccustomed to possessiveness, he wanted to gouge out the eyes of all of his friends at the table.

Laurie was equally affected by him as well. She could feel her heart beating faster every time he leaned over to hear what she was saying. She glanced at his profile, her breath catching in her throat as she admired his masculine beauty. Dark black hair trimmed very short on the sides and slightly longer on top framed his square jaw, and he had piercing eyes. And that body. She knew she was petite, but his large frame dwarfed hers. But instead of feeling intimidated, she felt surprisingly protected.

As the evening was winding down, Carol and Tom were ready to head back to his place while Laurie was saying her goodbyes. Rob, anxious to escort Laurie home to have more time with her, was about to ask her if he could follow her to make sure she arrived home safely.

They stood facing each other, her head leaning way back to look up into his eyes. *God, he looks like the man of my dreams. Like all the ones in my romance novels.*

Rob, while towering over her, had a gentle look as he peered down. *She looks like a princess,* he thought.

Leaning down, he was getting ready to offer his arm to escort her out when Amber came rolling over. "Guess you've fucked everything else in town, so I'm not surprised you're going for new blood. This one looks too virginal for you, though, Rob. Sure she can handle you?"

Laurie gasped, jerking away from the drunken woman grasping at Rob's arm. Rob, rage pouring off him, growled, "Get out of here, Amber." He turned towards Amber, shaking her hand off his arm as he propelled her away from their table.

Jake, coming to the rescue, took Amber's arm directing her over to Bill at the bar. "Come on, girl. Let's get a cab to drive you home."

Rob turned back around to apologize to Laurie only to find her walking rapidly toward the door. *Damn!* He started to take off after her but found his arm pulled back by Tom. "Rob, let her go, man. I think enough damage has been done tonight," Tom said.

"Come on, Tom," he replied, then looked down at Carol and apologized. "Carol, I'm sorry. I just... want to make sure…. I just need to …. Damn."

Carol couldn't help but giggle at Rob's inability to

complete a sentence. *Hmmm, Laurie may just be the one for him after all.*

Tom, letting go of his arm, watched as Rob jogged out of the bar after Laurie. He looked down at Carol, tucked under his arm, and leaned down to kiss her the way he had wanted to since she first showed up. "Let's go, angel, and head back to my place."

Carol, looking uncertain, asked if he thought Laurie would be all right. Tom assured her that Rob would make certain she got home safely.

"She doesn't seem to trust men, Tom. I don't want to see her hurt."

Tom kissed her gently this time and said, "I know, angel. But I think maybe they both just need to find their way." He threw his arm around her tiny shoulders and with a head jerk to Bill and Jake, he led her out of the bar.

Rob saw Laurie getting into a pale-yellow VW bug, and he couldn't help but grin. He'd never be caught dead in a car like that, but it seemed to fit her perfectly. He made it over to her window just as she started the car. She tried to ignore him, but with his large frame filling up her window as he tapped on the glass, it was impossible to pretend that he wasn't there. Taking a deep breath, she forced a smile on her face as she rolled her window down.

"Yes, Rob?" she asked formally.

Knowing he needed to rectify the situation, he tried

to turn on the charm. "Hey darlin', just wanted to make sure you got home safely. I thought I'd volunteer for that duty."

Laurie, completely unfazed by his charm, simply replied, "No, thank you. I'm perfectly able to see myself home." With that, she started to roll up the window.

He realized for the first time that his charm was not working and was actually glad it didn't. He wanted more from this sprite of a girl than someone he could charm into his bed for the night. Grabbing the edge of the glass before it closed completely, he called out her name. Looking frustrated, she stopped the movement of the window.

"Laurie, I'm sorry. Really. Truly sorry."

She looked back up into his face, sensing the sincerity in his voice. No longer sounding like he was trying to charm her out of her pants, he seemed sorry. "Rob, you don't have to apologize. We were just enjoying each other's company, that's all. No harm was done. I'm a big girl; I assure you my feelings weren't hurt by what she said. We can still be friends."

"No!" he said forcefully, causing her to look sharply up into his snapping eyes. Running a hand down his face in frustration, he forced his voice to calm. "I mean, I don't want to just be friends. I'd really like to get to know you. I felt something tonight, something I haven't ever felt. I know you felt it too. Can't we just forget that drunk girl and move forward?" he pleaded.

"Rob, can I ask you a question and you give me an honest answer?" Laurie asked softly, staring into his handsome face.

Encouraged that she was still talking to him, he readily agreed.

"Have you ever slept with Amber?" she asked looking into his eyes.

Damn! Goddamn Amber and her mouth.

Not knowing what to say, he said nothing for a moment, hanging his head.

Laurie continued, "And have you...um...you know...with a lot of women here in town?"

His eyes jerked back to hers, and for the first time in his life, he wished he had been more discriminating and that he had left his fuck-and-run philosophy behind in college. Looking deep into her stormy grey eyes, which were staring back at him expecting honesty, he knew he couldn't lie.

"Yes, although not as many as you've probably heard. But I have a reputation.... and it's probably deserved. But every woman I was with knew it was only physical. I never made any false claims or pretenses. I never made promises. I never met anyone I wanted to spend time with until tonight. I never met anyone who captured my attention until this evening." He could hear the desperation in his voice. "Please give me a chance."

She gave him a soft, sad smile. "Thank you for being honest, Rob. I know that I can't hold anything against you that occurred before tonight, but I just can't trust a player. You have no idea how much pain can come from a one-night stand. A lifetime of doubt."

He had no idea what she was talking about, but he could feel her slipping away. "Laurie, please."

"Goodnight, Rob. Goodbye." And with that, she

finished rolling up her window and pulled out of the parking lot.

He couldn't see the tear sliding down her face. *There really are no princes,* she thought ruefully.

Jumping into his truck, he followed at a discreet distance all the way to her apartment. Watching to see her enter safely, he parked outside, needing to think. Getting out of his truck, he walked over to a park bench near the building. It was an odd feeling, evaluating his life and not liking what he saw. In college, when he, Tom, and Jake had been football players, women had thrown themselves at him. The three of them had always enjoyed the favors coming their way, but he was the only one of them that continued that lifestyle when they moved back to Fairfield. Jake did not date often, and when he did, he preferred to meet women that did not live in town. Tom hooked up a lot but taking a cue from Jake, he tended to have his hook-ups out of town. Both being policemen, they did not want to hinder any cases by having slept with possible witness or suspects.

Shaking his head, he thought of his own stupidity. He realized now that his actions over the past years had reflected poorly on his parents as well as kept any possible relationship from happening.

Light appeared at an apartment on the third floor. Looking up, he recognized Laurie standing at the window looking out. She was looking into the distance, but even if she looked down, she wouldn't be able to see him in the dark. He stared at her. Even from where he sat, he could see her beauty. That hair – glossy, thick, long. Funny, instead of thinking of how he would wrap it around his hand when pounding into her, he found himself thinking of a fairy tale from his childhood that his elementary teacher would read. Rapunzel. The one who saved the prince.

Shaking his head, he thought he must be losing his mind. Never had a woman had such an effect on him. *Damn, I hope the guys don't ever get a hint of what I'm thinking!*

Laurie stood at the window, lost in her thoughts. Rob, the man she had been dreaming about, the man she thought might be someone worth getting to know, was nothing more than her father. A man who gave in to his baser instincts with no care as to the repercussions. A man not to be trusted. She wiped a tear from her cheek as she stood at the window looking out into the darkness.

Rob, looking back up as he acknowledged to himself that she was unattainable, was preparing to walk away when he noticed her wiping away her tears. *She's crying, you prick. You did this.* But then that thought gave him hope. *If she's crying, that means she's affected too. Time to change, man. Time to become worthy of her.*

6

The next week flew by as Laurie went into the school to get ready for the beginning of the academic year. She immediately fell in love with the older, two-story, brick building. Fairfield Elementary had served as the junior and high school about fifty years ago. Once the town built a separate middle school and high school, the large building became the elementary school. The ceilings were high, and each classroom had large windows letting in natural light. The kindergarten and first grade were housed on the second floor near the stairs leading to the cafeteria while the older students were housed in a separate wing. With the downstairs partially below ground level, the second floor was only about one-and-a-half floors above the ground, giving her a perfect view of the playground in the back of the building.

She felt an acute anticipation as she and the grade level chairperson walked up the stairs to her classroom, while she turned the room key over in her hand. Moving through the door, her heartbeat pounded as she viewed her room for the first time. Little tables with four chairs at each sat in the middle of the room. Low bookshelves lined the wall under the windows. Cubbies filled the opposite wall, and her desk sat in the corner facing the classroom. Walking over to the windows, she viewed the playground below stretching to the fence guarding the property. *My first classroom. My home away from home.*

She attended several meetings with other teachers, liking them immediately. She developed an instant rapport with Lucy Darby, the principal. There was so much for her to learn: procedures for lesson plans, the first-grade schedule, curriculum requirements, safety drills. Her mind was whirling every day by the time she got home.

She got home about the same time that Carol walked through the door, and they enjoyed their time together. They settled into a congenial camaraderie, cooking dinner and watching TV in the evenings. Occasionally, Tom would join them for dinner and other times he would pick Carol up and they would head out for a date.

Several days after the night at the bar, Carol and Laurie settled on the couch and tried unsuccessfully to find something worth watching on TV. Carol tossed the remote onto the coffee table and turned towards Laurie, tucking her legs under her. She seemed as though she wanted to talk but was having difficulty getting her thoughts together.

Laurie, staring at Carol quizzically, asked, "What's on your mind?"

Carol, blushing, looked at her roommate. "That obvious?"

Laurie just laughed, saying, "You've been trying for ten minutes to think about how to ask me something. I think we're friends enough by now that you can just ask."

Sighing, Carol spoke hesitantly. "I was just wondering what you thought of Rob. Well, to be honest, Tom was also wondering. I mean, I can see where you'd think he was such a player. I even told you that. But well, there is just something about Rob that is really likable when you get to know him. And... well... Tom says Rob really likes you." Carol knew she was rambling, but she wanted to get it all out before Laurie had a chance to shut her down. She glanced back up at Laurie's thoughtful face, pleased to see that it did not look as though she was angry.

Laurie was thoughtful for a moment, not sure how to answer. Taking a deep breath, she looked back into her friend's troubled blue eyes. "Carol, I have no right to judge Rob. If he's a player, then that's his business. But I assure you, I'm not ever going to be someone's one-night stand."

Carol rushed to say that she knew Laurie wouldn't, but Laurie continued, "And it is more than that. When I'm ready to settle down, I need someone stable. Someone who just has eyes for me. Someone who makes me feel as though their whole world is me." She hesitated, then looked into Carol's eyes. "Is that too much to ask?"

Carol leaned over and embraced Laurie. "No, that's

not too much to ask." Leaning back, she asked, "But do you think that Rob is incapable of that?"

Laurie, quiet with a sad, faraway look in her eyes, replied, "I don't know, Carol. But for now, the Rob I met the other night is still too much of a player for me. I would get hurt, and I'm going to protect myself from that."

"But what if, in protecting yourself, you don't allow yourself to possibly find that love?"

Laurie, still with a sad look in her eyes, looked away as she said, "It won't be the first time the handsome prince got away."

Carol, curious about her cryptic comment, knew that Laurie was not going to explain further. Picking the remote up again, they finally found a movie to watch as they enjoyed the rest of the evening.

Rob left work and headed to Tom's apartment. He felt like he was in middle school but convinced Tom to have Carol question Laurie to see what he needed to do to prove that he deserved a chance. Walking into Tom's house, he settled at the kitchen bar reaching for the beer that Tom was handing to him.

"Okay man don't make me beg. What's the word about Laurie?" Rob asked.

Tom sighed and looked his friend in the eyes. "You know, jerkoff, if you'd kept it in your pants more often or at least with some discrimination, you wouldn't be in this situation."

Rob looked up at Tom incredulously. "What the hell, man? You've slept with just as many women as I have, so how come you're so sanctimonious?"

"'Cause when I came back to town five years ago, I took a page out of Jake's book. No town hookups. Too much drama on the job and kept life cleaner!" Tom answered.

"Man, I haven't hooked up with anyone in a month. Not since I first laid eyes on Laurie," Rob confessed.

Tom looked surprised, but Rob continued. "Yeah, I saw her at the grocery store the first day she was in town. I didn't know who she was then, but one look at her rocked my world. I was actually ready to bang some girl I met in the bar after that, but one real look at *that*, all I could think of was how much of a princess Laurie looked like and, man, I swear my dick shriveled!"

Tom, with a raised eyebrow, stated, "Bro, I do not need to know that much about your dick!" The friends shared a laugh. Then silence ensued.

"Seriously. I can't think of anything else but her. Please tell me there's some kind of a chance."

Tom looked thoughtfully at his childhood friend, realizing how much he really wanted to see Rob happy. "The only thing that Carol said was that Laurie had been interested, but it appears that some other dickwad got to her first."

At that, Rob's eyes snapped in anger. "What do you mean by that?"

Tom, putting his hands up in front of him, replied, "Don't shoot the messenger! It's just that Laurie seemed to indicate that she had been burned before. Don't know the details but, Rob, you'd better be sure. Laurie's a great girl; nice, sweet, wholesome. The kind that someone wants to create a forever with. She doesn't deserve to have you dick her over." Tom could tell that Rob was about to retort when he continued. "Nor does she deserve to have every pussy you've dipped into, constantly in her face when she's out."

"Damn!" Rob cursed. "So, I'm screwed. I can't be judged on who I am or who I'm going to be, but constantly judged on who I've been?" Jumping up from the bar stool, he paced Tom's living room in frustration.

Tom, now sure of Rob's genuineness, walked over to his friend, placing his hand on Rob's shoulder. "Rob, give it time. You keep being real, keep proving to her that you're changing and interested, it'll happen. Won't say it'll happen fast. But it'll happen. Carol and I'll help."

Rob looked into the eyes of one of the men he trusted with his life. Nodding in agreement, he thanked Tom and headed out into the night. There was only one place to go when life was kicking him and he needed perspective. Rob drove down the streets to a familiar house. Walking to the door, he knocked rapidly, not ashamed to need the arms of the woman inside. The door opened, and he peered into the eyes that knew him best. Reaching out and pulling him into a hug, the beautiful woman knew exactly what he needed.

"Come on in Rob. You look like you need this," she said smiling up at him and handing him a beer.

"Thanks, Mom. What I really need is you. Is Dad home too? I need to talk and sort some things out," Rob said, affectionately looking at his mother.

Smiling, she called into the den. "Mac, turn the TV off. Family time!"

Rob sat with his mom and dad and talked for hours. He confessed what they already knew about his reputation. As hard as it was to discuss his sexual transgressions with his parents, it was more difficult to realize how selfish he had been. It never occurred to him that his mother had had to listen to snide comments over the years from some women coming into her shop. Or that his dad had heard comments as well.

He sat in the den with his parents, feeling completely ashamed and embarrassed. Looking up at them, all he could offer in his defense was, "I never slept with as many women as my reputation. I swear that I would hear of women claiming to have been with me, and I knew that had never happened. But I never said anything to correct the misconception. I also never saw it as using anyone. Honestly, whenever I had sex with someone, I always made it clear that it was physical only, and if they weren't on board with that, then I left."

Hanging his head, he admitted, "I guess that seems like very little doesn't it?" Then raising his head back up, looking his parents straight into their eyes, he said, "But making excuses for my past is piss poor. I'm over thirty years old; it's time to man up."

Bernie looked at her son with pride, thinking how much he looked like his father. Mac was the best of men and even though Rob didn't realize it, he was like his father in all ways. Once he gave his heart to a woman, that would be it for him. "Son, it's not a crime for a man to sow his wild oats. For that matter, it's not a crime for a woman to do the same."

This statement brought raised eyebrows from both her son and her husband. Laughing, she just added, "Well, what's good for the goose is good for the gander!"

Mac and Rob just shook their heads laughing, as Bernie relieved a lot of the stress and tension of the conversation.

Mac, looking at his son, asked, "Rob, what has brought about this sudden desire to see the kind of man you've been and what you want to be? You're a good person; kind, caring, loving, friendly, competent, loyal. Why the sudden self-doubt?"

Bernie, looking over at the two men in her life, leaned over and patted Rob's hand. "I think it has everything to do with a long-haired beauty."

Gazing at his mom, Rob smiled. Mac grumbled that he was the last to hear anything and demanded to be brought into the picture.

Rob began to share about Laurie. He explained about seeing her at the grocery store; then Bernie interrupted to share how she met Laurie with Carol at the shop one day right after Rob had left. He continued on to the night at Smokey's. He shared everything with his parents, desperately needing their insight. When he got to the part about Amber, both parents winced as though in pain. "Yeah, it went downhill after that," he admitted. He even told them what Tom had said about Laurie having been hurt before.

"She just needs a chance to see the real you. The part that's not a player, no longer a player," his dad interjected. Bernie just rolled her eyes at her husband.

"Honey," she said. "It sounds like she's practical. Once burned, she's not looking to get played again. Your dad is partially right – she does need a chance to see the real you. But that may take time. Are you serious about her? I would encourage you to befriend her first. Then that will give her time to see the real you."

Rob sat for a few minutes digesting this advice. *Friends. Could he be friends with a girl that he wanted to wrap himself around and protect from all hurt? And what if he was the one that caused the pain?*

Knowing he had to give it a try, he kissed his parents goodnight and headed home.

Laurie greeted the opening of school with great enthusiasm for her class of twenty-four first-graders. Each day she headed off to work, satisfied with the knowledge that she was doing something she loved. For the first month of school, they were required to have a fire drill every week, and she wanted to make a good impression on the principal. She taught the students exactly what they were to do, how to act, and where to go. In the second week of the new school year, she was not surprised to hear the fire drill alarm. Her class immediately lined up and proceeded outside.

She was surprised though to see a fire truck outside with firefighters around. Her eyes immediately landed on one particular firefighter. Rob. Trying to be unaffected, she couldn't help but notice his eyes staring straight into hers and his smile directed at her.

Her students began to talk with excitement, seeing the fire trucks. She quickly brought them back to order, and they continued on to their assigned location. At the end of the fire drill, Ms. Darby announced that the class with the best behavior would get to visit the fire truck and talk to the firemen. Laurie was pleased when her class was called. Leading the children over to the fire truck, she tried to keep them in order.

Seeing that she was losing control of her class, Rob quickly stepped up. Looking impressive in his fireman's uniform, he towered over the six-year-olds.

"All right, everyone, listen up," he boomed. The children immediately quieted, looking at him with awe. "Only the children who listen to their teacher will get to climb on the fire truck and meet Mr. Mac, the Fire Chief."

The children all looked to Laurie for instruction. Shooting him a grateful look, she divided them into three groups to rotate among the firefighters and the fire truck. The firemen took each group and began giving tours.

Rob maneuvered Laurie over to the sidewalk. "How have you been?" he asked sincerely, smiling down into her beautiful face. Her long hair was pulled back, and the wind was blowing tendrils all about. In the sunlight, he saw that her hair had strands of light brown, dark brown, reddish brown all swirled together. He realized that he had never actually noticed a woman's hair before. Not like this. Not memorizing its color. Or how the wind swept the loose strands around her face. He fought the urge to bury his hands in it, just to see how it felt. *Jesus, get a grip, man.*

Laurie, suddenly feeling shy after how their last encounter ended, smiled and replied, "Fine. I've been fine." It was as though her brain stopped working and she simply couldn't think of anything else to say.

He acted as though he didn't notice her discomfort and continued. "How are your kids? I have to admit, I never had a teacher that looked like you." Even though she was wearing comfortable slacks, he noticed how they hung perfectly off her ass. Her blouse was prim and proper, but it did nothing to hide her shape. He was suddenly glad for the large fireman's uniform that could hide his hard-on.

"The kids are great," she admitted, smiling up at him. "I really like them. They haven't learned to be cynical about school yet."

He noticed the smile that made his breath catch had reached her eyes, and they seemed to sparkle.

Reaching over she laid her hand on his arm. "Thank you so much for doing this for them. It's a great way to teach them about fire safety and such a treat."

Rob, feeling the spark from her tiny hand on his arm, looked into her face and noticed that she seemed to feel it as well. She jerked her hand from his arm and once again looked disconcerted. Not willing to lose momentum, he dove right in.

"Laurie, I'd really like it if we could be friends. I'd love to take you to dinner." Seeing that she was about to object, he quickly continued. "It would just be dinner. Just two friends having dinner. I've been in this town for most of my life and could fill you in on anything you'd want to know." Seeing her hesitate, he pushed his luck. "Come on, Laurie, just like friends. What have you got to lose?"

At this, she looked deeply into his blue eyes and began to smile.

"Well, okay. But just as friends."

Feeling as though he could breathe again, he grinned his famous panty dropping grin. "Well, all right then. I'll pick you up at six tonight."

She was startled. "Tonight? So soon?"

"No time like the present to get to know each other!" he replied.

Laurie, biting her lip, looked as if she was trying to decide. Continuing to press his advantage, he convinced her to give in. By this time, the children had made their rounds of the fire truck and were lining up to go inside again. She walked over to the fire chief to offer her thanks. He was a big, handsome man with a booming voice and a cheerful personality.

"I would like to thank you so much for letting my class get to see the fire truck and your men up close," she said sincerely, smiling up into his face.

Stepping forward, he took her hand in his, carefully perusing her face. "Call me Mac – everyone around here does. Except for Rob. He calls me Dad," Mac said smiling broadly.

Laurie, glancing between Rob and Mac, saw the familiar look the two men shared. Laughing, she shook Mac's hand and turned to take her class back inside.

"See you tonight, Ms. Dodd," Rob said softly, so as not to embarrass her in front of her students. She turned and gave him a smile before herding her students inside.

"Dinner?" Mac asked.

Rob nodded. "I have to start somewhere, Dad. The truth is, I haven't had dinner with a woman in a long time. But at least, she didn't say 'no'!"

Mac slapped his son on the back and boomed out for men to pack up their equipment. As Rob turned back to the school, he noticed Laurie standing at the door looking back at him. Giving her a wave, he headed back to the station, feeling lighter than he had in a long time.

Laurie tried on multiple outfits before flopping down on her bed in frustration. Carol came in, viewed the fashion disaster covering Laurie's room, and took over.

"Okay, what look do you want to go for? Sultry, come hither, I'm in control, I'm unattainable—"

"None of those!" Laurie jumped up from the bed, looking into Carol's laughing face. "What are you laughing at?"

Carol, still giggling, apologized. "I'm sorry, but for someone who is just going out with a new friend, you certainly are worried about what you look like."

Laurie huffed in exasperation. "I know," she said, looking back into Carol's understanding eyes. "I wish I knew what was going on. I mean, he can get any girl he wants….and probably has! What does he want with me? I've made it perfectly clear that I'm not going to be his next conquest. Is he one of these guys that just can't believe that someone is not going to hop into bed with him?" Laurie stopped her rant, sat on the edge of the bed and put her head in her hands.

Sitting down on the bed next to Laurie, Carol put her arm around her friend. "Laurie, I don't think Rob has any agenda other than getting to know you." Laurie looked up into Carol's eyes, seeing nothing but compassion. Carol continued, "I know you see Rob as a player and there's no denying that he has had his share of hookups. I also know that his reputation is worse than what it really is. And I know that he hasn't slept with anyone since he first saw you in town, the day you arrived." At this, Laurie looked confused.

"Yep, according to Tom, Rob saw you at the grocery store that first day you were in town, and he hasn't been able to think of being with anyone else but you since then."

Laurie quietly took in this information. "He said just friends, Carol. He promised we were going out as just friends."

Carol smiled and nodded. "Yes, but for Rob that's also new. He's never tried to be friends with a woman and hasn't taken anyone out to dinner for years." Letting this information sink in, she then winked at Laurie and said, "Okay, now let's find a going-out-with-a-friend outfit!"

An hour later, Rob sat in the parking lot of Laurie's apartment building. Nervous... he couldn't remember the last time he was nervous. Nor could he remember the last time he had wanted to take a woman to dinner. Taking a deep breath, he got out of the truck and headed inside. Knocking on the door, Carol opened it and greeted Rob warmly. He glanced down at Carol, noting her beauty and was glad that Tom had met such a wonderful woman. Carol smiled up at Rob, laying her hand on his arm. Awareness filled him that with Carol, he did not feel a spark at her touch as he did when Laurie touched his arm.

"I hope you have a good time, Rob. I really do," Carol said sincerely.

Rob smiled down at her, "Thanks, Carol. That means a lot to me. I know you're worried. It's just dinner as friends, I promise. For now, at least," he added with a wink.

Right then Laurie walked into the room, and Rob wasn't sure how the oxygen left so quickly. She was wearing skinny jeans with a soft yellow shirt that wrapped around the front. On her feet were yellow sandals with heels. Her hair was loose, falling down her back, and her makeup was subtle, showcasing her natural beauty. The smile on her face reached her eyes, and Rob wanted nothing more than to take her in his arms and kiss her.

While Rob was looking over Laurie, she was feasting her eyes on him as well. She stared at his magnificent physique, overwhelmed at the sheer masculinity of him. He was wearing jeans that, as usual for him, were stretched tightly over his thighs and cupped his manhood. Averting her eyes from his crotch, she noted the dark green button-up shirt that also stretched over his chest. The sleeves were rolled up at the wrists, showing his tan skin.

"Ready to go?" he asked, holding out his arm for her to take.

Laurie stepped up to him, looked up into his smiling

face, and placed her arm on his. Feeling the sparks again, she looked disconcerted as they headed out of the door.

"Hey guys," Carol called after them. "I'm heading to Tom's place, so if y'all end up wanting a place to talk after dinner, you're free to come here."

Rob nodded to Carol, smiling down at Laurie as they walked to the parking lot. Reaching the truck, he opened her door, and before she could climb in, she felt strong hands circling her waist and lifting her up to be seated. Before she could protest, he leaned in across her chest to buckle her in.

"I'm completely able to buckle myself in," she protested.

Chuckling as he closed her door, he rounded the front of the truck to hop in the driver's side. Starting the truck and backing out of the parking lot, he looked over at her face. "Darlin', I know you can buckle yourself in, but as long as you're in my truck, I'll take care of you." Knowing she was about to protest further, he quickly added, "That's what friends are for."

Driving down the road, she wondered where they were going for dinner. They drove out of town to an elegant restaurant by a lake. "Oh, how beautiful!" she exclaimed. The sun was just starting to set over the lake and the water glistened with the sparkling colors of the sunset.

He circled around the truck and lifted her out. He lowered her slowly to the ground, keeping his eyes on hers as her feet touched the ground. Continuing to keep his hands firmly planted on her tiny waist, he was unwilling to let go.

She looked up at him. "Are we going in?" she asked with a smile.

Startled out of his musings, he just grinned and offered his arm again. She placed her hand on his arm as they entered the restaurant. They were seated in the back facing the lake, and she was thrilled with the view. The pretty hostess attempted to catch Rob's eye, but Laurie noticed that he did not pay attention to anyone other than her. In fact, it seemed as though he only had eyes for her. *We're just friends. We're just friends,* she kept telling herself.

"So how did you end up in Fairfield?" he asked after they ordered, smiling the dimpled smile that made her heart feel as though everyone in the restaurant could hear it pounding.

Peering into his face, seeing only sincerity in his blue eyes, she couldn't remember the last time a man seemed genuinely interested in her. She had always considered herself to be very open and friendly, but dating was never something she was comfortable with. High school boys just wanted to see how far they could get, and now that she thought about it, the college boys weren't much different. Determined to never be anyone's fling, she realized that she had held herself away from trying to find an actual relationship. *And of course, the first man to make my pulse race happens to be a notorious player. Just my luck.*

Returning his smile, she noticed how his eyes twinkled as they looked at her face.

"Do you really want to know or are you just making idle conversation?" she asked, watching his expression. He looked hurt, and she immediately felt contrite. "I'm sorry," she said quickly. "I guess I'm not very good at this sort of thing."

A confused look crossed his face. "Not good at what thing?"

"This," she replied, motioning her hand back and forth between them. "Having a dinner conversation with a friend that I don't really know very well." She could feel the blush creep from her neck to her hairline, feeling the heat searing her face.

Rob, understanding her discomfort, reached across the table and took her hand in his much larger one, giving it a squeeze. "Hey, this is just you and me, having dinner, getting to know each other. No pressure." He hesitated until she raised her eyes to look into his once again. "Laurie, I just want to get to know you. I've never met anyone that I wanted to talk to, enjoy being around, you know? You're...different. You make me want to be a better person. And I just...well...I just want to know you. Is that okay?"

She looked up in surprise as this generally self-confident, handsome man sitting in front of her seemed to be humbled. She couldn't help but smile, thinking how much he looked like a little boy at that moment, unsure, wanting to please. "Yeah," she said softly. "That's okay."

He smiled as though the weight of the world was lifted off him. "Well, all right. So, how did you end up here?"

She began to tell him about her life, hesitantly at first and what she considered to be the abbreviated version. But the more he listened, the more he asked questions. His interest was genuine, and for the first time in her life, she felt at ease discussing the death of her grandfather and then the accident that claimed the life of her grandmother and mother.

He realized he was holding his breath as her story unfolded, as though he were watching a movie waiting for the climatic ending that always shocked the viewers. *How could she be so positive having so much happen to her?* Wanting to reach across the table and pull her into his lap, he had to fight the urge to blanket her in his arms, keeping everything painful away from her.

She continued her story about her Aunt Emma becoming her guardian, the tiny apartment they lived in, making their way through college and working at the restaurant. She glowed when talking about those times, as though the joy of those memories resonated with her very being. She even laughed when telling him that the apartment she shared now with Carol was the first time she had a bedroom to herself.

Chuckling at the thought, she looked up into his face, and immediately the smile left hers. He was staring at her as though she were some alien creature— one he couldn't comprehend. Embarrassed, she looked back down at her food. *I shouldn't have talked so much. I shouldn't have told him about my life.* Her embarrassment quickly morphed into anger. *Well, screw him if my life seems weird! It was my life.*

Realizing that she was now feeling awkward, he

cursed himself for making her feel that way. He reached across the table to grasp her hand, desperate for contact. She tried to pull it away, but her smaller hand was no match for his much larger one.

"Oh no, babe, you don't stop now," he said. "That story was incredible. You have so much to be proud of, so much you've done." He gently rubbed tiny circles on her hand, willing her to feel what he was feeling. *I've had everything given to me. She's had to work for everything. I've never known living without. She's never had a bedroom to herself*

She raised her eyes back to his warily. "I probably bored you. I did most of the talking during dinner."

He shook his head vigorously. "No, Laurie, I wasn't bored. Amazed, impressed, awed. But bored? Never."

Smiling up at him again, she noted the way her body was reacting to what he was doing to her hand. *He's barely touching me. How is it that I can feel it all the way through me?* The electric current running from his hand through hers continued its path right to her very core. She could feel her panties getting wet and her nipples hardening, and all she could think about was ....*Stop!* She jerked her hand away from his, needing to be back in control. As soon as she did, though, she felt the loss and found herself wanting to reach back out and grab his hand again to reconnect the current.

Rob grinned, knowing what was going through her mind. *She does feel it. She's as affected by me as I am her. Thank God. But go slow. Go slow.*

Knowing that she had shared more than she was comfortable with that evening, he steered the conversation back to general subjects. She asked him about growing up in Fairfield, so he regaled her with tales of him, Jake, and Tom as boys. She laughed at their antics, thoroughly enjoying herself. As he settled the check, she excused herself to go to the ladies' room.

Looking at herself in the mirror, she wondered what he thought of her. *Just friends. Just friends,* she kept telling herself. *It doesn't matter what he thinks, we're just friends.* Raising her eyes back to the mirror, she realized, *oh yes, it does matter. I wish I didn't care, but I like him.* Sighing to herself, she left the ladies' room and walked back toward the table.

Approaching the table, she saw the hostess leaning over, her pert breasts perilously close to Rob's face. Disappointment flooded her as she realized that he couldn't even stop being a player for one night. *Friends, we're just friends. It doesn't matter if he is scoping out Miss Perky Tit of the Year!*

Determined not to be affected, she made her way over to the table, coming up behind them. She could hear his voice, speaking softly, but with an edge.

"If you don't back away right now, I'll report you to the manager," he was saying. He turned his head to the side, and Laurie could see that his eyes were on the woman's face, not her tits. And he looked...embarrassed. "And furthermore, you should have more pride than to come onto a man who is so obviously with someone else. Someone so beautiful on the inside as well as the outside. So, take this check, keep your phone number, and count yourself lucky that I don't report you!"

Laurie came to a stunned halt, frozen in place by his words. The hostess, glaring back at him, stalked off, her heels clicking on the tiled floor.

Rob cursed as he turned looking towards the ladies' room afraid of what Laurie might have seen and misinterpreted. He was startled to see her so close, standing anchored to the floor.

He jumped up from his chair, ready to defend himself, but before he could speak, she ran the few steps separating them, threw her arms around his neck, and squeezed as though her life depended on it. Stunned, he wrapped his arms around her lifting her feet off the ground.

Pressed tightly together, her face was tucked into his neck, and she could feel his heartbeat against her breasts.

His massive arms wound around her tiny body, and he was filled with a sense of rightness. He wanted to protect her, keep her safe, take care of her. *So, this is what it means to crave more than just sex.*

He could feel her arms starting to slip from his neck, and he gently set her down. Keeping his eyes on hers, he smiled. "Let's get out of here, okay?"

Smiling shyly back at him, she just nodded. He reached down, grabbed her hand, linking their fingers together as he led her outside to his truck.

This time, she did not protest as he assisted her up into the seat and buckled her in. *What am I doing? It just feels right. Friends? Or more?* Shaking her head to clear her whirling thoughts, she watched him lift his muscular frame into the driver's seat.

Looking over at her, not wanting the night to end and praying she felt the same, he asked, "Where to?"

Laurie looked down at her hands, unsure of what she felt but knowing that she was not ready for the night to end. Raising her eyes to his, she said, "We could go back to my place." He raised his eyebrow at this suggestion. She quickly explained, "I mean, Carol is gone, and we could...keep talking...I mean, that is... um, if you wanted to." Heart pounding, palms sweating, she felt the words stick in her throat.

"Babe," he said softly. He held her eyes as he reached over to cup her face with his massive hand. "There's nowhere else I rather be, than with you."

Leaning her face into his hand, she could feel the current that was becoming familiar when he was around.

Back at her apartment, he hesitated at the door. As she entered, she turned questioningly. "Don't you want to come in?"

Running his hand through his hair, he suddenly felt as awkward as a teenager, fumbling on his first date. Giggling, she grabbed his hand and pulled him in. She led him over to the sofa, sitting on one side tucking her legs up under her. He sat on the other end, twisting his body to face her.

"You haven't told me about being a fireman," Laurie inquired. "It seems exciting and yet dangerous. Have you always wanted to do that? And work with your dad?"

Rob looked over at the gorgeous woman looking expectantly at him. *When was the last time a woman wanted to sit and talk to me? When was the last time one actually asked me about me?* Feeling as though he was entering uncharted territories, he found that talking to Laurie was as natural as breathing.

Relaxing, he leaned back and answered. "My dad was the most influential person in my life. I grew up seeing him go off every day in his fireman's uniform. One day, we were out at a store, and a man came running up to him carrying a little boy. The man shook my dad's hand, thanking him over and over for saving his child's life. Other people were gathering around," he chuckled at the memory. "At first, I was embarrassed. But then I realized that my dad had rescued that man's son in a fire. That was when I realized that my dad didn't just have a job. He was a hero. I always knew he had been *my* hero. But that day, I realized he was a hero to others."

Rob sat quietly for a moment then looked back into Laurie's grey eyes. "That was the day I knew what I wanted to be when I grew up...I wanted to be my dad."

Fighting the sting in her eyes of unshed tears, she looked at the man in front of her and saw the little boy, proudly worshiping his father. Leaning over to touch his hand, she said, "Rob, you did it. You became your dad. You became a hero."

He jerked his hand out from under hers angrily. "My dad? I'm nothing like my dad! He's honorable, lives his life for others – Mom, me and my sister Suzy, the people he saves, his men." Shaking his head in disgust, he continued, "I've been a selfish prick. Went to college on a football scholarship, being the big man on campus, living the life. And I've spent the past ten years continuing that all-about-me-lifestyle." The room was blanketed in silence, neither knowing what to say.

He reached back out to take her discarded hand, locking his fingers through hers. "But being around you makes me want to be a better man. Makes me want to be more like my dad. Makes me feel like I can be something other than what I've become. And if that is just friends, then so be it. But babe, gotta put it out there—I'm hoping to become worthy to see if we've got more."

His eyes bore straight into hers, Laurie feeling their power straight to her soul. Reminding herself to breathe, she felt a pull forward as though they were magnets unable to stay separated. They both leaned forward, stopping only when their lips were barely touching. Rob stopped, allowing Laurie to be in control.

She closed her eyes, feeling his breath wash over her face. Leaning in, she softly touched her lips to his. The kiss was gentle, full of emotion. Pulling back, she looked at his handsome face, such a combination of remorse and hope. "Rob," she spoke in a whisper. "I think you're more like your dad than you realize. You have the best of him in you. It's just taken you a little while to understand it."

He moved in quickly, capturing her lips in a soul-searing kiss, moving his lips over hers in a timeless dance. Her lips were soft and pliable. He ran his tongue over her lips, and as she opened her mouth, his tongue slid in. Forcing himself to hold back, he slowly followed the contours of her mouth, discovering, exploring, memorizing. He could feel her hesitation at first before her tongue began its own journey. *I want this to be the last mouth I ever kiss.* Rob had never been so moved by just a kiss. For him, kissing was the necessary action to get a girl ready for sex, not the part that made him ache and long to just continue the kiss.

He pulled back, causing confusion to war with passion in her eyes. Rob knew that she was not ready for anything more, and for the first time, he was willing to stop at just a kiss, although he was having a hard time convincing his swollen dick of that. He gently placed his hands on her shoulders, pushing her back just a little.

"We're going to take this slow, Laurie. I want to get to know you, and you have just found out a helluva lot about me that I've never told anyone. This," he said, pointing back and for between them, "is going to happen, but at your pace."

Laurie peered into his eyes, seeing not only sincerity but vulnerability, and nodded thoughtfully. *He just shared his most inner thoughts with me.* Wanting to give something back, she blurted out, "I don't know who my father is."

He jerked back, surprise and confusion crossing his face. "What?" he asked, not understanding what she was trying to tell him.

She blushed and looked down at her hands. "Well... you shared with me...something that you haven't shared with anyone else. I just...thought...um...that I would share back. You know…something that…um…no one else knows." Suddenly feeling exposed, she tried to jump up off the couch wanting to get away before he saw tears fall.

Rob, stunned by her admission and touched by her generosity, grabbed her around the waist and pulled her onto his lap. "Oh no, baby, you shared, and I want you to share more. But face to face. Not running away." He wrapped his arms around her, pulling her in tight against his chest. For the first time, he realized that he was thinking with his head and feeling with his heart… not his dick. And the warm feeling that penetrated deep inside was welcome. He could feel her stiff body begin to relax as he rubbed her back gently.

"So, tell me, baby. Tell me what you meant," he prodded.

"It's silly, really. I don't even know why I suddenly felt like crying because I've never cried about it before. It simply is what it is." She let out a huge sigh. "I mean, I can't miss what I never had, right?"

Rob, not understanding, turned her body around so that she was facing him, straddling him with her legs on either side. He wanted her close but wanted to look into her eyes as she was struggling to reveal something.

"What have you never had, baby?"

"A father. I mean, my grandfather was basically my dad, but I always knew that he wasn't really." She sighed again, looking up into his eyes. "I'm probably not making much sense, am I?" Not waiting for an answer, she quickly added, "Never mind, it isn't important. We can talk about something else." She started to move off his lap, nervous at the closeness.

"Laurie, you starting to share means the world to me. That tells me you don't think of me as some colossal fuck-up. So don't stop now. Keep sharing. What's going on behind those stormy grey eyes of yours?"

"It's just that as you were talking about your dad, how great he is, how you always looked up to him, how you wanted to be like him, how he was such an influence on your life. Don't you see, Rob? Even though you felt like you didn't measure up, at least, you had that. You had that influence. You had that measuring stick. You had that love." Laurie paused, taking a big breath then shrugged slightly. "I never had that. I never had a father."

Rob sat perfectly still except for continually rubbing soft circles on her back as she continued her story.

"My mom was only sixteen years old when she got pregnant with me. When I was growing up, she used to tell me that they met, fell in love, and before he went away, he left her with a wonderful present – me." Her lips curved up in a tiny smile at the memory. "When I was eighteen, my Aunt Emma gave me a box that she had found among Mom's possessions that had a note saying it was for me on my eighteenth birthday. Even though Mom had no idea she wouldn't be around to give it to me herself, it was so important that she set it aside just in case something happened."

He found himself holding his breath, waiting to hear what was in the box. He fought the desire to tighten his grip on her hips, continuing instead to slowly rub her gently.

"It was a T-shirt," she stated plainly. His eyes narrowed in confusion, encouraging her to continue. "It was my father's T-shirt. It appears that he was a soldier on leave, and while she fell head over heels in love, she was only a fling to him." She sat, letting her words sink in. "So...I'm the product of a man's one-night stand...a fling."

Her words poured over Rob with the effect of a bucket of ice-cold water. *That's why she hated what I was. She looked at me and saw her father. Damn him for walking away and damn me for living that life.* He let go of her hips, allowing her to slide from his lap. He stood up and paced the room, furiously rubbing his hand through his hair.

Laurie watched him, her chest feeling squeezed as though in a vice. *He is ashamed of me. Of who I am. Of who I come from.* The stinging of unshed tears in her eyes made her angry. She never cried over not having a father, and she sure as hell wasn't going to start now. Jumping off the couch, she walked purposefully toward the front door, pulling it open. "Thank you for dinner, Rob, but it's late," she said with her head held high while motioning towards the open door.

He looked over, seeing she was pissed and knowing his reaction was not what she needed. Stalking over to her, he leaned his much taller frame around her and slammed the door shut.

Indignant, she looked up into his face. "Look, Rob, I've spent my whole life not having a father in my life.

And guess what? That is fine! I was raised by a phenomenal mother, grandparents, and then my aunt." Her chest heaved with emotion and the tears that she had held back began to slide down her cheeks. "Maybe my being a bastard to a man who never hung around long enough to see an obligation or to be born to a teen mom is something that you can't handle in a friend, but that's who I am." She dashed the tears off her face as she unashamedly looked directly into his eyes. "And if you can't accept that or me, then screw you!"

He pressed his fingers to her lips, effectively shushing her. "Laurie, you got me all wrong. You shared, and I took it in. Babe, I'm not ashamed of you. I'm awed by you."

Her eyes registered doubt at his words and yet her traitorous body noticed how it felt to have his fingers on her lips. She fought the urge to pull his fingers into her mouth.

He hung his head, breaking eye contact as he admitted, "Honey, it's just that I'm ashamed of me. Don't you see, even though I promise you that I've never fathered a child, I was like your dad. Your words hit hard. I know they weren't directed at me, but I felt them."

At that, he leaned his body down, removed his fingers, and replaced them with his mouth. As his lips touched hers, she thawed. He felt the tension drain from her body as he moved closer. Reaching down, he lifted her up in his arms, his lips never leaving hers. The kiss was filled with longing, promise, hope. His arms wrapped around her securely, and he felt her grasp his biceps. *Please let me take care of you. Please feel this.*

Drowning in the feelings of his lips on hers, she felt the anger drain away, replaced by desire, longing. His kiss was so gentle, and her breasts felt heavy, and her nipples hardened as they were pressed against his chest. He moved his muscular thigh upwards between her legs, and she felt the pressure against her core. The tingling deep in her core seemed to connect her lips, her breasts, and her swollen clit. She heard moaning and was surprised to realize that it was coming from her.

Rob slid his hand upwards from her hip to the bottom of her breast. She was beginning to squirm on his thigh, trying to ease the building ache. He pulled his lips away from hers, and she mourned the loss. He gently lowered her feet to the floor, slowly separating their bodies. She looked up at his face, questioningly.

He leaned over and touched his forehead to hers, breathing her in. "Laurie, I want to stay. I want to take you back to your room and make love to you."

At that, her eyes opened wide. He smiled down into her beautiful face.

"Yeah, I know what I said. Make love. Not screw. Not fuck." He paused to let those words sink in. "I'm ready but know you're not." He took her hand and led her back to the sofa where he pulled her down next to him. "We've covered a lot of territory tonight," he said in awe, realizing he had never divulged so much to any woman before.

Smiling back at him, she nodded. "Yeah, we went to dinner as friends just getting acquainted and somehow ended up telling our deepest secrets." Laurie reached out and laid her hand on his. They both looked down at their hands together. Hers... small, white, dainty. His... large, tan, rough. Clasped together, harmonious.

"Rob, tell me what you're thinking," she begged. "I need to know what's in your mind. I don't want to have to guess what you're thinking."

He nodded, agreeing. "Let's make a pact right now. Honesty. I'm not going to lie to you, baby. Ever. No secrets."

Smiling the smile that took his breath away, she entwined her fingers with his.

"I was telling you the truth earlier, Laurie. Never met a woman I wanted to get to know until you. I want you in my life. If we can only be friends, then I'll take that. But I want more, and I'm going to work at us being more. But I know I'm not worthy of you yet. I need to work on that, babe. You make me want to be a better man. A man like my dad."

Rob, standing and pulling her up from the sofa, kissed her goodnight then walked to the door. Glancing back over his shoulder, he called out, "I'll see you tomorrow, babe. Lock up."

Laurie shut, locked, and leaned against the door, smiling to herself. She couldn't decide if she was exhausted or elated. Heading to bed, she realized it was both. It was time to call Emma.

8

"Miss Dodd, how can you tell if a boy likes you?" little Josie asked. Laurie looked down at the red-haired pixie, smiling as they were walking out to the playground.

"Do you have a boy that you think likes you?" Laurie asked, bending down to be at Josie's level.

"Well, Billy says I have freckles and says they look funny. But my mom says that means he likes me." Josie wrinkled up her freckled nose, deep in thought. "But if he really likes me, he wouldn't tease me, would he?"

Tossing her long braid over her shoulder, Laurie pondered how to answer her little charge. "Well, I know that sometimes when little boys like girls they do tease them because they haven't learned how to say something sweet yet. Maybe you should just ask him."

Josie and the other little girls around burst into giggles as they continued their way outside. "Miss Dodd, Miss Dodd!" the girls began to shout. Turning around, Laurie looked to the other side of the playground and saw Rob walking towards her with a huge bouquet of flowers. Blushing, feeling the heat crawl up from her chest to her scalp, Laurie tried to control her class. Clapping her hands, she sent them over to the playground equipment. Rob walked over with a broad grin, not pausing until he was a respectable couple of feet away and looked down at her. Her eyes did not leave his as he approached, as though she had no will when he was near.

"Miss Dodd, you look lovely today," he greeted holding the flowers out towards her, his grin evolving into a huge smile.

Still blushing, Laurie took the flowers in her hands looking at them with awe. The riot of color burst forth in a dazzling array. Raising her eyes back to his, she replied, "Thank you, Mr. MacDonald. These are beautiful. I've never gotten flowers before."

Rob was shocked and yet secretly pleased. Knowing he was the first to bring her such a pure pleasure made him want to be the one to always bring a smile to her face. Looking down, he took in her silky braid, flawless skin, pink T-shirt, cute denim skirt, and simple sandals showing off her painted pink toes. Taking her all in, he wished he could tell his dick to behave, but it seemed to have a mind of its own when she was around. Knowing she was working and determined to be a gentleman, he gave her a wink and a quick bow as he turned, walking back to his truck.

"Mr. Fireman," a voice called from the playground. Rob turned back around, facing a group of little girls all standing with Laurie looking at her flowers.

"Do you like our teacher? She says you should just ask a boy whether or not he likes you."

Rob threw his head back and laughed and then looked directly into Laurie's eyes. "Why yes, ma'am, I do like your teacher." Still laughing, he trotted over to his truck, feeling lighter with each step.

———

"What's on your mind?" Emma asked. Laurie had been calling her almost every day since arriving in Fairfield.

"Can a leopard change his spots?"

Emma laughed, and she couldn't help but laugh along with her. "I sound stupid, don't I?" She continued, "It's just that I feel like I've been all over the place since meeting Rob. I thought he was gorgeous and interested, then saw him as a player and wanted nothing to do with him. Then he seemed to want to just be friends. Then we had a friend date, and everything changed that night. Now, I have no idea."

"Laurie, what does your heart say? Honey, you have to trust your judgment," Emma answered.

"My heart says he's funny, handsome, caring, strong, protective, wonderful and seems to really like me. In the past couple of weeks, he's taken me out, made me feel that he is only interested in me and been a perfect gentleman. But my head keeps thinking that he's been a player for so long, can he just change? What if I get hurt?"

Emma sighed, choosing her words carefully. "Laurie, you can't control what he did before he met you. You have to decide what kind of man he is now. And sweetie, you cannot judge every man by your father."

"My father? I never even think of my father. I never knew him, so how could I judge any man against him?"

Emma could hear Laurie's anger searing through her words. "You've always said that you never think of him, but do you realize that every time you have gotten close to someone, you always pull back? You've never had sex because you're afraid of being someone's one-night stand. You've never made that step into an adult relationship, fearing hurt and eventually being left behind. Stop living in your mom's time or your dad's time. If you don't take a chance, you'll never find your time."

Emma's words poured over Laurie slowly, dripping into the corners of her mind. The corners where she did not like to look. Those words from anyone else would have brought immediate denial, but from Emma? Her aunt knew Laurie's every thought, feeling, heartbeat.

Sighing heavily, she knew Emma was right. She did hold herself back. Doing so kept her from being hurt. It also kept her from finding love.

Hanging up the phone with new resolve, she decided it was time to give Rob a chance.

"Miss Dodd, Miss Dodd!" The kids, jazzed up on Halloween candy, were the unruliest she had ever seen. Another teacher popped her head into the classroom to let Laurie know that they were going to the cafeteria about fifteen minutes later than usual.

"Why?" she asked in frustration. "These kids are about ready to chomp on each other if they can't get to lunch and eat something besides candy," she moaned. "And quite frankly, I'm hungry too!"

"I hear you," the other teacher agreed. "Rumor is something is wrong with the ovens in the kitchen. My kids have headed on down to the music room.

Forcing a smile on her face, she turned back to her class to give them an activity to last until lunch. Several minutes later a loud blast roared through the building, shaking the entire room like an earthquake. Ceiling tiles fell, books tumbled from shelves, chairs were knocked over, and the lights overhead went out. The children, in a panic, began to scream, and she frantically tried to calm them. The fire alarm sounded, and Laurie rushed to get the children lined up to go outside. As she opened the door, the smoke billowing down the hall had her shutting the door quickly.

Oh, God. The stairs are blocked. Shit, shit, shit!

Grabbing the phone in the room to check for directions, she found there was no dial tone. Running to the door one more time to ascertain the condition of the hall, she could tell the smoke was right outside the door. Slamming the door again, she turned to the windows.

The windows. It has to be the windows!

The school's fire alarms were tied in directly to the fire station just down the road. As soon as the bell sounded, the men jumped into action not knowing initially where the fire was located. The dispatcher came over the speaker announcing the location of the fire being at Fairfield Elementary School, and the firemen quickly and efficiently rolled out.

Rob's heart pounded with fear upon hearing their location. Never had he headed out to a fire located where he knew someone. Mac glanced over at his son, knowing full well the emotions that were overwhelming him. A fireman who cannot concentrate on his job could put others at risk and Mac was too good a chief to allow that to happen.

"Son, you need to stay focused. Can you do this?"

Rob's eyes cut over to his dad. Giving him a curt nod, he forced his heartbeat to slow, going over the elementary school's fire plans in his mind. *Oh Jesus, keep her safe.*

Laurie could already hear the sirens of fire trucks pulling next to the school, and running over to the windows, she could see that most of the teachers and students were getting out of the building. If the classroom next to hers was already emptied, that only left her classroom trapped on this end of the building where the fire was closest.

Pulling open the small window, she leaned her head out and began to yell. Torn between trying to calm the children and making enough noise that someone would see them warred inside. She could see Ms. Darby running around the corner with a crew of firemen.

Looking up, they motioned for one of the fire trucks to pull closer to the building. Turning back around, she squatted down momentarily to reassure the students. Gathering them quickly around her, she spoke calmly.

"Okay, guys, we're getting ready for an adventure, but we have to be careful; we have to stay calm and quiet so you can hear my instructions. Okay?"

The children, frightened and crying, nodded in understanding. Right then, she heard a man's voice calling to her. "Laurie."

Rob. He came. His voice washed over her, sliding deep inside, soothing her fear, calming her nerves. Whirling around, her eyes immediately found his.

"What do I need to do?" she asked running over to the window, seeing him standing on a ladder coming from the fire truck below. She could see fire hoses spraying off to her right where the flames were coming from the kitchen.

"Laurie, look at me. Babe. Look. At. Me," he ordered. Her eyes, large in fear, cut back over to his. "Stay with me, Laurie. Got me?"

Focusing, she nodded. "Okay. What do I do?"

"Line the children up and start helping them through the window. It's a small window, but these kids will fit through. Let me know if there are any injuries or special needs. We've got plenty of help as soon as we get them through the window."

She turned and clapped her hands to get the children's attention. Twenty-four little faces looked up, fearful but sure in the knowledge that she would take care of them. She picked up the first child closest to her and held her to the window. Helping the child to sit on the windowsill, holding them tightly, she supported them until Rob took the little girl and handed her to the next man in the chain. The window was small, but the children fit through easily, and the firemen worked quickly and efficiently. Eyes stinging and arms aching, she continued helping the children out of the window into the waiting arms of the heroes.

"Rob, this is Sammie. He's partially deaf but has a hearing aid."

Rob's calm voice continued to encourage and soothe, as though he knew exactly what she needed each moment. Glancing down at the ground, she could see her children being cared for by a community of firemen, volunteers, teachers, parents, and rescue workers.

"Rob, this is my very *special* friend, Carla."

He noticed the little girl with down's syndrome looking terrified. He held her gently and carefully, talking to her calmly as he passed her to the next fireman.

Rob turned back to Laurie. His eyes were constantly on her, measuring her emotions and physical strain. *Do the job. Do the job,* he kept telling himself. In all of his years as a fireman, he had never been so personally involved in a rescue. Heart pounding, he continually handed down each child to the next man on the team.

"That's it. That's all," she announced, unsure what to do next.

"Baby, I want you to back away from the window. I'm going to break several windows to make a larger space for you to get out."

Nodding in shock, she ran to the other side of the room. She watched in silent fear as Rob and another fireman on a separate ladder smashed several windows and the metal panels between them.

"Laurie, come on babe."

She ran over to the window dubiously looking at the shards of glass. Turning back to the classroom, she ran to the rubber mats in the reading corner. Grabbing a couple of them she ran back to the window.

"Good thinking," he said with pride as he watched her lay them on the windowsill to protect herself from the broken glass. "I want you to get up on the bookcase and then stick one leg out of the window. I'll get you and then we will slide you out."

After assisting in the rescue of all of her children, she hesitated. Heart pounding, sweating, stomach churning. Rob looked up questioningly.

"I'm afraid. I'm scared of heights," she confessed tearfully.

He knew the adrenaline rush was fading, and exhaustion paired with fear was going to make her rescue more difficult. "Come on, baby. Just come to me."

She focused on his beautiful face and just nodded. She climbed up on the mat covered bookcase and sat on the windowsill, hiking her long skirt up as far as she could.

"Don't look down, Laurie," he ordered. "Keep your eyes on me."

Breathing deeply, she swung her leg over the windowsill and put her tiny hand in his much larger one. At his touch, she felt warmth slide over her skin, easing her fear. She felt his fierce grip holding firm as he gently attempted to pull her from the building. *Oh Jesus, Oh Jesus, Oh Jesus. No! I can't!*

He could feel her body trembling and knew the instant that panic set in. Arms clawed their way toward him, grasping at air as her eyes were tightly shut.

"Babe, eyes on me. Eyes. On. Me," he ordered. She snapped her eyes open wide, staring straight into his. "Just look at me. Only me." Her body stilled as her eyes never left his.

Continuing to pull her away from the building, he cradled her body close to his, motioning for the truck lowering them.

The bulky fireman's uniform kept Laurie from feeling his skin, but being nestled in his arms, she never felt more sheltered. What she couldn't feel was how his arms were shaking. As they were lowered to the ground, she raised her head to look into his eyes. Seeing an emotion in them she could not identify, his piercing stare reached into her and wrapped around her heart as much as his arms surrounded her body.

Landing on the ground, the EMTs tried to take her from Rob, but he wouldn't let go. Tugging on the hem of her skirt to make sure she was well covered, he carried her away from the building over to the waiting ambulance. Tossing his hat to the side, he sat her carefully down on the edge of the ambulance. Jerking his coat off, he swept her back into his arms, firmly setting her on his lap while the EMTs came over to assess her injuries.

"I'm all right. Really, I'm fine," she protested, trying weakly to push off him. "I have to see about my kids."

Rob, not yielding, barked orders to the EMTs before gently speaking to her. "Laurie, the kids are well taken care of now. You sit here and get checked out." He felt the resistance leave her body, and he tightened his grip. Several minutes later, the EMTs declared that she did not need to go to the hospital. Ms. Darby came around to check on her, letting her know that she was released for the day, assuring her that all of the children had been picked up by their parents. The large fireman she had noticed earlier came around next. She looked up into the twinkling eyes of the fire chief, noting the resemblance to Rob.

"Well, Miss Dodd, you're the hero of the hour little missy," he boomed. Eyes wide, she just smiled at his commanding voice. Mac looked at his son, holding her firmly in his arms. Grinning broadly, Mac clapped his hand on Rob's back, "Looks like she's a keeper, son."

Giving his dad a head nod, he just tightened his arms securely around her.

9

Driving home, Rob called Tom to fill him in, knowing Carol would be concerned. "Tell Carol she's okay. She's with me. Yeah, going home. Yeah. Will do. Later."

Laurie looked wearily over at Rob not under-standing any of the conversation he just had with Tom. He had been so quiet since they left the school. Too tired to ask, too tired to care, she just laid her head back on the truck headrest. The truck came to a stop, and he walked around to help her out. Reaching in, he pulled her into his arms. She knew it was useless to protest and found that she really didn't mind being pampered at the moment.

"Where are we?" she asked, realizing he had not taken her home.

"My apartment," he answered. Looking down at her exhausted face, he kissed her forehead as he entered his place. Setting her feet gently down on the floor, he held her until he felt sure she was steady. Eyes reaching hers, he queried, "Hungry?"

"Kinda," she answered back truthfully. "We didn't get lunch. But I'm almost too tired to eat."

Nodding, he led her into the kitchen, sitting her on one of his stools. Getting out a couple of eggs and a frying pan, he quickly made scrambled eggs and toast. Serving it with a glass of milk, he set the plate in front of her.

She managed to get several bites of food in before the exhaustion overtook her. She could feel her chin begin to quiver. Eyes swimming with tears, she looked up at his firm profile. He circled around the kitchen bar and grasped her in his massive arms once again.

"Oh Rob, what if you weren't there? What if I couldn't have gotten the kids out?" She began to cry. "You saved me. You came for me."

He held her carefully, slowly rubbing circles on her back, kissing the top of her head, allowing her the release of pent-up fear and anxiety. "Baby," he said softly, "scared the shit out of me today. No lying. We got the call about the school, and my heart stopped. We pulled up outside, and I saw you hanging out of the window yelling– girl, I couldn't breathe. The whole time all I wanted to do was get you in my arms."

"But Rob, you're a hero. You got all those kids out and saved all of us. What you are and what you do is amazing," she said, looking up.

Leaning down so his lips were near hers, he could feel his breath mingling with hers. "*You* got those kids out. *You* kept calm, and *you're* the reason every one of those families tonight can tuck their kids in bed knowing they are safe."

At those words, tears began to fall freely, and sobs started to shake her whole body. He scooped her up and carried her back to his bedroom, crossing through it towards the bathroom. He set her down gently and turned on the water in the bathtub.

"Baby, you're exhausted. I want you to take a hot bath and relax. I'll be back with something for you to wear."

Pulling off her sooty, sweaty clothes, she climbed into the tub. Sinking into the water, she allowed the soothing warmth to lull her to sleep. Waking as the water cooled, she got out, cracked open the door to the bedroom and saw clean boxers and an FFD T-shirt lying on the bed. Quickly snatching them, she ran back to the bathroom and put them on. Self-conscious, she didn't know what she was supposed to do. Sneaking back out into the bedroom, she heard noises coming from the kitchen. She walked to the door and looked down the hall, just as he was coming around the corner.

He halted in mid-step, his eyes doing a body sweep then coming back to settle on her eyes. *Never wanted a woman in my shirt before. Jesus, I want her in nothing but my shirts!*

"Thanks for the clothes," she said, not knowing what else to say.

He took three steps to get to her, took her face in his large hands and brought his lips down to hers. The kiss seared her down to her toes. She immediately threw her arms around his neck to pull him down closer. He responded by lifting her up, never releasing the torturous kiss. She granted him access on a moan, and he plunged his tongue into her mouth. Desperate, needy, his tongue plundered every crevice of her mouth as though longing to memorize the feelings.

Emotionally drained from the day's traumatic events, she no longer cared if she was going to be his next conquest. She only cared that his mouth never leave hers, his body stay pressed up against her breasts, his hand continue to knead her ass. To hell with guarding her heart, she wanted all that he had to give at that moment.

He slowly let her body slip down his until she could reach the floor while continuing to keep his arms wound tightly around her. He began to lift his head, separating their lips. She felt the loss immediately and tried to reach back up to pull him in. He continued to lean away from her, and the realization that he was distancing himself finally made its way through her lust-filled mind.

"Babe, we can't," he said with such regret, she could have sworn there were tears in his words. "We have to stop now."

"Why?" she asked, not understanding his rejection.

He looked into her expressive eyes, seeing her pain. "No, Laurie. I'm not saying no to us. I'm saying no to us *tonight.*" Seeing the confusion in her expression, he continued. "Laurie, you've had an ass-kicking day. You're tired and vulnerable right now. When we do this, it's going to mean something to me. And when we do, you're going to know exactly what it means to me, so you don't walk away with any doubts about us."

Placing his hand on the back of her head, he pulled her back against his chest. She felt his heart beating next to her face, its tempo keeping time with hers. *Care. He's taking care of me. He cares for me.* Closing her eyes, doubts slipping away, she gave in to the moment. Feeling herself being picked up and cradled in his arms, she was carried over to the turned-down bed and tucked in.

He leaned down to place a light kiss on her lips before backing out of the room.

"Rob," she called softly. She lifted the covers next to her, eyes beckoning. Grinning, he dropped his jeans and slid under the covers next to her. Pulling her back up against his chest, he blanketed her with his embrace. Secure, safe, protected, cared for. Laurie had never slept with a man but was totally at ease with Rob. Eyes heavy, she drifted off to sleep, resting in the arms of the man she was falling in love with.

He lay there watching her sleep for hours. Her beauty and courage seeped through him, slipping into the cracks of his soul. Thoughts racing, he knew this was different. She was different. For a moment, he allowed a parade of faceless women to pass through his mind. He had never brought a woman to his apartment. He never slept through the night with a woman. He always made sure they knew the score. Once the deed was done and both were satisfied, he left with a smile thinking how great it was to be free.

Now, he saw that freedom as a chain, one that kept him from experiencing feelings of care, support, trust, love. *Love? Is that what is happening?* Funny, he thought –

that word no longer frightened him. Pulling her in close, he slept.

Laurie began to awaken but was disoriented and felt immobile. Glancing down, she recognized the large arm wrapped around her chest and the muscular leg thrown over hers. *Rob.* Smiling, she snuggled her back deeper into his chest, feeling his deep breathing.

Eyes popping open, she realized that she was feeling more than his deep breathing if the bulge pressing into her ass was any indication. *Oh, my.* She may have been innocent, but she was not ignorant, and the size of the bulge made her wonder how that would ever fit. The light of day made her choice clear. No fear. No second guessing. No turning back.

She wiggled around to face him, his eyes now open wide, taking her in. Her sleep-tousled hair, pale complexion, expressive grey eyes. Eyes looking directly at him. She leaned over, placing her lips on his. Gently, at first, she moved her lips over his, as though exploring the texture, the feel, the movement of them together. The kiss became deeper, giving in to more longing, holding more promise. He rolled so that his large body completely covered hers, holding his torso up by his arms while allowing his erection to continue to press into her.

The kiss, having a life force of its own, consumed them as their tongues began to move together, twirling around each other in an erotic dance. She could feel her

hips rising to press harder against his, searching for...
something. Something she needed, wanted, desired.

He raised his head from her lips, questioning, "Are
you sure, baby? You better be sure 'cause this is no fuck.
This happens, you're mine. No turning back, no regrets.
I don't deserve you, but I'll sure as shit work every day
to be the man you deserve to have."

Her eyes held warmth as she stared into the handsome face that rested only a few inches from hers.

"You with me, Laurie?" he asked once more. *Please,
baby, be sure. Please let me love you. Please let me work every
day for the rest of my life deserving you.*

Speaking in a whisper, she answered, "I get you, Rob.
I want this. I want you. No turning back. No regrets."

"Thank God," he said, his mouth claiming hers once
more. Startled, he felt her small hands on his chest
pushing him away. Leaning back, he raised an eyebrow
at her. She seemed nervous, not looking at him. "Babe,
eyes on me." Her eyes immediately shot to his held there
by his gaze. "What's going through that beautiful mind?"

Licking her lips, sending him to distraction, she
faltered, "I need to...well, it's just that...I...don't really
know...well, you..."

"Babe, whatever it is, just say it. If you don't want to
do this now, it'll stop. We're going at your pace, Laurie."

"I'm a virgin," she blurted out.

The words, like water over a dam that once out
cannot be pulled back, hung between them in silence.
Looking to the side, she could feel the blush burning
from her chest to her hairline, flaming everything in
between.

He was stunned at her words yet strangely at ease with her confession. In fact, he felt the oddest feeling of pride. *I may be a caveman, but damn – I'm the first.* He looked back down into her innocent face. *And I sure as hell will be her last.* Sensing her embarrassment, he quickly lowered his lips back to hers.

Speaking against her lips, as softly as a whisper, he told her, "I'm so glad you shared before this happened. I wanted it to be perfect for you, but now I know to make sure it goes slow and gentle as well."

Taking her lips back in a soft kiss that quickly spun into world-shattering territory, she gave in to the feelings. Leaning to one side, he slid one hand under the T-shirt she was wearing, halting in its path on her breast. Kneading the heavy weight in his hand, he captured her moans in his mouth. Encouraged, he gently pulled on her nipple, eliciting squirming from underneath him. Smiling, he slid her shirt over her head, rising back up to look at her stunning breasts. They were full and pale, with rosy peaked nipples, aching for his mouth.

Obliging, he lowered his mouth to the closest nipple, sucking hard, swirling his tongue around the hardened bud. Pulling it deeply into his mouth, his hand continued its exploration, over her stomach, down her hips, and into the boxers she was wearing. Jesus, she was so wet for him, he could feel himself almost lose control. *Focus man, focus. Go slow.*

Her head was swimming with sensations she had never known. The feeling of his mouth on her nipples had her wanting to push her breasts upwards toward his face for more. His hand slid down to her folds moving around in the moisture that had pooled there. Her hips began the age-old mating dance pushing upwards towards his cock. Suddenly, she felt him slide a finger in her slick folds creating a sensation that began to overtake her. His tongue moved in and out of her mouth mimicking the action of his finger.

The pressure deep in her core began to build, to what end, she had no idea. It was as though she were running towards a goal knowing the finish line would be the ultimate high. Feeling him add another finger to her dripping sex, crooking it deeply inside, she crossed the finish line, bursting into flames that threatened to consume her as her inner muscles grabbed at his fingers. The sensations reverberated from her sex outwards in all directions. Breathing heavily, she panted, trying to suck oxygen into her lungs. As the tingling subsided, she felt weightless in the aftermath of her race. Opening her eyes, she looked up at his face staring down at her.

"Is it supposed to be that way?" she wondered out loud, unsure of his reaction.

Emotion overtook him as he realized he had never experienced that – watching a woman come apart in his hands for the first time and knowing that he truly cared about her. Not just did she get off. Not just was she ready for the next one. Not just is it time to do it and get on my way.

Saying nothing, he dove in for another toe-curling kiss. Plundering her mouth, he explored each crevice while bringing his hand back up to her breast, kneading it in his palm. Feeling her hips begin to undulate again, he leaned over to grab a condom from the nightstand. Feeling her stiffen, he looked down knowingly.

"Babe, no woman has ever been in this bed."

Her eyes shot to his in doubt.

"It's true, Laurie. There are no ghosts here in this apartment. No ghosts in this room, in this bed. Just you. You're the first and only woman I ever wanted to be here. And you're going to be the last."

Looking into her face, relieved when he saw her smile, he tore off the edge of the condom wrapper. She slid her hands down to his cock feeling the silky hardness there. Her hand would not circle it completely, but she worked it up and down as best as she could, trying to remember what she had learned from her romance novels.

"Whoa there, Laurie. This'll end before it begins." He rolled the condom on and placed his cock at her entrance. Hesitating, he wondered what to do. *Jesus, how can someone who has fucked as much as I have not have a clue how to do this. Fast, hard, unemotional is the only thing I've ever done. Slow it down, ease it in.* In the past, Rob only cared that his partner got off, but he had never cared if they were comfortable, nurtured - all the things that he wanted for Laurie.

With his cock at her entrance, he slowly pushed, easing himself in. *Oh man, she is tight.* The sensations that felt so amazing to him, he realized would make it uncomfortable for her. Keeping his eyes on hers, he used her facial expressions to see how she was doing.

Wincing, with her eyes shut tight, she tried to relax as the sensation of fullness and pressure built.

"Laurie, don't want to hurt you, babe, but I don't know how not to."

She just nodded, keeping her eyes tightly closed.

He continued to push his cock deeper, unsure how far to go. *I've always just slammed it in, knowing the woman could take it.* His partners never seemed to mind as they would moan loudly or scream, "oh baby"!

"Need your eyes on me. I've got to know how slow to go to make this better for you."

She answered him by pushing her hips up as far as they would go, impaling his dick in her. Gasping at the fullness and momentary pain, she felt him halt his motion. Looking into his deep Irish blue eyes, she smiled. "I'm okay, honey."

Rob began sliding in and out of her tight channel stroking her gently then with a little more force and watching her face carefully. Gratefully, he saw no pain but a look of contentment crossing her expression. Emboldened, he leaned down to take her lips again.

Laurie felt her bottom lip being nipped by his teeth, the pain quickly being replaced by his gently sucking. The feeling she had earlier with just his fingers was amplified by his cock, its thickness sliding in and out of her core, also pressed on her clit, driving her mad with longing. The fleeting thought of her romance novels swept through her mind. *I want to do this right. I need to make sure I do everything I'm supposed to.* The thoughts were quickly forced out as she gave herself over to the sensations she was feeling deep inside.

"Rob, I need...."

"What do you need, babe?" he said.

"I...don't...know...just...More!"

Grinning, he began to move faster, her tight muscles grabbing at his dick as he pumped deep inside. *Never. It's never felt like this.* He reached down between them pinching her nipple and rolling it between his fingers.

That was all it took to bring Laurie hurling into oblivion, electricity sparking from deep inside her core outwards to every corner of her being. Screaming his name, she felt her sex tighten over and over, wanting to drag out the sensations to the end of time.

Rob, completely blown away by the power of her orgasm, pumped a few more times then joined her. Head raised, neck tight as he powered through his own release, he pulsated deep inside of her. Crashing down on top of her, he was vaguely aware that he was crushing her but felt unable to move.

Laurie, feeling his massive weight, gently massaged his back not wanting him to move. Rob, awareness returning as his ragged breathing eased, slid out and moved to the side. Hearing her mewling at the loss, he chuckled in pride.

"I'm not gone, babe, just letting you breathe." After a few minutes of letting the warmth spread over them at the enormity of what they had just done, he rolled off the bed and stalked to the bathroom.

She watched his ass as he stalked away. She couldn't help but smile as she realized that it was his ass that first grabbed her attention in the grocery store. *God, that's a beautiful ass.*

He returned, having disposed of the condom, carrying a warm washcloth.

Embarrassed, she tried to pull up the sheet.

"Let me take care of you," he said, pulling the sheet back down. "And never hide that beauty from me." He gently wiped the cloth between her legs, noting the slight smear of blood. Shaking his head, he felt the air leaving his lungs. It was one thing to be told the woman you love is a virgin, but seeing the physical evidence was overwhelming. *Love?* He smiled to himself. *Yeah, Love. That's what this is.*

Rubbing her hands on his chest, marveling at the expanse of muscle underneath her fingers, she looked into his eyes. Licking her lips nervously, she asked, "Is it always like that?" She hated having to be compared to all the other women he ever had, but she was so afraid she fell short of his expectations.

Rob, seeing the doubt in her beautiful eyes, knew she felt insecure. *My reputation is making her feel this way.* Cupping her face in his hand, he stroked her cheek with his thumb. Leaning down so that his lips were almost touching hers, breaths mingling, he said, "Laurie, it's never felt like that for me. Blew me away. You're my dream, Laurie, and I need to say it upfront. I'm in love with you. Never said that to anyone either. I know it's too soon for you, but a man like me, I feel it, I say it."

He looked into her expressive eyes that filled with tears.

"I love you too, Rob. I was just afraid...."

He interrupted, "Laurie, from the moment I met you, months ago, there's been no other woman. Told you I was going to work every day to make sure I deserved you, but you also need to know there is nothing standing between us. No other woman exists for me. Not in the past. Not in the future. I can't change my screw-ups from the past, but they have no place in what we have. Understand?"

She listened with her whole heart. *He loves me. He wants me.* Nodding, she placed her hand on the side of his face, pulling his lips in close to hers. "I got you, Rob."

Rising from the bed, he pulled her to a standing position, holding her close as their bodies touched from chest to knees. Feeling his dick rising to the occasion again, he sent her to the shower alone, knowing if he spent any more time with her naked, he wasn't going to be able to stop himself from claiming her. She may not know it, but she was too tender to be taken right now.

He watched her walk out of the bathroom, once again dressed in one of his T-shirts and boxers, rolled several times at the hips to keep them up. Her wet hair was slicked back from her face, grey eyes clear and shining up at him as she walked across the room. She looked so natural in his apartment. *I want this every day. I want her here every day. I want her in my life forever.*

He hopped into the shower while she cooked breakfast for them. Turning on the large flat-screen TV while they ate, the local news was full of stories about the school fire and the heroic actions of the new first-grade teacher and the fireman that risked their lives to save the children.

His phone pinged with an incoming message, and he looked down. "Laurie, it's Tom. His text says Carol's been trying to get hold of you."

Grabbing her phone from her purse, she looked up

in shock. "I have thirty-seven missed calls." Most were from Carol and Emma, but several were from the newspaper and local television station. Calling Emma first and then Carol, she assured them she was fine and had spent the night with Rob so that she could be cared for. Both women read between the lines and knew that something had happened. Promising to talk to them later, she hung up.

Rob smugly looked over. "Your girls wanting details?"

Giggling, she just vaguely answered, "Maybe."

"Well make sure you tell them I was awesome!" he joked, kissing her quickly.

She just smiled, knowing those words were exactly what she would be saying to them.

10

The rest of the week was busy as Laurie and the other teachers met to find out what to do about their classes. The fire was contained in the kitchen and stairwell, but there was smoke and water damage to the classrooms nearest that area. The city's building architects declared the rest of the building to be safe, but the school remained closed while the school board came up with a plan for the clean-up and feeding the children during lunches. It was finally determined that the town's middle school, which was just down the street, would provide sack meals for the elementary children until the kitchen was repaired.

Laurie walked into her classroom, looking at the plywood covering the broken window. Drawn to it, she reached out, her hand resting on the windowsill that she had lifted the children through. Heart pounding, she took a step back. The knowledge that Rob was her savior gave her comfort, but the memories of that day still caused her palms to sweat.

"You okay?" Jean asked, slipping into the room behind Laurie. Jean Roberts was the school social worker.

Smiling, Laurie turned and leaned over for a hug. "You here to check me out?" she asked, only partially joking.

Jean looked back and smiled. "Nah, I'm here as a friend."

Laurie laughed. "I'm okay. I was just having a moment there – remembering how lucky we all were. And I really miss the kids; I can't wait till they get back."

"You're a great teacher Laurie. That's a gift you know," Jean said, peering deeply into her friend's eyes. Laurie felt herself blush. Jean continued, "I'm serious. You care, you give, you have a great capacity for putting others first. Your parents must be proud."

At this, Laurie's eyes jerked away.

Apologizing, Jean realized she touched a nerve. Laurie squeezed Jean's hand. After having told Rob about her father, the secret seemed to no longer have the power to choke her as it once did.

"It's fine, it really is," Laurie assured her. "Quite simply, my wonderful mother was a teen mom, and both she and my grandparents showered me with love. I lost them all by the time I was twelve, but then my Aunt Emma stepped in and became my mom, sister, and aunt all rolled into one. So yes, they would be proud." She hesitated then, feeling comfortable with Jean, she continued. "My mother was a one-night stand to my father, and he never knew I existed and never wanted to."

Jean was thoughtful for a moment then boldly asked, "How do you know he never wanted to know about you if he never knew you existed?"

Shocked, Laurie stood as though rooted to the floor. *What? Of course, he didn't care. A fling - isn't that what Mom's letter said. But...if he never knew I existed, how can I be sure?* After her childhood years of imagining her father as a prince that her mother loved, then to have the image of him as a player who used her as a fling, maybe she had never seen the real man.

"I'm just curious. Have you ever tried to find him?" Jean asked.

Laurie decided that since Jean knew some of her history, she might as well tell her the rest. She told her of the stories she heard growing up, about the prince her mother fell in love with and then the T-shirt with his name on it that she received when she was eighteen. Jean listened in fascination to the story.

"I just never thought about finding him. I never needed to. I never missed what I never had," Laurie told her, hearing the words that she had said countless times over the years whenever Emma would ask if she wanted to search for her father.

Jean stood to leave and patted Laurie's hand. Looking down, she replied, "Sometimes knowing what we missed is painful. But often not knowing our past chokes up our future. I wonder... your mother gave you his shirt, but she was hoping she would be the one to give it to you. What answers would she have given you to the questions you have? She never sought him out but must have known that it was something you might want to do once his name was revealed."

With that, Jean left the room, leaving Laurie staring at her friend's back. Knowing her mom's adolescent reasons for keeping his name a secret, she wondered what purpose her mom had for sharing once she was an adult. Shaking her head, trying to remove the tangled thoughts crowding in, she stood and headed home. *Time for another chat, Emma.*

Laurie and Carol stood in her room looking into her closet once again. Now that she had a steady paycheck, Laurie had been able to purchase more clothes, but she was still clueless as to what to wear to meet Rob's parents.

"Augghhhh," she cried out, flopping down on her bed. "What do you wear to meet the parents of your boyfriend? I have no idea how to do this!"

Carol laughed, both at Laurie's indecision over clothes and hearing Rob being called her boyfriend. She knew Tom's player ways had ceased once they began dating, and she was sure that Rob would be the same. Tom had been doubtful that Rob would ever settle down, but she kept telling him that when the right woman came along, Rob would realize what he wanted and how to get it.

"No idea how to dress or no idea how to be Rob's girlfriend?"

"Both." Laurie, still lying back on the bed, raised her

head up to look at her friend. "It's happened several times, you know?"

Carol, with a questioning gaze, sat down next to Laurie on the bed. "What's happened, honey?"

Laurie stared at the ceiling, feeling tears starting to slide down her face. Taking a deep breath, she explained, "Running into some of his old fuckbuddies."

"Oh, Laurie. I'm so sorry." Carol paused for a moment, lost in thought. "The same thing happened a time or so with me, but at least most of Tom's old conquests were out of town, so I didn't have to be constantly reminded."

Laurie lay still, wiping the tears before sitting up. "I know Rob feels horrible when it happens. I even tell myself that it will eventually stop. Oh, I don't know," she said with exasperation as she shook her head.

"You want to tell me about them?"

Laurie barked out a noise of frustration, ruefully shaking her head again. Sighing in resignation, she looked up at Carol's sympathetic face and agreed. "Last week we were coming out of his mom's bakery, laughing at something she had said. God, Carol, I felt so happy at that moment. His arm was wrapped around me, and everything just felt so...right. So...real. Then two women came out of a shop, took one look at Rob and walked over as though I wasn't even there. One tried to press her boobs right onto his arm, and the other was placing her hand on his chest before he could pull us back. You want to know what happened next?"

Carol, almost afraid to agree, feeling nauseous, just nodded her head.

"They asked if he wanted to do a threesome again! Again! Jesus, that means he did it before!"

"What did Rob say?"

Taking a cleansing breath, Laurie admitted, "He was angry. Embarrassed. Upset. Afraid I was upset. He jerked back from them, saying that he was with me now." Hanging her head, she continued the torrid story. "One of them just said that I was welcome to join."

"Oh God, honey, I'm so sorry," Carol said as she placed her arm around Laurie.

"Of course, Rob was beyond furious at that time. He called them a few choice names, told them to get away from him and said that he had better never hear of them speaking to me again. Then he literally pulled me down the street away from them." She paused again, collecting her thoughts. "It was awkward as hell. He didn't know what to say. I didn't either. I mean what do you say to that? 'Gee honey, are you sure you don't want a four-some tonight?' I finally told him to take me home – the day was ruined, after all. He was afraid I would walk away from him."

Looking back into Carol's face, she continued, "I thought about it. I found myself wondering if I could be the girlfriend of a reformed player. I feel as though whenever we're out somewhere, I'm constantly on guard. When a girl walks near us, I feel sick to my stomach wondering if she is coming over to start some-thing. There have been a couple of other times like that, but that was definitely the worst."

Squeezing her friend's shoulder, Carol replied. "Lau-rie, you're the only one who can decide if Rob is what you want. If he's worth the fight. If he's worth the trouble."

Laurie, eyes flashing, said, "Oh, I know he is worth everything. He's so much more than what those skanks see. He's so much more than what everyone sees. Hell, he's so much more than what he even sees in himself!"

Carol smiling, "So is he worth the trouble?"

Realizing what her friend had done, Laurie laughed. "Yeah, he's worth the trouble. I know he is true to me. And I know eventually the other women will all fade away." Then with a smirk, she added, "To hell, preferably!"

Laughing in agreement, Carol turned back to the closet, rummaging through Laurie's clothes again. Carol had some perfect clothes, but she was much too slim to be able to share them with Laurie.

"Go casual, but classy," Carol advised. "Bernie and Mac are down-to-earth people, and you don't want to appear stuffy. But since you're being introduced as Rob's girlfriend then you also want the classic look." She pulled out dark jeans, a hunter green sweater with a modest V-neck, and Laurie's black boots.

Glancing at the clock on the nightstand, and realizing that she was running late, she jumped into her clothes and had Carol do her makeup. Standing with their arms around each other, the two women looked into the mirror. Carol's blonde beauty gave her an angel-like quality, almost otherworldly. She was slim with a delicate look about her that belied the strength underneath.

Slightly shorter than Carol, Laurie knew she looked

much more like Emma and her mom. Petite, but with the curves she knew Rob liked, her flawless face was framed by her dark hair that hung down her back.

Their eyes meeting in the mirror, they laughed just as the doorbell rang. Opening the door together, they looked up at two of the most handsome men in Fairfield. Tom's Nordic-God looks had Carol's eyes sparkling. Laurie's pulse was racing just looking into Rob's Celtic appearance with his black hair and blue eyes.

The men were equally entranced by the vision in front of them. Tom's protectiveness came to the forefront whenever he looked into Carol's angel eyes, and Rob was always stunned that his beautiful Laurie wanted him, faults and all.

Both couples headed out into the night, promising a double date soon. With that, Rob escorted Laurie to his parents' house. He noticed that she was unusually quiet. Chancing a glance over at her profile, he could see she appeared tense.

"What's up, babe?" he asked.

Exasperated, she looked over at him. "Can you always tell what is going on with me?"

Chuckling, he replied, "Laurie, first I don't want you to hide shit from me. No matter how little you think it is, I want to know. Second, if you haven't figured it out by now, I make it my business to keep a pulse on you. That's what being with me includes. Me knowing you. Me watching out for you. Me taking care of you."

His words moved over her, wrapping around her as tightly as his arms when they lay in bed at night.

Smiling to herself, she almost forgot that he had asked a question.

"Babe," he asked gently. "What's going on in that beautiful head of yours?"

"I'm nervous about meeting your parents."

"Laurie, honey you've had coffee at my mom's shop dozens of times, and you met my dad at the school. What's to be nervous about?"

"Rob, that was different. At the coffee shop, your mom just sees me as another customer, and your dad just saw me as someone you rescued. What if they don't like me for your girlfriend? What if I don't meet their expectations?"

He pulled over to the side of the road, putting the truck into park. Pushing his seat all the way back, he gently pulled her over the console of this truck and placed her in his lap, wrapping his arms around her.

"I'm going to tell you like it is. Don't like bringing up past shit, but it's the only way to make you feel better. Fairfield isn't a huge town, and it was no secret even to my parents how my reputation was gained."

Laurie could feel herself stiffen at the reminder of his past. His arms tightened around her again.

"Eyes on me, Laurie," he gently commanded. She raised her eyes to his, relaxing at what she saw there. His blue eyes held nothing but concern.

"My parents despaired of me ever meeting someone that could love me for me and give me a chance at a future like the one they had. And it wasn't until recently that I pulled my head outta my ass and realized how my behavior reflected on them." Shaking his head at his own folly, he continued. "Mom met you months ago and was bowled over. She couldn't say enough about how pretty and sweet you were. I never told you that I spoke to my parents about you before we ever went out on that first date. So, they knew you were special. They knew I was falling. And they are over the moon about it. So, babe, you've got nothing to worry about. They already love you and approve of you."

Smiling, she cupped his face in her small hands, bringing her lips in for a gentle kiss. The kiss began to build as their tongues mated, and she sucked on his lips. Pulling back, he groaned. "Oh girl, we gotta stop. I don't want to have a hard-on walking into my mom's kitchen."

Giggling, she crawled back to her side of the truck, and he headed them back down the road. Rob's parents had moved to just outside of town when he was in college. Their home was a large, refinished farmhouse with a small barn in the back yard that they had transformed into a big rec room. The weather had gotten colder, and when they exited the truck, Mac threw open the front door ushering them inside. As soon as Laurie crossed the threshold, Mac grabbed her in a bear hug, picking her up off the floor.

Rob slapped him on the back, growling, "Dad, let her go. You're going to break her!" Laurie laughed as Mac set her gently on the ground.

"Ah, Laurie, darlin', seeing you with Rob is a sight for sore eyes! Good to have you here."

Bernie came walking in from the kitchen, with her typical apron around her waist. Pulling Laurie into a gentle, although just as heartfelt, hug, Laurie felt accepted. "Make yourself at home. I'll bring out some appetizers in just a minute."

As Rob escorted Laurie into the large comfortable family room, she noticed pictures on the fireplace mantle. Walking over, she saw several pictures of three boys at various ages from about five years old to mid-twenties.

"Oh my goodness, this is you, Tom, and Jake! You all were so cute!" Laurie exclaimed.

Rob laughed in embarrassment. "Yeah," he answered.

Mac spoke up then. "Those three were inseparable. We all lived on the same street when the boys were little, so they were friends from preschool. Played football together in high school and college. Quite the athletes, all three. Tom and Jake went on to the police academy, and Rob came home to follow his old man here with the fire department."

"Dad, I hardly think Laurie wants a dissertation on the three of us."

Laughing, she admonished Rob. "It's fine, Mr. MacDonald. I love seeing these three cuties." She wandered down the mantle looking at the other pictures. These were all of the MacDonald clan. Mac lovingly looking down at his wife and children. Rob with Suzy when she was a baby.

Rob watched her carefully and saw the exact second that a wistful look passed over her face. Knowing that she had become more sensitive about her family, he stood behind her wrapping his arms around her. Looking over her shoulder up at him, she smiled.

Right then, Bernie came in with the appetizers followed by Suzy, Rob's much younger sister. Suzy was a beauty at only sixteen, with the same coloring as Rob. Her glossy dark hair and sparkling blue eyes would surely turn the heads of the boys at her school. Laurie quickly found out that she was a sophomore in high school, had straight A's, and was interested in a boy named Brad Evans.

Rob rolled his eyes. "Not happening, Suzy."

Suzy huffed, and Laurie could sense an argument brewing between the siblings. She looked quizzically at Rob.

Suzy looked at Laurie asking, "Did you have an older brother? 'Cause sometimes they suck! He tries to tell me I can't date until I'm twenty!"

Laurie couldn't help but laugh at Rob thinking he was going to keep Suzy from dating. She loved the banter among the family, wishing more than once that she had known that.

The conversation flowed, and she found herself completely relaxed and accepted by the MacDonald family. After dinner, she and Bernie cleaned up the kitchen. Looking directly into Laurie's eyes, Bernie said, "Sweetie, I have to say how glad I am that you're with Rob. He came months ago to tell us about this amazing girl he met, and I knew that night he'd met someone special. Mac and I could not be happier."

Family. Belonging. Friends. Love. As they drove back to his apartment, she realized how glad she was to have moved to Fairfield.

"Rob, can I ask you a question?" she asked hesitantly.

"Sweetheart, you don't have to ask if you can ask. Just ask."

"I was just thinking about Emma."

"You miss her, don't you?"

"It is difficult to explain. From the time I was about two years old, we shared a room. She was my aunt, my roommate, my pretend sister, my friend, then my guardian. We talk almost every day and well, I miss her. She works as a high school counselor, but I know she would love to change schools. It's just I've found a place where I belong, people that I love. When I came here, she told me that it was my time." Looking into his eyes, she continued, "My time to get out on my own. My time to have my own place. My time to discover me. My time to fall in love."

Entwining his fingers through hers, he encouraged her to open up more as they sat in the parking lot.

"I would like to ask her to try to get a job here. I'd like her to move to Fairfield, but I wanted to know what you thought."

"Honored you want my opinion, Laurie, but you don't need my approval to have Emma come here, whether to visit or live. What are you really thinking, babe?" he probed.

"Well… you and I are still kind of new. And I don't want you to think that you're not enough for me. Or that she would intrude into our lives."

Rob placed his fingers on her lips to silence her fears. "Laurie, I've got my parents and sister and best friends in this town. You're here by yourself. Finding your time as you say. I want you to have your family where they make you the happiest, and if that's Emma moving here, then I'm all for it."

Breathing a sigh of relief, she wrapped her arm around his waist as they walked inside. Sliding her hand down on his firm ass, she gave it a squeeze as they crossed the threshold.

Rounding on her quickly, he picked her up and walked forward until her back hit the door and her breasts were pushed up against his chest. Up until now, their sex had been very active but tame, only missionary and in the bed. Wanting to make sure she was comfortable, Rob had not attempted anything more adventurous. Leaning his head back to look into her eyes, he quickly asked, "You okay, babe?"

"Oh yeah," was her response.

That was all the encouragement he needed. Slamming his lips onto hers, he kissed her hard and possessively. Nipping her lips, sucking her tongue into his mouth, slanting his head to get a deeper angle, his kiss owned her. Delving into her mouth, he explored every crevice as his tongue danced with hers.

She answered back with her tongue, stroke for stroke. Her fingers dug into his muscular biceps as she held on tightly, feeling as though she were drowning, and he was her rescuer.

She felt her panties becoming wet and couldn't resist squirming desperately against his engorged cock pressing into his jeans. The need for friction was overwhelming, and she couldn't think of anything else but wanting to have him pumping inside of her, satisfying that need.

He lowered her to the floor just long enough to unzip her jeans and pull them off her body. Without breaking the kiss, he picked her back up and continued to press her against the door. He held her easily with one hand on her ass, and the other pushed up her sweater. Jerking down the cups of her bra, freeing her breasts, he sucked one nipple deeply into his mouth, swirling the swollen bud with his tongue.

Rubbing her aching core on his jean-clad dick, she could feel him press into her. "Rob, I need more. Please," she begged.

He moved to the other breast, giving it the same attention that he gave the first. He reached down and grasped her panties in his hand, tearing the fragile material and tossing them to the floor. He unzipped his pants freeing his enormous cock. "Need to get a condom, baby."

"I'm on the pill to control my periods. I'm safe," she answered.

He looked carefully into her eyes. "I've never gone without a condom, and I get tested for my job. I'm clean, I promise."

She looked into his blue eyes, seeing honesty shining back. "I trust you, Rob." With those words, she gave him everything she had to give.

Hearing those words, he felt them wrap around his heart and into his very being. He'd had women give him many things over the years but never their trust. Those precious words were the most important gift he had ever received. Cupping his hand on her cheek, he stared into the grey eyes that captured him the moment he first saw them, promising, "I'd never put you at risk, Laurie. Never."

His lips barely grazed hers in a kiss so soft she wasn't sure it was real. All she knew was that she needed him, body and soul.

Lowering his leg, he pushed his jeans to the floor along with his boxers. Fingering her folds, he found she was more than ready for him.

"You're soaked, babe. You ready? Can you take it?"

"Rob, please, take me now," she commanded. "Hard."

He pushed his dick into her dripping folds, slamming her against the door. Looking at her quickly to see if she was all right, he saw her head thrown back, eyes closed, and a smile on her face as she took all of him into her body. Satisfied that she could take it, he began to pump harder and faster, pounding into her as though his life depended on it. Sucking on her nipple again, he lightly bit down, causing her to gasp.

She had never felt so full, so complete in her whole life. The friction was setting her core on fire, releasing sparks that she recognized as being close to exploding. "Rob, I'm close. Oh more, more, I'm close."

Pumping furiously, he reached between them, pressing on her clit. That was all she needed to go over the edge. Sparks igniting, she felt her inner muscles clenching around his still pumping cock. He continued to ride her, pushing in as far as he could go before throwing his head back, neck straining as his dick released his seed deep inside her willing body.

God, it has never felt like that. Skin to skin. With someone I love. Panting, he held her tightly as he drew in one ragged breath after another, with his head resting against the door next to hers. *She owns me.* He realized this thought did not scare him but instead fulfilled him.

His breathing finally slowed down, and he gently lowered her to the floor. Keeping his hands around her waist until she was steady on her feet, he kissed her swollen lips gently, softly. "You're mine, babe. And I gotta tell you. You have all of me. Heart, soul, body."

Carrying her back to the bathroom, he turned on the water. Placing her down, he let the water get warm before moving her under the spray.

Having him wash her gently was the most relaxing thing Laurie had felt in a long time. Smiling shyly, she said, "You don't have to do this, you know?"

"I take care of what's mine. And *you're* mine," he replied, smiling down into her beautiful face.

Taking the shower gel, he gently washed her body starting with her feet and working his way up her toned legs. Spending a great deal of time lathering her luscious ass and between her legs, his cock answered the call of the wild again. Wanting the shower to be about her, he tried to talk his dick down, but where Laurie was concerned, it had a mind of its own.

She had been soaping his impressive body starting with his wide shoulders and moving down his huge arms and chest muscles as he was concentrating on her lower half. As they met in the middle, both standing under the warm shower spray, she couldn't help but notice his dick, eager and ready again.

"Sorry, babe," he said, with a smirk. "He just knows what he wants when he's around you."

Smiling, she just moved her slick hands over his cock, alternating between his shaft and his balls. "Anytime, honey," she replied.

Rob continued his lathering of her breasts, focusing on both with equal enthusiasm, by this time knowing his dick wasn't going to behave. Not with a soapy, naked Laurie in front of him.

Shyly looking up, she asked softly, "Can we try shower sex?" He gave her a questioning look, so she quickly added, "Oh, we don't have to. It was just a thought." Feeling the embarrassment engulf her, she knew she was blushing furiously.

Raising her chin with his fingers, he gazed into the grey eyes that were now stormy. "Babe, anything you want. Anytime you want it."

Lifting her up again, settling her on the tip of his cock, he guided her onto him gently this time. Unlike earlier, this was about slow. Gentle. Easy. Care. Comfort. Pressing her back against the shower wall so that the water was on his back and out of her face, he moved her up and down, letting the sensations flow over both of them.

Taking a wet nipple in his mouth, he sucked gently, circling his tongue around the beaded tip. Knowing this was a new experience for Laurie, he realized it was new to him as well. *It's all new with her. Everything. The sex. The feelings. Everything.*

It didn't take long for her to feel the familiar pull of her impending orgasm. Climbing higher and higher until she knew she was ready to jump off the edge, she felt him press against her clit and that was all it took for her to fly apart. Throwing her head back, she felt her orgasm roar through her as her inner walls grabbed at his pulsating cock.

With just a few more pumps, Rob joined her, as she milked every bit of seed out of his straining dick. As he emptied himself into her waiting body, he knew this was it for him. She was his forever. Lowering her carefully onto the shower floor, he leaned back to turn off the cooling water.

She placed her hands on his face as his hands came up to cup hers. "I love you, Rob," she admitted. "I love who you are. I love how you make me feel. I love who we are together."

"Laurie, I love you too. Never felt this. Never thought I would. But you're it for me."

They slept that night tightly tucked in, both dreaming of a future together in Fairfield.

11

The holidays swept in separating Rob and Laurie for the first time. Since he was volunteering to stay at the station over Christmas Eve and Christmas Day to relieve the firemen who had families, she decided to go visit Emma. The girls spent three days talking, sharing, laughing, and planning. By the time Laurie had been there for one day, she had convinced Emma that Fairfield was the greatest place to live. Emma confessed that she would look for a job there, also feeling the stress of living away from her only relative.

On Christmas Eve, they sat on the floor of Emma's apartment, drinking wine and looking through old photo albums. The two women looked so similar both as children and adults. And of course, pictures of Sarah brought back many memories. Laurie couldn't help but wonder what her life would have been like if her mother was still alive. But knowing that the past cannot be changed, she looked ahead with enthusiasm.

Reminiscing about Christmases past, they laughed and even cried a little, sifting through the memories. Looking at the pictures of her mom, Laurie became pensive.

"What's going through that mind of yours, Laurie?" Emma asked.

Laurie smiled. "You always could read me, couldn't you?"

"Let's just say I've had years of practice!" Emma retorted. "Come on, spill it, girl. I can tell something is on your mind. Is it about Rob?"

"Oh no, everything is fine there," Laurie said, her smile lighting up her face. "It's... well, it's about my father."

Emma looked at Laurie in disbelief. For the past six years, Laurie had not talked about her father. She never spoke of him in anger; she just simply never spoke of him. Having read that Sarah was just a fling to him seemed to close the door on that relationship. "Okay," Emma said slowly. "You've definitely gotten my attention."

"I was talking to Jean, our school social worker and counselor, after the fire and she mentioned that my parents must be proud. I'd just told Rob all about my parents and it no longer seemed forbidden to tell someone I trusted about them. But after I explained the situation, she brought up that if Mom never told him about me, then how could I ever be sure that he actually rejected me? Let's face it, the only two people who actually know what happened were Mom and Brock."

Laurie looked at Emma and just shrugged. "I mean, I don't plan on finding him, but well...let's just say that it gave me a different perspective."

Emma leaned over and hugged Laurie. "I'm proud of you, girl. You really are coming into your own time, aren't you?"

Going back to their wine and memories, they talked well past midnight and into Christmas Day.

Mac came in to relieve Rob so he could have a few hours away from the station. "Got any plans, son?" he asked.

"Yeah, Tom and Jake are meeting me at Smokey's for a drink. I'll just be a couple of hours, and then I'll be back."

Mac eyed his son, proud of the change in him. Mac knew that for years a trip to Smokey's with the boys would usually end up with Rob tangled in the sheets with some nameless woman. He was always proud of Rob but knew he had a lot to offer a good woman and felt like he was wasting years chasing skirts. Now that Rob was with Laurie, his son seemed so much happier. Mac walked over and clapped Rob on the shoulder. "Tell the boys 'Merry Christmas' from Bernie and me."

Rob walked into Smokey's a little early and sat at the bar to wait for Tom and Jake. Bill and Wendy Evans walked over to greet him.

"Where's that gorgeous girl of yours?" Wendy asked.

"She went to visit her aunt for Christmas, and I'm working at the station, so it was a good time for her to go."

"Well, she certainly has made a believer out of me," Bill said cryptically.

Rob, looking at his friend, raised one eyebrow in question.

Bill chuckled. "Never thought anyone could reform a player like you, but she sure did."

Wendy slapped her husband's arm, calling him an old coot. "Ignore him, Rob," she said. "I always knew that the right woman was all that you needed. And Laurie is a keeper!" She looked up smiling. "Well here comes the rest of the crew. Tom here has found his darling, so I just need to work on Jake."

Rob greeted his friends, and they made their way to a table. The three men presented a wall of masculinity as they walked through the bar. The room was somewhat empty on Christmas Eve, but the three handsome men turned the heads of the usual women there.

Tom looked at his two best friends and declared that he had an announcement to make. Jake and Rob looked over, confusion written on both of their faces.

"You two need to mark your calendars for May 20th. I've asked Carol to marry me, and she said yes."

Jake and Rob enthusiastically congratulated Tom, then called Bill and Wendy over to celebrate with them. Wendy bounced over, hugging Tom, declaring that Carol was the best thing for him. Bill bought another round of drinks for the friends, congratulating Tom as well. Pressed for details, Tom admitted that he and Carol were ready, but that her parents were difficult people to please.

"Carol has tried her whole life to please them, even though years ago she decided to take charge of her life. I just think that she used to think that things would get easier with them. She finally realized that it's her life, and she's going to have to please herself. So we decided that it didn't make any sense to wait. I gave her the ring this morning and we agreed to get married in May. Neither of us wants a big wedding, although that'll be a battle with her parents," he said shaking his head. "But May it is, and well, I want you two to stand up with me at the wedding."

The three friends continued their annual Christmas Eve get together, toasting their friendship. They were getting ready to leave when two of the local barflies sauntered over. Jake was well known for not being a player in town, and while most of the women had learned that Rob and Tom were off the market, a few just couldn't believe that he would be faithful.

Roxie, a busty blonde with her boobs falling out of her shirt, plopped down quickly on Rob's lap, shoving her almost naked breasts into his face. Her giggling, drunken friend, was over to the side making eyes at Jake. Rob had slept with Roxie several years ago and now looked at her in disgust. Snarling, he hauled her off him.

"Oh, come on, Robbie," she whined. "We had fun once. We could always have a good time again. That little girlfriend of yours couldn't possibly give you a blow job as good as me."

Rob, full of fury, more at himself than her, lowered his face to hers and growled, "We never had fun. We had a fuck. That was it. No emotion. No next time. Just. A. Fuck. At least I now know what I want. I suggest you move on and do the same."

Stalking over to the bar to say goodbye to Bill and Wendy, he was tempted to down another whiskey, but he knew he had to go back on duty. He, Tom, and Jake walked out into the December night, the cold wind barely cooling off his anger.

"You okay?" Jake asked.

Rob, tight-lipped, just hung his head for a moment. Looking back up into the faces of his oldest friends, he replied, "Yeah, but it sucks to have your past keep getting shoved back at you. I was a fuck-up, guys, and you knew it. Hell, even last summer I called myself a fuck-and-run." Shaking his head at the memory, "Just wished someone could have knocked some sense into me years ago. I love Laurie. She's it for me." Sighing, he said, "At least this happened when she wasn't around. I'd be pissed as hell if Roxie had played me in front of Laurie."

Rob, rubbing a hand over his face, looked away for a moment. "I keep wondering if she's going to get tired of this shit. Figure I'm not worth it." Looking back at their faces, he continued, "It's happened before. We're out having a great time, and someone from my fuck-and-run past comes up trying to start shit. Jesus, I see the look in her eyes...it's like she's devastated. I swear I'd prefer anger over hurt."

Jake smiled at his friend. A man of few words, he clapped Rob on the back and just said, "What's important is what you know now. You got a good thing. She's a strong woman, and she knows you love her."

Tom agreed. "Just keep doing what you're doing. Same thing happened a time or two with Carol. It sucks, but I just kept letting her know she was it for me. The only one. And eventually all the others slink away leaving you with just pure gold."

Rob smiled, and they parted as they always had, friends and brothers. Rob headed back to the station house.

Laurie returned two days later excited to see everyone. She pulled into her parking space, sorry to have left Emma but glad to be back home. Running up to her apartment, she noticed an envelope taped to the mailbox with her name on it. Grabbing it, she ran up the stairs and went inside. Carol greeted her enthusiastically.

"Well, let me see it!" Laurie exclaimed, reaching for Carol's hand.

Holding her left hand out, Carol showed off her gorgeous diamond engagement ring. Squealing, jumping up and down, and hugging, the two friends celebrated. Laurie could not look at the ring enough. The center diamond was not overly large but was surrounded by a circle of smaller diamonds. On Carol's tiny fingers, the ring was perfect.

"Sooo, I want to ask…will you be my maid of honor?" Carol asked.

"Oh my God, I've never been in a wedding before!"

"Well, since you and I have been living together, you've become my very best friend. And we're dating best friends, so it is perfect!"

The girls continued to talk and plan for a while until Carol needed to get ready to go to Tom's. Laurie walked back over to her purse to get her cell phone when she came across the envelope again. Opening it, a sheet of folded computer paper was inside, with nothing more than a print of a picture. Holding it in shaking hands, she saw that the image was of Rob holding a woman whose breasts were shoved in his face. There was a time stamp on the photo from two nights ago. Carol walked over and looked at the picture.

"Oh Laurie, there must be an explanation. Rob would never cheat on you."

Looking at Carol, she answered calmly, "I know. Really, I do. But why would this slut send this to me?"

"Laurie, you know Rob was a player before he ever saw you last summer. But since that time, he has only had eyes for you. I know it was hard at first for you, with women still throwing themselves at him." Carol looked off to the side with a rueful look on her face. "Believe me, I know the feeling. When Tom and I first got together, I never knew what we might run into… there was an occasional old hook-up of his around to make sure I knew she had him first. But we worked through that, and eventually, everyone got used to us being *us*."

"Carol, I know Rob has been faithful, but we promised to not keep any secrets from each other, so I have to tell him about this. I was going to head to the station anyway, so I'll head on over there now."

Hugging each other goodbye, Laurie walked out, hopped into her car and drove to the fire station. Knowing she trusted him, her mind still raced with the possibilities of what could have happened. Shaking her head in frustration, she pulled into the parking lot.

As she got out, several of the men saw her and yelled back for Rob. He came around the corner, stopping dead in his tracks as he saw her. Standing next to her cute yellow bug, she looked adorable in her winter boots and funny knit hat. He came running out at full speed, swooped in to grab her up, and swung her around. Laughing, she brought her lips down on his, relishing the feel of him pressed against her. She just wished that they didn't have so many layers of clothing between them but knew that evening they wouldn't.

"Missed you," he said between kisses. He immediately noticed that she was distracted. Setting her down, he escorted her inside where it was warmer. Walking to a secluded corner, Rob leaned down, looking into her eyes.

"What's up, Laurie?"

Blushing, she looked straight ahead at the massive chest pressing into her.

"Eyes, babe," he quietly ordered.

She raised her eyes to his, seeing concern staring

back at her. "Rob, generally I would just throw this out, but we promised to never keep secrets from each other. I know nothing happened and I'm not upset. I just don't want to keep anything away from you."

His eyes narrowed as he looked down to see that she had a piece of paper held out in front of her. Taking it in his hands, he unfolded the picture and stared at the photo.

She looked up nervously as the expression on Rob's face went from disbelief to pure, unadulterated rage.

"Damn!" he exploded, shoving backward, twisting his body as he stalked away. Anger poured off him filling the air with fury. "I can't believe this shit!"

She stood quietly looking down at her feet knowing it was best to let him have his moment.

He suddenly turned back around, seeing her tiny body completely still in the corner staring at her feet. *Jesus, what is she thinking? Why would she believe me over this picture? Goddamn it! What did she say? She didn't believe it?*

Stalking back over, he placed his shaking hands gently on her face, lifting them so that he could see into her eyes, wanting to take the pulse of her emotions. "I swear to you that picture is not what it looks like." She started to interrupt, but he slid his thumb over her lips silencing her.

"You said you don't believe it, and you got no idea how happy that makes me. But you deserve to know how that picture came about." She stood quietly her eyes warm in the knowledge that her man needed to give her reassurances.

"Jake, Tom, and I get together every Christmas Eve for a drink. Just us three, no one else. It's been a tradition for a long time. The bar was almost empty. Talked to Bill and Wendy for a bit, then it was just us. Tom shared about the engagement. We were just finishing up. This ...," he spit out while holding the paper, "came over with one of her cronies, already drunk, and plopped herself down on my lap. Babe, I immediately pushed her off me and told her to get lost, but that other bitch must have snapped this Goddamn picture in the process. Honest to God, that was all. Jake was there, he knows."

He continued to look deeply into her eyes, fear crawling around his heart. All of the other girls he ever banged, he never cared about their feelings. But this small princess in front of him held his heart in her hands. She had the power to crush him...or the power to save him.

Her eyes began to light up as a smile formed slowly then spread to her whole face. She raised her arms to cup his strong jaw, feeling the stubble under her fingers. "Rob, I know. You don't need to explain anything to me. I never believed anything happened." Looking into his piercing blue eyes, she continued, "Rob, I used to feel jealous of your past. Of the women you were with. And it hurt when we were first dating to feel that every time we went out, there was always someone wanting me to know they had you first."

His eyes closed momentarily, his heart continuing to hurt as he realized how hard this had been for her.

Never a coward to face fear, he forced his eyes back open, looking into her face as she continued.

"But I'm no longer jealous. You see, Rob, I know now. They never *had* you first. None of those women ever *had* you. I'm the only one to have held your heart. And you're the only one to have held mine."

Touching his forehead to hers, he felt the fear loosen its grip from around his heart, replaced by a spreading warmth. *What did I ever do to deserve this woman?*

"Rob," she spoke softly, and his eyes sought hers again. "I've been gone three days, and it feels like forever. The only reason I showed this trash to you was because of our promise. I know you're mad, but honey, I want you with me. With *me*. Not being mad at her in your mind."

He knew he was going to handle Roxie, but he had to admit Laurie made sense. He couldn't stand that someone had messed with his woman, but she deserved his attention right now. Breathing deeply, clearing his thoughts, he nodded.

"You got it. Don't mistake me, I'm dealing with this shit later, but you got all of me now." Taking her lips in a possessive kiss, he put all his emotions into the moment.

Mac came out to greet her boisterously, interrupting the kiss.

"Son, you can go ahead and leave. We've got this here."

"Appreciate it, Chief," he replied, grabbing Laurie's hand. "Leave your car here, babe. We can pick it up tomorrow."

"Why can't we just drive my car?" she asked, already knowing the answer.

Rob looked at her and said, "Yellow VW bug? Me? We don't work. Your ride looks cute for you, but Laurie, not being seen in town in that yellow bug."

She laughed, "I knew that... I just wanted to get a rise out of you."

"A rise?" He swatted her ass as she hopped into his truck. "I get you home, and you're gonna' see a *rise* out of me!"

She leaned over the console to give him a quick kiss. "Rob, you can give me anything you want!"

"Oh hell, girl, let's get home."

Rob and Laurie barely made it home before tearing their clothes off. She slipped out of his grasp as he shucked his jeans off and ran down the hall to the bedroom. Suddenly lifted off the ground and tossed onto the bed, she screamed in delight as he grabbed her ankles and pulled her to the side of the bed. She raised her head to watch as he laid a trail of open-mouth, wet kisses from her breasts down her stomach, ending between her legs. Her legs spread wide, he feasted on her wet folds, sliding his tongue deep inside. *She tastes sweeter than anything I could have imagined.*

Her head fell back on the bed as the sensations swept over her, threatening to drown her in their intensity. Her sex throbbed as his tongue continued its ministrations. She began to rock her hips up as though they were seeking more contact, more pressure, more …anything.

He chuckled and placed his large hand on her hips to keep her still. He continued to lick her folds, pressing his tongue inside her core, then moved up slightly to pull her clit into his mouth. His hand slipped up towards her breasts, lightly pinching a nipple at the same time.

She cried out as her world exploded in a shower of sensations, sparks flying out from her core in all directions. He lapped up her juices as the orgasm created the flow he had been waiting for. She lay boneless, not sure she could move until he stood and leaned over her, dragging her body up higher on the bed. Lifting herself up, she admired the body towering over her. She would never get tired of seeing him naked, his muscular body proudly on display. Over six feet of sinew, bulky shoulders, biceps, and pecs from years of weight training for football and now carrying fire equipment. His six-pack abs led downward to his massive legs with his cock standing out ready to meld his body with hers.

He crawled up her body. With the scent of her sex filling the air, he nipped at her flat stomach and suckled her breasts. He loved her natural breasts, the feel and texture of them as he palmed one while deeply sucking the nipple of the other. He lowered his hips between her legs feeling his dick straining to enter her as though it had a mind of its own. Rob looked down at the face of the woman he loved marveling that such a perfect creature wanted him. Her eyes were closed allowing her thick lashes to touch her cheeks. The pale complexion was reflected in the moonlight shining through the blinds. And her hair. That shiny mass of thick hair lay across the pillow and down the sheets.

"Eyes, babe," he softly ordered. She smiled as her grey eyes met his blue ones.

"Love you, Laurie. All my heart," he whispered.

"I love you too, Rob. Always."

With that, he plunged his straining cock deep inside her, fully seating himself in one thrust. Laurie's hips moved upwards to meet his as the thrusts became more forceful. With wild abandon, he pumped furiously inside, reaching some secret place that he wanted to touch. With that intensity, it did not take long until she was screaming his name as her climax roared through her.

He pumped until her sex had stopped milking him, then he quickly pulled out much to her dismay. Before she could question him, he flipped her over on her stomach and grasped her hips to pull them up and back.

"On your knees, babe," he ordered, voice raspy with need, as he placed a pillow under her hips.

She quickly obeyed, loving his take-charge-mood. He held a handful of her hair in one hand, pulling gently. A loud crack sounded as he slapped her ass with his other hand, the pain sharp and quick, but then just as quickly, he rubbed the spot gently, soothing the reddened area. Immediately, she felt her inner walls clench and moisture pooled again. She moaned involuntarily, and he leaned over her back.

"Is that okay?" he asked, still smoothing her ass.

Moaning in pleasure was the only answer she was

able to give, and he just chuckled again. Several more ass slaps came in quick succession each followed by a soothing touch. He slid his fingers into her warmth feeling the wetness that dripped over her folds.

"You're soaked for me, babe. You okay with this? Won't do anything you don't like."

"Please, Rob, just do it. Take me now."

Grinning, he replied, "My momma always taught me to listen to a lady." And with that, he plunged his engorged dick into her waiting core.

This angle brought new sensations for Laurie, and she felt as though her world was tipping on its axis. His fingers gripped her hips, digging in to hold her as he pounded in fiercely.

She rocked back and forth as his body slammed into hers over and over. *How can these different positions feel so amazing?* She loved the feel inside but wanted the friction on her clit. Slowly moving her hand down between her legs, she fingered herself, hoping he wouldn't notice.

"Oh, babe. Seeing you touch yourself is going to make me harder," he panted, between thrusts.

Embarrassed, she quickly removed her hand, placing it back on the pillow.

"Don't stop. Keep doing it," he ordered.

Sliding her fingers back to her clit, she rubbed and pulled on the swollen nub, feeling herself race to the end, desperate for the finish line.

Wanting her to come again before he did, he reached around pinching her nipple, sending her moaning.

"Are you close?" he asked roughly.

"Yes," she panted. "Yes, yes." The friction sensations from her sex were sending sparks outward as the pressure began to build. Like a volcano that needed to erupt, she was so close, straining to find her release. Her hands went back to the bed as his hard thrusts pushed her forward.

His hand slapped her ass once again before sliding forward and pinching her clit. That was all it took for her eruption, as the lava flowed over the edge in all directions.

Her sex convulsed around his cock, and with a few more thrusts he felt himself give over to his own release. Head thrown back, thick neck muscles straining, he pulsated into her waiting body, experiencing a release unlike one he had ever felt in his life.

They both fell forward onto the bed, his large body completely covering hers. Sweating, breathing heavily, Rob had never felt so sated in his life. Awareness slowly came back, and he realized that Laurie was crushed under him.

Rolling to the side, he pulled her gently to him. "Babe, sorry. Didn't mean to crush you. You okay?" He brushed her hair away from her beautiful face peering deeply into her eyes. What he saw stunned him.

Tears, shining in her eyes, glimmered back at him. Her face was lit with a smile that dazzled. Reaching her small hand up to cup his strong jaw, she gently rubbed the stubble.

"I'm fine, Rob. That was so amazing. It was as though we were truly one person. One movement. One body. One soul." Looking deeply into his gorgeous eyes, she leaned in to place a chaste kiss on his lips. "I love you, Rob. Always and forever."

He closed his eyes momentarily, wondering once again how this amazing creature ever came into his life. "Love you back, Laurie."

With that, he tucked her in tightly, arms and legs tangled, breaths mingled, hearts beating as one and slept.

12

Winter settled in Fairfield, often resulting in recess time being spent inside due to the cold temperatures. Laurie found herself having to be more creative in ways for the students to release their excess energy. As they were playing games on the floor of the classroom, Jean came to the door with a little girl in tow. Laurie walked over, smiling at the child, noticing her shy demeanor and her big eyes staring out at the other kids in the room. After introducing herself to Cindy, the boisterous students in her class ran over to meet the new girl, immediately pulling her into their games.

Jean leaned over telling her they needed to talk at the end of the day. Laurie just nodded and turned back to her class. After the last school bus had left, Laurie headed to Jean's office.

"Hey, what's up?"

"Hey, girl. I need to have you read the records that came in with Cindy. She's in foster care having been taken from her abusive home."

Eyes snapping, Laurie swore. She hated the abuse that some children faced, and while she was glad that Cindy was in a good foster home, it always made her thankful once more that Emma had stepped up to be her guardian.

Jean continued, "It appears that her uncle was abusing her, but the parents didn't believe her. Her former school discovered it, and she was taken from the home. The uncle is in jail awaiting trial, but DSS and the judge decided, for her own protection, she would be placed in a therapeutic foster home."

Eyes skimming the report, Laurie looked back up at Jean's kind face. "She's with the Carlsons?" Jean nodded, and Laurie sighed in relief. The Carlson family was a well-known foster family in town. The mother had a psychology background, and the father was a special education teacher. They were loving, friendly and had assisted many children over the years as incredible foster parents. The Carlsons would be perfect for Cindy.

"Anything special I need to know?" Laurie asked, closing the report.

"She just doesn't feel comfortable around men. Even Mr. Carlson has to be very careful around her. Keep an eye on her; she may have to stay with you instead of going to art class for a while." Their art teacher was phenomenal but was a male; therefore, Cindy may not take to him immediately.

"No problem," Laurie answered.

She and Jean continued to talk casually for a little while. Jean was funny, warm, and so genuine. Laurie always enjoyed spending time with her. They decided to head to Bernie's Bakery for a treat and to continue their conversation.

Bernie greeted Laurie as a daughter already, hugging her tightly and yelling out her favorite coffee order to the barista. Once seated, Bernie brought over their coffees and pastries. Patting her hand, Bernie told her the treats were on the house.

Jean and Laurie sat quietly for a few minutes, the luscious indulgences taking all of their attention. Laurie carefully perused her coffee partner. Jean was a beautiful, single, forty-year-old woman. Laurie realized that she always felt comfortable with Jean because she reminded her so much of Emma. Caring, wise, intelligent, protective.

Jean looked up from devouring the scrumptious treat, laughing about the calories she would need to work off.

"Can I ask you a question, Jean?" Laurie asked. "You don't have to answer if you don't want to."

"Sure, fire away," Jean replied. "I honestly don't have any secrets."

"I was just wondering if you were seeing someone. You never talk about dating anyone, so I was just curious."

"I was married once, many years ago," Jean answered thoughtfully.

"What happened?"

"We were young, early twenties, just out of college. I was working in a school system, and he was a contractor, building houses. We were happy, saving money and hoped to start a family soon. But life has a way of sometimes changing your plans."

Laurie, having told Jean her own story, was well versed in how life can throw all your plans into a tailspin.

"He was killed on a job site. One morning I kiss him goodbye, and the next thing I know I get the phone call to go to the hospital. A truck filled with wooden beams was being unloaded at the job site, and a cable snapped. The beams landed on him, crushing him." Jean looked into the distance, as though the memory from fifteen years ago was as fresh as if it had just happened. "At least I was told that he would have died instantly and not suffered."

"Oh Jean, I'm so sorry. I should have never asked."

Jean patted Laurie's hand. "Don't be silly, Laurie. Talking about Rick allows me to remember him. I've moved on but will always remember. And no, I'm not dating anyone now. I've occasionally gone on dates, but just never found anyone that interested me for longer than a few dinner dates." Grinning at Laurie, she joked, "But who knows? My handsome prince may come riding up someday!"

Right then, Carol walked in and joined them. The conversation turned to a happier subject as they discussed Carol's upcoming wedding.

"My parents are being difficult as usual, but Tom is encouraging me to do things my way."

"Absolutely!" Jean stated, and Laurie agreed. Bernie came over and joined in the plans. Before they knew it, the winter sun was setting early, and the friends parted with promises to get together again soon.

By the time Laurie got home, she was exhausted. Carol was spending more and more evenings with Tom, so Laurie had the big apartment to herself. She decided to lie down for a nap since Rob wasn't expected until later. He came in using his key, noticing the lights off and Laurie's purse and shoes left in the living room. Walking through the apartment turning on lights, he made his way to the bedroom. There he found her on top of the comforter, still dressed in her work clothes, sound asleep. He was concerned. She had been getting increasingly more tired but insisted that she wasn't sick. Grabbing a blanket off the end of the bed to throw over her, he noticed her feet. Flipping on the light to get a better look, he saw that they were bluish in color. He touched them, and they were freezing cold, turning white where his fingers pressed. *Jesus, her toes are cold.*

Feeling her feet being wrapped up, she began to stir. Opening her eyes to the sight of Rob sliding onto the bed with her made her smile. "Hey, honey," she said sleepily.

He gently rubbed her back then pushed her hair from her eyes. "Babe, you're hot. You may have a fever. Your cheeks are kinda red."

She rolled over, wincing as she sat up.

"Darlin', you need to go to the doctor," he said, concerned. He leaned back against the headboard, pulling her carefully back toward him, and tucked her into his front. "I wrapped up your feet - they were blue."

She laughed. "I've had cold, blue feet for years. It gets worse in the winter." She rubbed her neck and winced again.

He replaced her hand with his, massaging the area. "Is Carol coming home tonight?" She shook her head, so he pulled his phone out of his pocket.

"Oh, honey, I'm okay. Please don't interrupt Carol and Tom's evening. Carol is so stressed with the wedding planning. Her parents are horrible to deal with."

He looked down at her. "Laurie, I'm not playing around. You've been tired lately, lost a little weight off that gorgeous ass and now this. Maybe you have the flu. I want you at the doctor's tomorrow."

Laurie pouted, but one look at his face and she knew he wasn't going to give in. Sighing, she agreed then moved to get out of bed. He pulled her back in for a hug, kissing the top of her head.

"Worried about you, sweetheart."

Leaning up and kissing him quickly on his lips, she headed to the kitchen. He followed close behind, capturing her hips as she bent over to look into the refrigerator. "Laurie don't cook. Let's go out or order in."

"Chinese?" she asked with a smile.

Grinning back, he grabbed the phone and called it in.

Sitting at the table, eating Chinese, Laurie told Rob about Cindy. He listened, jaw tight in anger, to the tale of the little girl who had been abused. Cursing, he asked how her parents could have ignored what was going on in their home.

"I don't know, honey. It's bad enough to be abused, but when your parents don't believe you, then you lose hope. Thank God her former school recognized problems and stepped in. I think she'll do well in my class, but she is very wary of men."

Cleaning up the remains of the dinner, she commented, "I almost forgot, but Jean said that her parents are mad about her being taken from them. They don't know where she is right now, but I have to be careful to make sure no one picks her up other than her foster family."

Rob, always in protective mode where she was concerned, wrapped her in his immense embrace. "Laurie, you're not in any danger with them, are you?"

"Oh no, there are too many people at school for them to try any contact there. I would be more fearful if she were taking the bus, but the foster family will always be picking her up."

Twisting around in his hug, she faced him, bringing her arms up around his neck. Rising on her tiptoes, she pressed her lips to his, desire flooding through her. Mewling as Rob pulled back, she opened her eyes, disappointment replacing desire.

"Babe, don't want to do anything if you're sick."

Stamping her foot, she retorted, "I'm not ill! I was tired and took a nap. I feel fine and want my man!"

He raised his eyebrow. "Did you just stomp your foot?"

Wiggling to escape his embrace, she huffed, "Fine, don't make love to me. See if I care!"

Throwing his head back laughing, he exclaimed, "Laurie, you want me, girl, you got me. Just let me know if you're not feeling it." Then scooping her up into his muscular arms, he headed back to the bedroom. He slowly removed her clothes, peeling away each layer as though unwrapping a delicate present.

Both naked, he smoothed his large hands over her body, worshiping each inch. Holding her eyes with his, he slowly made love to her, letting all of his love pour into each action. By the time they both climaxed, they lay sated, Laurie tucked into his loving embrace, his heavy arms wrapped around her chest, his legs over hers.

She fell asleep almost immediately. He lay awake for a while, worry for her creeping into his consciousness.

Laurie sat in the doctor's examining room feeling foolish for having come in for the appointment.

"This seems so silly. I know I don't have the flu, but my boyfriend insisted, and I talked to my roommate who is a nurse and she agreed. So here I am."

Dr. Alexander smiled at Laurie after looking over her list of symptoms. "Well, let's see if we have everything. You have had a low-grade fever for a few days, your neck is stiff, and you have lost a little weight. Is that it?"

"I also have a little redness on my face, but it just looks like I used blush when I didn't." Giggling, she also confessed. "I know this sounds dumb, but my feet are always cold."

Dr. Alexander did the physical examination but admitted that her diagnosis was incomplete. "You have some flu-like symptoms, but I don't think it is the flu. Unfortunately, your symptoms could also be indicative of a number of other things. I'd like to do a blood test so that we will have more information."

She hated blood tests but knew she couldn't get out of it. Thanking the doctor and making a follow-up appointment, she walked out to her car. Leaning against her bug was a gorgeous, imposing, dark-haired fireman, looking incredibly sexy. Running over to him, she jumped into his arms, wrapping her legs around his waist as he captured her in his embrace.

"What are you doing here, sweetie?" she asked.

"Didn't want to wait for you to call. Wanted to know now what's going on," Rob answered. "What did the doc say?"

"Well, she doesn't think it's the flu but said the symptoms could be anything. She is sending me to the lab to get blood work done."

"Leave your car here and I'll take you."

Laurie panicked, knowing that she always passed out when having her blood taken, and she did not want Rob around. "Umm, you don't have to do that. I...I can just go really quick and you can um… go back to the station."

"Darlin', you can't lie for shit. What's up?"

Pouting, she admitted, "Fine. I just hate blood work and needles, and I don't want you to see me pass out."

He laughed at her exaggeration. "Babe, you'll be fine. I'm taking you and no arguing." He helped her up into his truck, and they drove down the street to the lab at the hospital. Once there, he walked her into the lab and sat waiting with her until they called her back.

She had become quiet, her face pale and hands shaking. Rob saw her distress, realizing that she was getting worked up. Leaning over, he whispered, "You weren't kidding, were you?"

She just shook her head as she stood up to go back. He surprised her by joining her in the small room. The phlebotomist looked up at the massive man who seemed to take up all the space in her little room. As she pulled out her equipment, he noticed that Laurie was already beginning to hyperventilate.

"Babe," he called out. Her eyes shot towards his. "Breathe." Nodding, she focused on her breathing while her blood was being taken. Rob, not taking his eyes off her, noticed that even though the simple procedure was over, her face lost all color. Pitching forward in the chair, she slipped towards the floor.

"Damn," he cursed. Reaching forward, he grabbed her in his arms. The phlebotomist led them to a room across the hall with a hospital bed in it and ran off to get Laurie some juice.

Laurie quickly came to, embarrassed that Rob had

seen her faint. Bringing her hands up, she covered her face.

"Oh, Rob, I didn't want you to see me faint. This is so embarrassing. It happens every time I'm around needles."

He leaned down kissing her forehead. "I want to be with you in all things. I plan on one day being with you when you have our child." Her eyes opened wide with this declaration. "It has something to do with you, I want to be a part of it." Helping her to sit up to drink her juice, he continued. "No secrets, babe. Remember?"

She leaned her weight on him allowing him to help her out to his truck. Smiling up at this handsome, loving man, she knew that the truth was important to him.

13

As January snows were falling, everyone was beginning to get cabin fever. Carol texted Laurie to see if they wanted to meet the gang at Smokey's that night. After checking with Rob, she cheerfully agreed. Heading home after school, she met Carol in the apartment to get ready. Their lives had become so entwined with the men that they were dating that they did not get together as much as they would have liked. It felt like old times, commenting on their outfits, talking about wedding plans, and catching up on their jobs.

"I went back to shift work to make more money, but Tom isn't very happy about it," Carol confessed. "He hates anything that cuts into our time, but he also hates me being in the ER during the middle of the night."

Laurie knew that Carol's parents were wealthy, but also knew that Carol was completely independent. "Do you need the extra money?" Laurie inquired.

Carol shrugged but admitted, "My parents were being…difficult about the wedding, so Tom and I decided to pay for everything ourselves. It will be small, friends-only, and won't cost too much, but the extra money from the graveyard shift helps."

"I have no idea what I'll do when I get married. No parents, no extra money on a teacher's salary!" Laurie said without rancor.

Carol reached over to hug her friend. "Oh, I'm so sorry. Here I'm bemoaning my situation but wasn't even thinking about yours."

"Don't apologize! We all have our crosses to bear. Believe me, I'm very content with my life now. It hasn't always been easy, but it is what it is. Who knows when I'll get married anyway?"

Carol laughed as she pulled on her blue tunic over her black leggings. "Oh, I think that Rob may have something to say about that! I have a feeling that he may be planning to tie you to him before too long!"

Laurie couldn't help but smile at her friend's prediction. She chose her navy leggings paired with a pink cashmere off-the-shoulder sweater. Both women pulled on their boots and grabbed their winter coats and hats before heading out of the door.

Rob, not wanting to take a chance on running into any more barflies before Laurie arrived, sat in his truck in the parking lot. Jake tapped on his window looking surprised.

"You going to hang out all night in your truck?"

"Hell, man, the last time we were here, that crazy

Roxie had her friend take a picture of her falling into my lap and sent it to Laurie."

Jake, disbelieving, just looked at Rob. "You're shittin' me."

"I wish I was. I came over here the next day and confronted her. Told her that she ever even looked Laurie's way, I'd forget I was a gentleman and kick her ass." He chuckled. "Then Wendy came over and did kick her ass to the curb."

Jake started laughing. "Leave it to Wendy to do what we men couldn't do!"

Just then, Tom drove up with Carol and Laurie in tow. As Laurie came toward him, he once again stared at the beauty in front of him.

Greeting him enthusiastically by standing on her toes to grab his face and pull him in for a kiss, he couldn't believe his luck. The others laughed and Rob tucked her under his arm as the five of them went inside to join more of their friends. Several firemen and policemen were there with their dates. Bill and Wendy greeted them all and started serving drinks.

Rob helped Laurie take her coat off, but when he saw the pastel pink sweater that hung off her shoulder, he nearly had a heart attack. Her luscious shoulder was bare. *No bra strap. Damn, she's not wearing a bra.* He tried to get her to put her coat back on.

"Rob, I don't need my coat on the inside," she said, her eyes searching his face for the reason behind his stony countenance.

Leaning down so that his mouth was next to her ear,

he whispered, "You're not wearing a bra. Not having every dick in this place staring at your tits."

Putting her hand over her mouth to stifle her giggles, she leaned her head back so that she could whisper in his ear. "Honey, it's called a strapless bra. I assure you I'm covered up!"

He leaned over and discreetly checked out her breasts to make sure her nipples weren't poking through her sweater. He placed her coat on the back of her chair satisfied that she wasn't showing too much but frustrated knowing she was still too beautiful not to be looked at. Sitting down next to her, he scooted her chair over so that it was touching his, threw his arm around her shoulder, and pulled her in tight.

Tucked into him, feeling dwarfed, she complained, "Rob, I can't see anyone! How am I supposed to carry on a conversation? I told you I'm covered. Honey, I would never come out dressed to embarrass you!" Rolling her eyes and huffing, she finished her quiet tirade.

"I'm not pissed at you. You know how to dress like a beautiful woman, but you don't know dick about dicks."

Incredulous, she turned to look into his face.

"Men see a bare shoulder and that means that they're going to check out the tits to see if they're covered. You may be, but I don't want to fight off every man in this place 'cause he's staring at your breasts."

"You must be joking," she said, eyes narrowing. "Are you telling me that you're still checking out the boobs of every woman in this place?"

Rubbing his hands over his face in frustration, he replied, "No! Once a man has what I've got, what Tom's got, we don't check out shit. But if you'll look around, most of these men are single or just here with a casual date. That means they're checking you out."

"You give the most back-asswards compliments!" she snapped.

Releasing a sigh, he leaned over and brushed his lips against hers in a chaste kiss. "Just laying it out there, Laurie." Noticing that she slumped back against him, he slid his arm from around her and rubbed gentle circles on her back. "Please look at me."

She looked up into his blue eyes, once more getting lost in the depths of them.

"Don't want to take away anything from the night for you, Laurie. You're beautiful, and I just have to deal with the fact that men will look. But I'm proud of being yours. Still don't know what I did to deserve you."

She lifted her hand to cup his firm jaw. Barely touching her lips to his, she whispered, "I love you, Rob MacDonald." She felt his breath mingle with hers as though she needed his breath to live.

He pulled her in for a gentle hug, possessive but protective, then moved her chair so that she was not as hidden as before. Looking over at Jake's smirk, he knew his friend had heard the entire exchange.

"Fuck off, man, your time's coming," Rob joked.

Shaking his head, Jake just laughed. "Don't mind saying hope you're right."

The conversation flowed as much as the drinks did. Laurie loved meeting more of Rob's co-workers and hearing stories of their daring rescues. Tom and Jake joined in with tales of their youth. The dates that the other men brought were nice women and Laurie enjoyed their company as well.

Laurie had been around Jake often and always sensed a sadness about him. He was a quiet man, and she wondered why he wasn't married yet. Rob always said that Jake was waiting for just the right woman. *Emma. Emma would be perfect for Jake, and he was just what she needed. He needs a woman to take care of him. Emma takes care of everyone. But Emma needs someone to take care of her also. Hmmm. I'll talk to Rob later to see what he thinks.*

Her neck was stiff from sitting in one position, and she couldn't believe that she was already tired by ten o'clock. Rob noticed that fatigue was showing on her face. "Babe, you want to go home?"

"Goodness, no. I'll be fine. I think I'll go to the ladies' room though to move around a bit."

"I'll come with you," Rob said protectively.

"Rob, it would look silly for you to come. I'll be right back." With that, Laurie stood and walked down the hallway by the bar.

Walking into the ladies' room, she used the facilities then headed over to wash her hands. Looking up into the mirror, she noticed the redness on her face that her makeup was barely covering. Dark circles were under her eyes. *I sleep all the damn time; why the hell do I feel so tired?*

She rubbed her stiff neck trying to twist it from side to side. It was as though it did not want to move without the pain screaming at her. *I so don't have time to be sick.*

Looking at her pink sweater, she pulled it up so that it covered both shoulders and draped farther in the back. Smiling to herself, she pulled open the door. Standing right outside the door, leaning up on the opposite wall was the colossal hunk of the man she loved staring intently at her. His eyes cut to her sweater, and she saw the warmth in them. Walking over she placed her arms around his waist knowing she couldn't raise them without pain. "What are you doing out here, you silly man?" she asked softly.

"Only silly for you, woman."

She laughed and hugged him tighter. His arms encircled her, completely surrounding her with his body. *Warm. Protected. Cared for. Loved.*

She leaned her head back to look into his eyes, and she gasped in pain.

Immediately, he bent down to look at her without her moving her neck. Panic on his face, fear in his heart, he grasped her arms. "Laurie, what is it? Is it your neck again?"

Trying not to cry, she barely nodded.

"That's it," he declared. "We're leaving, and I'm taking you to the hospital."

She dug her heels in. "Rob, we're not going to the ER for a stiff neck."

He rounded on her quickly forcing her to take a step back. "Babe, I'm not kidding. We promised no secrets between us. I want to know exactly how you feel right now."

Just then, Carol walked over on her way to the ladies' room.

"Good, Carol's here. You can talk to both of us," Rob said to Laurie. Turning to Carol, he said, "She's not feeling good, and I want to take her to the ER."

Carol, immediately concerned, looked at her friend and went into nurse mode. "What are your symptoms?"

"Carol, I've been to Dr. Alexander. She ran blood work on me, but the results aren't back in yet."

"And..." Carol prodded.

"I'm just tired a lot, run a low-grade fever several times a week, and my neck is so stiff it hurts, but that's probably just from sleeping crooked."

Carol lifted an eyebrow at Laurie. "Stop trying to diagnose yourself by making light of the symptoms," she admonished.

By this time, Tom appeared in the hall to see what was taking Carol so long. "What symptoms?" he asked.

Laurie glared at all of them, feeling the sting of tears threatening to fall. Recognizing her stress and embarrassment, Rob reached over and pulled her into a gentle hug. "Just worried about you, babe."

Jake walked over, seeing his friends gathered in the hallway. Tom leaned over to him quietly letting him know what they were discussing.

Carol interjected, "I agree with Laurie, there's no reason to go to the ER now." Laurie looked over with gratitude. "But you definitely need to keep your follow-up appointment with Dr. Alexander. It could be something simple as stress, or it could be indicative of a lot of things. All are best if found early."

Tom laid his hand on Rob's shoulder in understanding. Rob looked up at Tom and Jake, giving a quick head nod to both of them. All three men had chosen professions that protected and served. It wasn't just their jobs. It was who they were. It was ingrained into every fiber of their beings. Since childhood, they had pledged their loyalty to each other, their brotherhood. And that commitment extended to their families and now their women. Rob knew that Tom and Jake understood his fear for Laurie. Their friend had found the woman of his dreams. The completer of his soul. The possibility that she could be sick brought fear to them as well as to Rob. Tom gave Rob's shoulder a squeeze before they all headed back into the bar.

Laurie was terrified that everyone at the table would comment on their absence. Thankfully, most of the group was on the dance floor or at the pool tables. They all sat back down and continued to enjoy each other's company. A little bit later, Rob knew that Laurie had reached her limit. Reaching behind her, he snagged her coat.

"Come on, sweetheart. Let's go home."

Laurie looked at him gratefully. Hugging all of her friends goodbye, they headed back to her apartment.

14

Laurie was making significant progress with Cindy. The tiny girl was playing with the other children, smiling occasionally, and as soon as Laurie was able to ascertain her reading level, she was pleased to find that she was reading above grade level. She was still wary around any males but according to the Carlsons, she was making strides with Mr. Carlson. Cindy did not speak very often, preferring to observe everything around her carefully.

Jean dropped by to follow Cindy in the classroom. She was receiving professional counseling outside of school and saw Jean twice a week in school. She smiled at Jean, having gotten used to her as well. But it was Laurie that held the little girl's confidence. She would often stand near Laurie. Jean had told Laurie that Cindy seemed to have an innate sense of who she could trust, and Laurie was definitely one of those people.

"You haven't had her parents try to contact you, have you?" Jean asked.

"Goodness, no!" Laurie exclaimed. "They don't even know where she is, do they? I thought that was in the court order."

"It is. The Carlsons haven't had anything suspicious either but keep a watch out. We don't want her found and snatched."

Laurie sighed. "You know when I went into elementary education, I thought I would just be teaching the bright little minds that passed through my classrooms. I honestly had no idea that I would have to deal with abusers, kids with alcoholic parents, fires in the school, and the host of other things that cross our doorsteps!"

Jean patted her hand and agreed. "I started out as a teacher and then went into social work. It is wearying but satisfying at the same time." She headed out of the classroom just as it was time to take the children to the playground.

The February day was cold but clear, and the students were running off their pent-up energy. Laurie liked to play with them, but her knee had been hurting ever since she got up this morning. *What the hell is going on with me? I'm twenty- four and feel like an old woman!*

Standing over to one side, she noticed a minivan with darkened windows driving slowly down the road. It stopped off at the side of the playground and sat in the street for several minutes. Ever attentive when dealing with young children and possible threats to them, she stood straighter, making her presence known. The van continued on down the road. *Probably nothing. You're being paranoid; this school is surrounded by minivans!*

The cold was seeping into her making her knee even

stiffer. Clapping her hands, she herded the children back inside.

"Miss Dodd why are you limping?" one of the students asked. She noticed that Cindy came immediately to her side, looking up at her with concern.

"Oh, I just have a stiff knee. I'm fine."

Reassured, the children sat down to get ready for their next activity. Cindy stayed at her side. Reaching down to touch her shoulder, Laurie nodded for her to move on to her chair. Limping over to her own chair, she looked at the clock. Only another hour to go. *I hate that I have no energy!*

As soon as the children were picked up or taken home on the buses, Laurie headed back to her room. After cleaning and arranging the lessons for tomorrow, she sat heavily at her desk. Her follow-up appointment wasn't until next week, but she wanted to talk to the doctor anyway.

Calling Dr. Alexander's office, she spoke to the nurse. "I was just checking on my blood work and to tell her of my new symptoms." The nurse wrote everything down and said the doctor would call her as soon as she was free.

Laurie spent more time working in her room and then her cell phone rang. Looking down, she was relieved to see it was Dr. Alexander.

"The good news is that you do not have the flu. The bad news is that I'm still not sure what is going on with you. I'm concerned that you have stiffness in your knee and that your neck is worse. If it was just your neck, I was going to have you see an orthopedist and suggest physical therapy. But with your knee involved, I'd like to see you sooner than next week. Can you come tomorrow after school?"

Laurie agreed and hung up the phone. Feeling frustrated, she headed home. *I don't want to have something wrong with me, but I'd like to know what is going on. Some kind of diagnosis is better than not knowing. At least with a diagnosis I can be treated and not in the dark!*

Tom and Jake stopped by the fire station to talk to Mac and Rob about an arson fraud investigation they were working on. After interviewing them about the case, Mac headed off leaving the three friends left to talk.

"How's Laurie?" Tom asked.

Rob shook his head in frustration. "I just can't get a good handle on it."

"She seeing a doctor?"

Rubbing his hand over his face, Rob looked up at his friends. "Yeah, but so far we don't know anything new. I don't know. I just keep thinking...I don't know. I..."

"What are you trying to say, Rob?" Jake asked.

"Look, you all know about Laurie's background. We've talked to her aunt about anything hereditary from her mother's side of the family and came up empty. So then, of course, the doc asks about her father's side. And we got nothing." Rob was silent for a moment, trying to put into words the thoughts that had been going through his mind.

Tom and Jake knew this and gave him time to pull his thoughts together. They waited patiently, as years of camaraderie gave them a unique bond.

Sighing, Rob continued. "I'm just going to say it. Been thinking that maybe it's time Laurie tried to find her dad. She has his name and knows he was in the Army at the time she was born. I think it wouldn't be too hard to find out if he's still alive."

Jake spoke up first. "What does Laurie think of this idea?"

The silence in the room was deafening. Tom and Jake exchanged glances but said nothing.

"When the doctor asked about her dad's side of the family, I hinted to Laurie later that if she wanted to try to find him, I'd take care of it for her." Shaking his head at the memory, he continued, "She was pissed. Said she had lived for twenty- four years without him, and she wasn't going to start looking for him now."

Rob was quiet again for a few moments. "I could find him privately, on my own." He sighed. "We promised there'd be no secrets between us ever."

Tom raised his eyebrows at this statement. "Bro, you know what you've got to do. You can't go find this man without her knowing."

"What if possibly trying to save her life is more important than keeping a secret?" Rob answered.

"Damn man, you're screwed no matter which way you go," Jake observed.

"Yeah, well, been thinking about this constantly. I've

hired a private investigator to do some preliminary scouting."

The three friends continued to discuss the pros and cons of trying to find Laurie's father for a while longer. Vowing to support Rob in whatever decision he came to, they shook hands and went their separate ways for the evening.

Packing an overnight bag, Laurie was getting ready to go to Rob's place. Deciding she needed to hear Emma's voice, she called her aunt. After chatting for a little while, Emma finally asked, "So what's the real reason you called?"

"I'm so easy to read," she moaned, plopping down on her bed, placing her aching leg up on her comforter.

"Only to me, Laurie. Well....and maybe to Rob," Emma laughed.

Laurie and Emma never beat around the bush. Having grown up the way they did, they supported each other in all things. So, Laurie dove right in. "Rob brought up finding my father the other day. He thinks I should because he's freaking out since the doctor asked for a medical history and I couldn't give any information about my father's side of the family."

"Laurie honey, what do you want to do?" Emma asked softly.

"I don't know. I mean, let's look at this realistically. One, this man may not even remember my mother. If she were a fling, she would have been one among hundreds of nameless faces." For a second, she closed her eyes tightly, trying to shake the image of Rob with all the women of his past. *Focus, focus!*

"Second, if he did remember her, I would be coming out of the blue twenty-four years later as a complete surprise. He may have a wife, other children, it would totally interrupt his world. Third, what if he refused to see me? I've told myself that I didn't miss what I never had, and that was easy when my father was a faceless figure of my mom's memories. I wasn't hurt because he never knew about me, so his not being in my life wasn't personal. But if he rejects me, then that is personal. Aughhhhh."

Emma's clear voice came through the phone as though she were sitting right next to Laurie with her arms around her. "Honey, you can't worry about interrupting his life. Yes, if he is married with a family, it would be a great crisis for them to deal with, but you do have a right to know who he is. But it sounds as though you're not ready to make that decision right now. You've said that Dr. Alexander doesn't feel that it is necessary right now, so you can wait. Don't rush to make a decision yet."

Sighing, Laurie leaned back on the bed and smiled. Emma always knew how to read her. She was simply not ready to take that step yet.

"And Laurie," Emma continued. "Just remember, you have to do this on your time. When you're ready. Not Rob. Deciding whether or not or even when to find your father must be done on your time."

"My time. You're right. This has to be done my way, at my pace, at my time. Oh, Emma, I love you!"

"I love you too, Laurie! By the way, do you want to hear some happy news?"

"Of course, anything to get me out of this funk!" Laurie replied.

"Well, the Fairfield School Board just posted a job opening for next year for a high school counselor and I applied."

"Oh my God!" Laurie screamed. "Oh, you must get it! Then we can be together and live in the same town!"

"Well, we'll see, but I'd love to move to Fairfield. It's been so good for you, so who knows? I may just be able to make my home there as well!"

Hanging up, Laurie felt lighter than she had in weeks.

Laurie drove over to Rob's apartment for the night. Tonight, he was on call, so since his apartment was closer to the fire station, they decided that she would spend the night there. She knew there was no way she could keep her stiff knee from him but also did not want it to ruin her night. *Maybe I can, at least, get into his apartment without him seeing me limping from the parking lot.*

She pulled her bug into the space and opened her door. Grabbing the door frame, she hauled herself out of the car and leaned against it to steady herself. Reaching back to grab the bag allowed her not to have to bend her knee. Having accomplished that, she shut and locked the bug then began the slow limp towards his apartment building. *Thank God, his building has an elevator!*

She had barely made it into the lobby, hobbling over towards the elevator, when the door to the stairs was thrown open with such force it banged loudly against the wall. Startled, she whirled around, nearly losing her balance. Looking towards the sound, she saw Rob stalking towards her, fury on his face. Like an avenging angel swooping down, he towered over her as he approached.

"Rob, you frightened me," she said, then squeaked as she was picked up in his massive arms. She threw her arms around his neck to steady herself, knowing he was furious but not knowing why.

"Rob—" she began.

"Not a word, babe," he ordered.

Huffing, she began again. "Rob, I—"

"Laurie. Not. A. Word."

Deciding that not speaking at the moment would be the best course of action, she allowed him to continue to take her up to his apartment. Once inside, she noticed that as angry as he was, he gently sat her down on the sofa, carefully placing a pillow under her knee.

After sitting her down, he stood over her momentarily, then began to pace around the room. She continued to sit quietly, knowing that he had to process whatever was going on in his mind.

Turning around to look at her sitting on his sofa, he ran his hand down his face as though to clear his head.

"Babe, I'm not happy," he stated plainly.

"Rob, I get that honey, but I don't know why if you won't tell me," her voice rose in anger.

"Been looking out my window for ten minutes waiting for you to drive up in your cute, little ass yellow bug. See you drive up, can't wait to get you up here. I look down, and you're barely able to get out of your car. I watch *my* woman, who never said shit to me about hurting today, try to limp into my building." His voice shook with anger.

She opened her mouth to retort, but he held up his hand, shaking his head.

"No secrets, Laurie. You don't feel like coming here, I go to your place. You hurt, I should know about it. You're mine to take care of. A man like me sees his woman barely able to walk, and he didn't know about it, that shit doesn't fly, babe."

Eyes stinging, chin wobbling, she stared at her hands clasped in her lap. All she wanted was to be held, not scolded like a child. She could feel herself getting angry but couldn't open her mouth or the tears would start to flow. So she just looked down.

He looked down at the tiny woman on his couch. The woman that represented forgiveness, repentance, understanding, care, love. The woman that held his heart. The woman he wanted to spend the rest of his life with. Taking a deep breath, he squatted down to her, took her small pale hands into his, leaned over and kissed her forehead.

That was all it took for the tears to come. He carefully lifted her up just enough to slide in under her, settling her on his lap. Head tucked in under his chin, she gave in to the tears that had threatened all day. He hated to see her cry, but he knew from his sister that sometimes a woman just has to get it all out. Holding her gently, rubbing his hands comfortingly along her back and arms, he kissed the top of her head.

Finally, she was calm enough to speak through her tears. "I'm sorry, Rob. I called the doctor today and am going back tomorrow. I wasn't trying to keep anything from you. I knew as soon as you saw me up here, you'd know. I'm just so tired of hurting. I'm tired of not knowing why this is happening. I'm tired of not feeling good." She paused for a moment. "I'm just plain sick and tired of being sick and tired!" she said on a sob.

He sat silently for a few minutes. *That's it. I'm calling the private detective to find her dad. Gotta know if there is something we're missing. God, I just hope she forgives me.*

As her sobs subsided, he continued to hold her gently. "I didn't mean to take my frustration out on you." Sighing heavily, he continued. "I just looked out of the window, not believing my girl wouldn't have called for my help. If you can't walk, I'll carry you."

Tears over, he placed her on a kitchen chair while he prepared dinner. Having taken something for the pain, she was feeling better, and the steaks he cooked were fabulous. Sitting on the sofa watching TV after dinner, Rob with his beer and Laurie with her water made her feel almost normal again.

Snuggling into his side, she began to nuzzle his neck. Kissing her way up towards his jaw and then over to his ear, she nipped his earlobe with her teeth then sucked it into her mouth. Sliding her hand down to his crotch, she found his dick ready and waiting.

Pushing her back, he looked at her sternly. "Babe, if you don't feel well, we don't have to do anything."

Grabbing his jaw in her hand, she pulled his face around to hers. "Rob, I'm not an invalid. The pain pill has kicked in and I. Need. My. Man." Then she latched onto his lips as though her life depended on it.

Growling in response, he picked her up and headed back to the bedroom. Standing her gently on the floor, he took her face in his hands and kissed her softly at first, then with more possessiveness. His tongue plunged into her receptive mouth, searching out each crevice, memorizing her taste, texture, feel. She responded in kind, sucking his tongue into her mouth, her need to feel him inside overwhelming.

He grasped the bottom of her sweater and pulled it over her head, their lips separating just long enough for the material to pass between them. Tossing it to the floor, he reached in front of her to unsnap her lacy pink bra, and it soon landed on top of the sweater. Now that she was standing topless, he palmed her heavy breasts, thumbing her nipples, eliciting the most delightful moans.

She reciprocated by pulling his T-shirt up, although she was too short to take it all the way off. She slid her hands over the muscles of his chest as he finished pulling his shirt over his head, tossing it on the pile of clothing on the floor. She loved the feel of his skin under her fingers. Tracing each bulge, she flicked his nipples as her fingers roved continuously up his chest, over his shoulders, and down his biceps. The sheer size and strength of his body never ceased to amaze her. Or turn her on.

As their kiss continued, her fingers found the button of his jeans, and she quickly unbuttoned it. Sliding down the zipper over his considerable manhood, she managed to push his jeans down to his knees, and he pushed them further and slipped out of them. His erection was tenting his boxers, and Laurie palmed him, sliding her hand down the waistband.

"Hold up, babe. I'm so hard for you, don't want this to end before it gets started," he rasped.

Laying her gently back onto the bed, he leaned over to undo her slacks. Sliding them down slowly, kissing the flesh of her hips, then her thighs, he reached her knees, and …

"What the hell?" he shouted.

Startled out of her sexual bliss, she jerked up in surprise at his exclamation. Looking down at his head and her body, she noticed that her left knee was huge with swelling.

"Jesus, Laurie," he continued to rant. Standing up, staring down at his beautiful woman, his heart pounding. He knew she had a stiff knee but had no idea it was in this shape.

Looking back at her face, he saw silent tears trailing down her cheeks. *Now she's more upset. Christ, what the hell is going on? Shit, man, pull it together.*

Rubbing his hand on his face, he leaned back over and kissed her swollen knee. Crawling up her body, he reached her face and kissed the tears from her cheeks.

Whispering softly against her mouth, "Sorry, Laurie. I just can't stand to see you hurt."

Continuing to kiss her gently, he felt her arms wrap around his neck and pull him closer. Aware of his large body, he wavered on how to make this work without causing her more pain. *Her riding me? No, she would have to be on her knee. From behind? No, that won't work either, 'cause she can't stand up. Shit.*

She felt the change in his kiss. His lips were against hers, but his mind was definitely *not* in the moment. Pulling away, she looked into his eyes, demanding that he look back at her.

"Rob, where'd you go, honey, 'cause you're not here with me."

He dropped his head then looked back up. "Just trying to make this work for you babe. Don't want to hurt your knee."

Nodding in understanding and ever practical, she thought for a second. "I just can't bend my knee or put pressure on it. If you can handle boring missionary, I should be good."

Grinning down at her, he replied, "Nothing boring about my dick being buried deep in you, in any position."

At that, he captured her lips again in a dominating kiss, plundering, sucking, nipping.

Carefully sliding down the bed, he kissed her stomach again then continued his trail of kisses down to her slick folds. Licking her wetness, he pulled her folds apart to allow his tongue deeper access. *God, I love the taste of her.*

His tongue delving in and out of her slick folds, he reached up with one hand to fondle her breast. Her hips rotated upwards pushing into his face.

She could feel the delicious pressure building in her core, smell the scent of sex in the air, desperately needed her release.

He moved his mouth up towards her swollen clit, sucking it into his mouth, allowing his tongue to swirl around it. At the same time, he pinched her nipple and felt her convulse against his face.

Her hips bucked as she begged for more. He added a finger deep into her core, and she exploded as waves of bliss pounded over and over. Throwing her head back, she allowed the sensations to carry her away. Away to a place where there was no pain. No worry. Just Rob. And her.

He watched her face carefully as the pleasure washed over, grateful to have been able to take her there. *Beautiful. Precious. Mine.*

She slowly opened her eyes, smiling up at him. Raising her arms, beckoning him, she needed to feel his body on hers.

He moved back up her body and carefully lowered his hips between her legs, positioning his dick at her opening. Sliding his hand between them he guided himself in and in one thrust was fully seated. *Warm. Tight. Welcoming.*

"Babe, I want you to feel every inch," he whispered.

She felt stretched as his huge cock pushed all the way up into her. He began a slow thrusting, pulling almost all of the way out before pushing back in again.

Rob, worried that his lower body would press against her swollen knee, raised himself up. Kneeling on the bed between her legs, he pulled her hips upwards toward his dick. Gently pushing her legs apart as wide as she was comfortable, he began his slow thrusting again. This angle produced a new sensation for her, and she began to moan as the friction deep in her core caused sparks to spread throughout her core.

He fought the urge to begin pounding, knowing that this needed to be about Laurie, about her comfort, her pleasure. *Never felt that way about a woman before I met her. Never gave a shit about the woman except to make her come first.* Now it was already second nature to put her needs before his.

Feeling his own release coming soon, he leaned down to grasp her nipple in his mouth. Sucking it deeply, he nipped at the hardened bud with his teeth.

"Babe, come for me," he begged. Right on cue, she felt herself lost once again in her release. The walls of her core grabbed his cock tightly, she felt wave after wave of pleasure crashing through her. Rob, losing control, pounded the last few thrusts deep inside, allowing her contracting muscles to milk him. Leaning up with her hips tightly held in his firm grip, he threw his head back, neck straining as his release poured deeply inside. Continuing to pump until the last drop was gone, he slowly pulled out. Gently moving to the side opposite of her injured knee, he lay down beside her, pulling her into his embrace.

They lay together, sated, and he pushed her hair from her face. Staring down into her eyes that were filled with love, he kissed her lips with the soft promise of forever.

Untangling himself from her, he rose from the bed. She watched as his muscular back and tight ass walked towards the bathroom. In a moment, the sound of water running in the bathtub could be heard. When he walked back in, he looked at her knee carefully. Having been around numerous sports injuries and trained as an EMT, he tried to ascertain exactly what was going on.

She held her breath, afraid that he was going to explode in frustration again. But he just gently probed the swollen flesh and then gently lifted her and walked to the bathroom.

"I could get used to being carried around by a handsome, well-built, naked man," she murmured in his ear.

Eyebrow cocked, he growled, "Just any naked man, darlin'?"

Laughing, she replied, "No, not just *any* naked man. At least as long as you're around."

Pretending to drop her in the tub, she screamed and held on to his neck tightly. Laughing, he lowered her gently into the hot water. "I want you to soak for a while. The warm water will help with the knee. Should have iced it earlier in the day, but the warmth will make it feel better now."

Still kneeling beside the bathtub, he looked at her beautiful face, kissed her forehead and said, "We gotta think about where you live."

She looked up at him, confusion showing on her face.

"Laurie, Carol is spending most nights with Tom,

and in a couple of months they'll be married. No sense in you trying to find a new roommate when you and I spend most of our time together and we can stay here. Right now, you need help with stairs, and I've got an elevator."

She looked up, a smile lighting her whole face. "Is that your romantic way of asking me to move in with you?" she teased.

He looked down with a shit-eating grin on his face. "I want you in my home, in my bed, and in my life. Now's as good a time as any!"

He stood and started to leave the bathroom. Turning back around, he asked, "Laurie, when is your appointment tomorrow?"

Looking up into his now serious face, she answered, "Three o'clock."

Nodding, he walked out of the bathroom, closing the door behind him to keep the warmth of the tub from cooling too quickly. Sliding down into the deep, warm water, letting her cares seep away, she felt his love surround her, keeping her safe.

15

The next day as Rob arrived at the fire station he immediately headed to the chief's office. Mac always had an open-door policy, and as usual, his door was standing wide open. Rob walked in, knocking on the door frame as he entered.

"Chief," he greeted.

"Son, what can I do for you?" Mac answered in his usual booming voice.

Rob looked down momentarily then focused back on Mac's blue eyes that seemed to notice everyone and everything around him. "I'm going to be taking some time off occasionally and may need to ask some of the others to cover for me."

Mac put down his pen and pulled his reading glasses off his face. "You all right, son?"

Rob realized that right now he needed to talk to his dad, not the chief, a distinction that he was always careful to keep. "Dad, Laurie's not well. Don't know what's wrong, but she's got a bunch of doctor appointments, and I want to be there when she goes."

Mac immediately stood up from his desk and walked around to stand in front of his son, pulling him in for a hug. Rob felt a lump in his throat as his father's large embrace encompassed him. Taking a shaky breath, he stood stoically for a moment, allowing his father to express his love and concern through the hug. Stepping back, Mac ushered Rob into one of the office chairs as he lowered himself down into the one next to it.

"What's going on, son?"

"Don't know, Dad. She's got all these weird symptoms. Tired all the time, neck so stiff she can hardly turn it, knee stiff and swollen, a slight rash on her face. Jesus, even her toes turn blue when her feet get cold."

Rob rubbed his face in frustration, sighing as he looked out of the window. Looking back at his dad's kind face, he said, "I just want to be available to go with her to the doc appointments when she goes."

"Son, you've stepped in for years, taking shifts for every one of these men here. You have covered for them at holidays, family events, when their kids were sick or just graduating from kindergarten. I think you deserve to be able to ask the same of them. You take what you need when you need it."

The two men sat quietly for a moment, Mac allowing his son a chance to get ahold of his emotions.

"What can we do, your mother and I?"

Rob looked up gratefully, knowing his parents would move heaven and earth to help him or his sister, and now Laurie. "Nothing right now, but thanks, Dad."

Rob and Mac headed out to the main area where a large group of firefighters and EMTs were working on the equipment.

Mac boomed, "Listen up!" The crew immediately gave their full attention to their chief. "Rob here has a personal problem where his Laurie needs to make some doctor's appointments. And no, she's not pregnant," he added, eliciting a few smiles from those who knew the chief was looking forward to grandchildren.

Rob continued the speech to his fellow firefighters. "What the chief means is that Laurie does have some doctor appointments coming up, and I want to be there. Don't know what is going on, but I take care of what is mine."

Immediately the others in the group clamored to assure Rob that they would cover any shifts he needed. Rob felt the emotion in the room, touched by the camaraderie. Mac clapped his son on the shoulder, and for once without booming, he whispered to his son, "You need us, you got us."

Nodding, Rob headed out to talk to Tom and Jake. He knew what he had to do. He just prayed that Laurie would see it that way.

Tom and Jake agreed to meet Rob at the diner for lunch and when he pulled into the parking lot, he was not surprised to see them already there. Walking inside, he waved to the owner and then headed over to their table.

Not one for small talk, Jake immediately asked, "Laurie?"

Rob nodded. "It's getting bad. Last night I lost my shit 'cause I look outside my window and her knee is so swollen she can barely get out of the car and walk inside. She's got another appointment this afternoon, and I'm going too." Shaking his head, he pushed his plate back in frustration. "Man, I'm a fuckin' mess worrying about her."

"Hate to have a Hallmark moment, bro, but that's what love will do to you," Tom replied.

"Tom, I talked to her last night about moving in with me. Carol is over at your place most nights, and if I'm working, Laurie will have a place with an elevator."

Tom nodded in agreement. "Yeah, Carol was going to help Laurie find a new roommate since we'll be married this spring, but she just said the other day that she wondered if you all would want to move in together. The lease is up for renewal next month anyway, so it's a perfect time to let it go."

Rob, relieved that one problem was taken care of, heaved a sigh of relief.

Jake, watching his friend carefully, noted, "You've decided to find Laurie's father, haven't you?"

Rob looked at his two oldest friends knowing they understood him more than almost anyone.

"Right now, I just want to find out if this man exists and is still alive. I know his first and last name and middle initial. I know he was in the Army about twenty-five years ago and was stationed near the Richmond base. Not going to let Laurie know about this right now.

The PI reports only to me. As soon as I find out more info, then I'll tell her."

Jake and Tom both nodded in agreement, knowing that Rob would support them anytime they needed it. Lunch finished, the friends shook hands as Rob headed down the street. Deciding to pop into Bernie's Bakery, he thought his mom could pick out the perfect item for Laurie to have before they headed to the doctor's office.

Opening the door to the familiar smells of the bakery, he was greeted by his mom flying across the room to pull him for a hug. Standing about eight inches shorter than her son, Bernie could still engulf him in a mother's hug. She had the ability to make anyone feel as though they were the center of her concern, especially her family.

He quickly recognized that his mother's greeting was more than her usual enthusiasm. "Dad call?" he questioned.

His mom raised her face to his, tears in her eyes. "Oh, Rob, I'm so sorry that Laurie is not well. Please," she begged, "if there is anything you or she need, let me know." Suddenly straightening up, she immediately declared, "You two need to come to dinner tonight. There's no sense in her trying to cook right now."

He chuckled. His mom was convinced that good food could make any situation better. Now that he thought about it, maybe she was right. *Good God, I've hit the age where I now think like my parents.*

"I did actually come in here to see if I can get something for Laurie to eat before we go to the doctor this afternoon."

Her eyes lit up, and she scurried off to the kitchen. In just a couple of minutes, she was back with a bag much bigger than Rob thought would hold one treat.

"I know she likes the strawberry cheesecake tarts, but I also wanted something that would not be messy before the doctor's appointment, so I included a bear claw pastry. So you don't have to worry about anything for breakfast, I included three different types of muffins."

"Mom," he started to speak.

"Now if you come over for dinner, I'll make sure to have some cake for dessert. And if there is anything you can think of that she also likes, just give me a call, and I'll bring it home."

"Mom!" he interrupted. She looked up in surprise. Rob laughed and pulled his mom into a huge hug. "I think you've got us covered. We're good."

Looking up into her son's eyes, she wrapped her arms around his waist, giving into the hug. "Son, your father and I've always been proud of you. We worried when it seemed like you were never going to find someone special, but I kept praying that one day you'd know what your dad and I have. Honey, we love Laurie. She is so good for you, and you're such a wonderful man for her. If there is anything we can do, you must let us know."

Rob held his mom closely for a few minutes, knowing she needed comforting as much he did. *I have this. A mom and a dad who have raised me, stood by me, and are still with me as an adult. Laurie never had this.*

Dropping a kiss on his mother's cheek, he took the large package from her and headed out of the door.

Laurie and Jean were standing on the playground watching the children. Jean had finished talking with Cindy and had brought her out to play. The other first graders ran up, grabbed Cindy's hand, and pulled her off towards the swings.

"Isn't it great how children are so accepting of new people and new experiences?" Laurie observed.

Jean agreed. "Yes, it's us adults that are afraid to step into unknown territory."

Laurie looked sideways at her friend. "You afraid? What are you scared of?"

"Oh, I think there are probably lots of things I'm afraid of. I would love to meet someone and have a real relationship again, but every time I do, it just never goes to the next level. Maybe it's the unknown that holds me back."

"That's very profound," Laurie admitted. Before she could continue the conversation, the same minivan that she had seen before drove slowly by again. Stopping by the fence that surrounded the school's property, it sat for a while. Laurie moved away from the wall she was leaning against and started limping towards the van. Suddenly, the van began moving down the street again. Still too far away to see a license plate, she watched it disappear.

"What's up?" Jean asked as Laurie made her way back.

"I know I'm paranoid, but there's a minivan with dark windows that I keep seeing around here, right after you told me about Cindy's parents." Laurie looked into Jean's worried face. "I know it may be nothing, after all this *is* an elementary school and minivans are always around here."

"Do you think we should let the authorities know?" Jean asked.

"I told the principal, and I also called the Carlsons. They said they would be diligent, and of course, they always come into the school to pick her up. I just wish I could get a license number, but with this damn limp, I'm not good for much," she said in frustration.

Jean leaned over and touched her arm. "I'm praying for you, Laurie. I know this is hard for you."

Laurie appreciated the sentiment and concern. Looking at her watch, she blew her whistle and called the children back inside. Several of the boys fought over who would get to hold the door for her.

"Why thank you, gentlemen," Laurie exclaimed as she went inside. The boys laughed and continued to hold the doors for the rest of the class.

Rob wanted to make sure he was at the school to help Laurie, so he got there early. Signing in at the office, he went to her room. As he entered, chaos erupted. "The fireman, the fireman," the children yelled. Rob laughed as the children swarmed around him.

"Is there another fire?" one little girl asked.

"No, no," he quickly assured her. "I'm just here to say hello to your teacher and to check up on all of you."

His eyes sought Laurie's and her smile dazzled him.

"Okay, children, we have five minutes to get ready. Find your red homework folders and make sure to put them in your backpacks. Tommy, I want your mom to send in a note if you're going on the art field trip. Josie, don't forget your hat and gloves today."

He noticed that the children immediately listened to their teacher and began to gather their materials. He looked over at a small girl who was standing very still staring up at him with huge eyes. Not afraid, but definitely wary. *That must be Cindy.*

Knowing his size made him too imposing, he squatted down so that he would be less frightening. Cindy watched him carefully as Ms. Dodd walked over to him saying hello.

"Cindy, would you like to meet the fireman that helped the children earlier this year?" Laurie asked.

Cindy walked over to Laurie and stood by her side, still staring at Rob.

Rob softly greeted Cindy, being careful not to reach out to her. Cindy stayed next to Laurie but smiled shyly at him.

"Run get ready to go home, sweetie," Laurie told her, and Cindy moved to get her coat.

He stood and looked at his beautiful girlfriend. Her

hair, pulled back away from her face, hung long down her back. Her red sweater, modest in appearance, could not hide her figure from his perusal. Wearing black slacks again, he noticed that she was wearing black tennis shoes. Cocking his eyebrow as he looked down, she just shrugged and explained, "I'm steadier with these shoes, and I can't wear heels and limp around all day."

Nodding in understanding, he wanted nothing more than to take her in his arms and kiss her pain away. But twenty-five pairs of eyes all around would not make that a good idea.

He watched in awe as she corralled all the students and limped out with them to the buses. He followed them as Josie wanted to hold his hand. Standing to the side as Laurie managed to get each student to their bus or into their parents' cars, he noticed that one lady came to Laurie to take Cindy's hand. At a discreet distance, he could catch part of their conversation.

"I wasn't able to get to the road to get a license plate number, but I've alerted our principal, and I wanted you to know."

She finished up with her children and turned to Rob. "I just have to finish in my room, and then we can head to the doctors."

He wanted to carry her but knew that she would not appreciate the gesture. He walked slowly beside her as she limped back to her room. Once inside and away from prying eyes, he swooped in and picked her up in his strong arms. She threw her arms around his neck and brought her lips to his. Aware of where he was, he kept the kiss gentle but wanted nothing more than to delve his tongue inside her warm mouth. Setting her back on her feet, he slid her body closely down the front of his. Giggling, she looked down as he adjusted the tightness in his jeans.

She went about quickly straightening the room, Rob helping as directed.

"Babe, what were you saying to Mrs. Carlson? Something about trying to see a license plate?"

"Oh, I was told that Cindy's parents might be looking for her even though the judge who placed her with the Carlsons temporarily took away their parental rights. Ever since then, I keep seeing the same minivan with darkened windows drive by. It pauses near the school, and when we're out playing, it stops for a while. So today I decided to walk over and see who was inside and what they were doing. But when I got closer, they pulled away quickly."

She said this so matter of fact that she never noticed a drop in the temperature in the room.

"Are you kidding me?" he asked, barely keeping his anger in check. "Babe, you think someone, *anyone*, is around who shouldn't be, you call the police. You do not walk over to have a chat!"

Laurie looked at his face, his tight jaw ticking and realized that he couldn't help but always try to jump in to protect her.

"Honey, there was a fence between me and them. They couldn't have hurt me, and I think it's important that they know that someone is watching out for the children." Taking a few halting steps over to him, she placed her hand on his chest right over his heart, looking up into his eyes. "Rob, we always have to be aware of child molesters and pedophiles hanging around elementary schools. Even if it had nothing to do with Cindy, I have to be diligent."

Hanging his head, silently praying for patience in dealing with his beautiful but headstrong woman, he looked into her eyes and saw her silent plea for understanding.

Placing his hands on either side of her face, he softly kissed her lips. "I get there is so much more about what you do than just teach. Never even realized. But I want you safe. What is your school's protocol for this type of shit?"

"Our school safety plan has me alert our principal of any and all concerns and observations, which I've done. It's up to her to inform the school safety officer who, based on the information, lets the police know. I often see the police cars drive by the school routinely."

He felt her fingers rub his chest over his heart, and he captured her hands in his much larger one. "Thanks for telling me, Laurie. I just want you safe."

Her smile spread across her whole face, and Rob felt it wrap around his heart.

"No secrets, Rob. Remember? Of course I'll tell you."

She turned to pick up her coat and purse, and he stood rooted to the spot.

No secrets. But damn. I need to do whatever I can to take care of you. Please forgive me when you find out.

He then escorted her to his truck, lifting her up comfortably to place her in the passenger seat. Handing her Bernie's bag, much to Laurie's delight, they headed to the doctor's office.

16

Rob sat in the waiting room while Dr. Alexander completed her physical examination of Laurie. The nurse brought him in when they were ready to discuss the possibilities.

Laurie sat holding his hand as Dr. Alexander began.

"Laurie, often when trying to find out what is going on with someone who has a variety of symptoms, the best thing we can do is start eliminating concerns. For example, here is what I do know. Your x-rays and scans show no abnormalities or tumors."

Laurie felt Rob's hand squeezing hers tighter with every word the doctor spoke.

"Your blue toes and fingers when you get cold are probably caused by Reynaud's disease. This is not a debilitating condition, usually more of a nuisance than anything else. Apparently cold affects it but so can stress. Some things you can do are to take care of your hands and feet. Keep them warm, don't go barefoot, and don't wear tight rings or shoes."

Laurie nodded. So far, so good. Nothing she couldn't handle. Glancing to the side, she wanted to see how Rob was handling everything. Eyes focused on the doctor, his jaw was tight, she could feel stress pouring off him.

"Your other symptoms do concern me. The low-grade fever, your severe joint pain and swelling, combined with the Reynaud's, all point to an autoimmune disease, possibly lupus."

Laurie and Rob stole quick looks at each other, neither knowing what lupus was. Looking back at Dr. Alexander, she admitted, "I don't know what that is."

"Autoimmune diseases cause the body's natural immune system to mistakenly attack and destroy healthy body tissue."

Rob suddenly remembered how Jake's mother had been diagnosed with rheumatoid arthritis and hearing Jake mention autoimmune. *Damn, why hadn't I paid more attention to what Mrs. Campbell has?*

"I have a friend whose mom has rheumatoid arthritis," he volunteered.

Dr. Alexander nodded her head enthusiastically. "Exactly! They are both autoimmune diseases. Where RA affects just the joints, well with lupus your body's immune system attacks your internal organs as well as joints."

Laurie sat in stunned silence. Taking it all in. Letting the news slide slowly into the corners of her mind. Glancing out of the window, she noticed the cars driving up and down the road. Her mind suddenly thought of how many people had sat in this very office hearing news that was going to change their lives. Not just here. But in all doctors' offices. All hospitals. We drive by them every day, but we never think of what news is being given that alters people's lives. *Lupus. Lupus.*

"Laurie are you all right, dear," Dr. Alexander gently asked.

Her eyes snapped back to the doctor's and then over to Rob's, seeing his concerned face. Letting go of her hand, he placed his arm around her shoulders and pulled her in for a hug.

"Babe?"

"Fine. I'm fine." Turning back to the doctor, she stoically asked, "So, do I have lupus and if so, what does it mean?"

"I'll be referring you to a rheumatologist for further diagnosis, but I think it is very likely that they will concur. They'll do more blood tests and have you complete a family medical history."

This statement grabbed Rob's attention and solidified his resolve to find Laurie's father. His thoughts were interrupted by Laurie's comment.

"I only have information on my maternal side; I never knew my father."

Dr. Alexander nodded and said that while they wouldn't have the whole picture, having her mother's history would be helpful.

"If I do have lupus, what exactly does that mean, and what is the cure?"

At this, Dr. Alexander took a deep breath, and both Laurie and Rob felt themselves on high alert.

"Laurie, there is no cure. The disease is unpredictable and difficult to control. Mostly the rheumatologist will treat the symptoms with a variety of drugs. Some days you will have no pain and feel absolutely fine. Other days, it will be hard to get out of bed. But Laurie," Dr. Alexander said when she was sure she had her attention, "Many people with lupus live healthy lives as long as they control the symptoms. They work, they exercise, they have fun, they have families."

At this last statement, Laurie looked quickly at Rob and then back to Dr. Alexander.

"So, lupus won't affect my ability to have children?"

Again, Dr. Alexander hesitated. *Why do doctors do that? Just tell me. Tell me the truth!*

"It shouldn't affect your ability to get pregnant, although it can affect if you can carry the child to term."

Feeling lightheaded, Laurie slumped onto Rob's shoulder. He grabbed her as the doctor called for the nurse to bring the ammonia capsules.

Pushing her head between her legs, he said, "Breathe, babe. Deep, slow breaths."

The nurse entered the room and quickly held the ammonia to her nose. Reviving, Laurie was embarrassed. Leaning back heavily on Rob, she looked at the doctor.

"I'm so sorry, Dr. Alexander. It's just a lot to take in, but I want to know it all."

Rob continued to stroke her arm as she leaned heavily against him. He wanted to hit something, rail against God, take this burden from her. *While I was concerned with nameless hook-ups, this woman was working, studying, living to improve her situation. She's a thousand times better than I ever was. Why her? Well, I sure as hell am going to take care of her.*

"My dear, no apology is necessary. You have been given a great shock. I'm going to give you some literature to take home, and then you will be more prepared for your rheumatology appointment. My nurse will make the appointment for you when you leave. I'll be working carefully with them on your treatment plan. I also want to start you on prednisone, a steroid, for the inflammation in your neck and knee."

Rob had seen enough football injuries to know all about using steroids to help with inflammation. *Finally, something I understand.* He also knew they worked quickly but wasn't sure if they could be taken indefinitely. *But thank God...it's a start.*

By this time, Laurie was just nodding without taking in any more information. He assisted her up and took the literature from the doctor. She leaned on him as they made the next appointment and went out to the truck. He kept glancing at her pale face, but she wasn't saying anything. He picked her up, gently placing her in his truck. Leaning over to buckle her in, he brushed her hair from her face. Wanting to kiss her, he held himself back as her eyes did not even seem to register his presence.

He swung his tall frame up into the driver's side. Placing his hands on the steering wheel, he just sat, not moving. Looking over at her, sitting stoically, his heart ached for her. "Laurie, I'm here for you, baby. Whatever you need, I'm here."

She turned her head towards the handsome visage in

front of her and felt his love. It was almost tangible. Smiling a small smile, she reached over and placed her small hand on his.

He lunged across the console, capturing her mouth in a gentle kiss, pouring all the love he could possibly give into the kiss. *Feel this, babe. Feel what I feel. Please let me take care of you.*

She spoke softly against his lips. "I love you, Robert MacDonald."

"I love you too, Laurie Dodd." Hesitating for a moment, he continued. "I was talking to Tom earlier about your apartment. Carol is practically moved in with him, and the lease is up in a month. Makes no sense to find a new roommate when we spend so much time together. My place has an elevator."

She gave a half-hearted laugh. "Honey, are you still trying to convince me to move in with you?" More somberly, she added, "It's a big step. Are you sure we're ready or are you doing this out of a sense of guilt or responsibility?"

He took her face in his hands, "I'm listing all these practical reasons. But the honest-to-God truth is that I love you. Loved you since I met you. You're my life. Before you, I was existing but not living. I want to wake up looking at your gorgeous face every morning and go to bed with you in my arms every night. Truth is, you make me want to be a better man. Hell, I'm a better man just by being with you." Kissing her lightly, he added, "Please, babe, move in with me. It's our time."

Tears flowed down her cheeks as she held him tight. He wiped her tears with his rough thumbs. Smiling up at him, she gave him her answer. "Rob, I've worked for so long just to make it in life. Always feeling like I was searching. But this place is it for me. You're it for me. My searching is over. I love you with all that I am. So, yes, I'll move in with you."

He dove in, plundering her mouth, their tongues clashing, tasting her, feeling her, breathing her. She felt the familiar dampening of her panties and ache between her legs. As she started to squirm to relieve the pressure, he chuckled. Pulling back, he said, "Babe, I swear I could take you right here. But the parking lot of the doctor's office is probably not the best place to bury myself deep inside of you."

Laughing, she agreed, moving back in her seat. Rob, adjusting his swollen dick in his jeans, started the truck.

"Laurie, my parents wanted us to come over for dinner, but I'll call them, and we can go another time."

She thought for a moment and then said, "I'm not going to go home and fall apart. The news today sucked, but we need to tell your parents about moving in together, and we can tell them what's going on at the same time."

"You sure?"

Shrugging, she admitted, "Honey, I'm not sure of anything right now. But I really don't mind seeing them."

"Well, all right. By the way, Mom's having some of your favorite cake."

"Now that's a reason to go!"

Dinner with the MacDonalds was just what Laurie needed. From the moment they walked in the front door, Mac and Bernie swooped in, surrounding them with hugs and comfort. Keeping the conversation light during dinner since Suzy was around, she was able to enjoy herself and the delicious meal. It was so obvious that their family loved each other dearly. Suzy even joked about being their 'oops baby', explaining the reason there were fifteen years between her and Rob.

"Well, you're the prettiest 'oops' I ever saw, baby girl," Mac said as he winked first at Suzy and then at his wife.

After dinner, Bernie suggested they take the cake and coffee into the family room to get comfortable.

"Let me help clear the table, Bernie," Laurie offered as she rose to begin gathering plates.

"No!" four voices shouted out at once, startling Laurie into dropping one of the plates back onto the table.

"You don't need to be on your feet or putting strain on your knee."

"Laurie, I'll help Momma. You go sit down," Suzy offered.

Bernie and Mac made similar excuses.

Rob walked over and tagged Laurie around the shoulders. "Come on, babe. You've had an exhausting day. Let's sit down for now."

"Mom, you go ahead in with them. I got this," Suzy volunteered. Laurie noticed Bernie lean over and kiss Suzy's head, whispering, "Thanks, sweetheart."

Family. That's how it works. That was always how Emma

and I were. And Grandma and Grandpa and Momma before they died. I've missed this.

Sitting down in the family room, Rob settled Laurie down on the sofa with her knee propped up. Sitting down next to her, he pulled her into his side, embracing her completely. Bernie and Mac settled in their chairs, after having passed around the cake and coffee.

Bernie spoke first. "Kids, I don't want to pry, but Laurie we know you went to the doctors' today. What do you want us to know?"

That opened the conversation as they informed Bernie and Mac of everything Dr. Alexander had told them. They spent almost an hour discussing what they knew, questions to ask the rheumatologist, and how to manage her symptoms.

Instead of being upset, Laurie found it strangely comforting to be able to discuss the diagnosis and how it might affect her life. It seemed to take the power out of lupus to realize that she was not alone.

Looking at Rob, she remembered that she hadn't told Emma yet. "I need to call her, but I think I'll wait until tomorrow."

Mac, having listened carefully to all that had been said, looked at his son, pride filling his heart. Was it just eight months ago that his son had continued his playboy ways but now sat with his arm around a beautiful, smart, caring woman, offering her care and comfort and love? Bernie, glancing at her husband, knew exactly what he was thinking and smiled to herself.

Turning back to the couple on the sofa, Bernie, ever practical, asked, "Laurie, what can we do to help?"

"Honestly, there isn't anything I need. I start taking the prednisone tonight, and that should immediately take the swelling down. I have meds for pain as well when needed. At work, the kids are great! They run and get things for me so that I don't have to jump up every two minutes. At home, well…." She looked at Rob shyly.

He looked down at her beautiful face and gave her shoulder a gentle squeeze. Looking back at his parents' quizzical looks, he said proudly, "Mom, Dad, Laurie and I are moving in together this weekend."

Bernie clapped her hands in delight, and Mac boomed in his exuberant voice, "Congratulations!"

Rob continued his explanation. "Carol's going to be moving in with Tom. Their lease runs out next month, and no need for Laurie to go through the stress of finding a new roommate when she'll be with me most of the time anyway. Plus, my apartment building's got an elevator." Kissing the top of her head, he added, "You guys know we're in love, so this is just the next step."

Bernie couldn't contain herself anymore. Already envisioning Laurie as her daughter-in -law, she rushed over to embrace both of them in a hug. Rob assisted Laurie to stand as Mac came over to congratulate them again. While Bernie held on to Laurie, immediately discussing ways to make Rob's apartment more comfortable, Mac grabbed Rob in a bear hug. Mac's eyes shined with unshed tears, and he just said, "Real proud of you, son. Real proud."

Soon afterward, Rob and Laurie said their goodbyes. He picked her up and carried her to his truck, and they headed to his apartment.

"Babe, I heard Mom talking to you about changing the apartment around to make you more comfortable."

"Oh, honey, I won't change anything, I promise," she rushed to assure him, imagining he thought she was going to run in and fill the place with girly things.

He jerked his head towards her as he pulled into the parking lot. "Laurie, listen up good. As of right now, this place is your home as much as mine. You want your pictures up, you put 'em up. You want different covers on the bed, fine. You got shit you're bringing over, that's fine too. And as soon as we can, plan on us finding a home together."

She looked over at her handsome prince with the moonlight shining through the windshield. "Rob, you didn't ask for all of this. I know this is a lot to take in. I would even understand if it's too much."

He looked at her sharply. "You'd better not be talking about you getting sick and me not wanting to stick around. If you even insinuate that shit, your bottom will feel the sting of my hand."

She giggled and found herself getting wet at just the thought of betting spanked by him. Her involuntary squirm to ease the fluttering between her legs was noticed by him.

"Damn, girl, we'd better get inside before this gets outta hand in my truck."

Still laughing, she hung on tight as he carried her upstairs into *their* apartment.

Settling her on the couch while he turned on the lights throughout the apartment, he found himself looking around. The apartment was clean although somewhat sterile. One family picture and one picture of him, Jake, and Tom sat on the end table next to the sofa. His bed was covered in a grey and navy comforter, but that was the only color in the room. Shaking his head, he realized that this apartment was just a place for him to hang out between shifts. And since he had never brought any women back to this place, it really was just a crash pad. *Maybe it's not too early to look for a house together.*

That night, as he curled his body protectively around her much smaller one, his mind raced with the events of the day. He had already made the call to the PI to start the search of military records to see if Laurie's father could be located. He hated to keep a secret from her, but the doctor said it was important to reduce her stress.

He was determined to read through all of the lupus material that the doctor had provided, plus get online and see what else he could find out.

Damn. He almost forgot that he needed to talk to Jake and Tom about the minivan that was driving around. The last thing he needed was Laurie worrying about a child in her classroom. *I'll see them tomorrow.*

Finally deciding that his mind had covered everything it needed to, tightening his grip on Laurie's peaceful body, sleep claimed him.

17

The next week brought a steadiness to Rob's and Laurie's lives. She was feeling better now that she was on medications and could walk without a limp. She had only seen the minivan one more time and began seeing the Fairfield police cars drive by the school more frequently.

Rob had spoken to Jake and Tom, explaining the situation with Cindy's parents. They agreed that there was a threat, and after discussing it with the police chief, patrol cars were assigned to increase their daily rotations around the elementary school.

Laurie's favorite time of day was when she left school and drove to her new apartment. Rob had cleared out half of the closet, although she insisted that she did not need that much space. His apartment was about the same size as what she shared with Carol, but the extra bedroom was used as a study/guest room. There was room in the study for her to set up her laptop to complete lesson plans and get work graded. His laptop was in there as well, but they generally weren't using them at the same time.

The kitchen was the area that she wanted to get her hands on. His cabinets were filled with old cookware and dishes that Bernie had given him years ago. She bought all new pots, pans, dishes, and glassware. At one of the second-hand shops downtown, she snagged an old spice rack that she filled with spices and olive oils, placing it on the counter.

The only decorations she added to the living room were a colorful blanket draped over the sofa and her framed family photos on the end tables. The antique coat rack by the front door now held her winter coat and hat. With a silk floral arrangement in the center of the table, she now felt as though when she walked in the door it was her place as well as Rob's.

In the bathroom, she tried very hard not to take up too much room, but there was no getting around it – women had more bathroom items than men. But finding a cute basket in the same downtown shop, she filled it with her makeup and hair products, then stored it under the sink.

Laurie had started a tradition of stopping by Bernie's Bakery and loading up on pastries and coffee to take to the fire station on weekend mornings when Rob and Mac were there. Since Rob left early for his shift, she popped into Bernie's. His mom greeted her with usual enthusiasm, and after checking to see how Laurie was feeling, she began packing up the treats.

Suzy was working in the shop, and Laurie was glad to get to spend a few minutes with her. A group of teenage boys came in, one tall blond constantly looking over at Suzy. Laurie couldn't help but tease her when she realized that Suzy couldn't keep her eyes off him as well.

"Who's the blond hottie?" she asked.

Suzy reddened and whispered, "Brad. That's Brad Evans. He's a varsity football player. He's a junior this year so he's one year ahead of me. His parents own Smokey's."

Laurie had to hide her smile as she listened to Suzy's dissertation on Brad. "Well, he certainly is cute and appears to have eyes for you."

Suzy's eyes grew wide, and her blush deepened. "Do you really think so? I like him so much, but I have to pretend not to, so I won't get teased."

Laurie took a quick trip down memory lane as she remembered her days from high school. Just then, Bernie headed back with all of the bags for the firemen.

"I'll help Laurie take these out, Mom," Suzy volunteered. Hugging Bernie goodbye, Laurie and Suzy headed out.

"Could you use a hand, ma'am?"

Laurie looked over her bags and saw the young man, Brad, offering to help while keeping his eyes on Suzy. Smiling, she agreed and handed her bags to him. She watched as he made small talk to Suzy as the three of them headed to her yellow bug. Thanking them both, she watched as Brad walked Suzy back into the bakery. *Hmmm, I wonder what Rob will say about that development?*

The yellow VW bug had barely pulled up to the station when it was surrounded by a group of enthusiastic firemen. They came to grab the bags from Bernie's, and Rob came jogging over to grab his girl. Her eyes met his as he came closer. *God, he is gorgeous.*

Her smile lit her whole face, and he wondered once again how he could have ever gotten so lucky. Picking her up in his arms, his mouth plundered hers as she answered right back with her tongue tangling with his. Remembering where they were, he slowly separated letting her slide down his front until her legs were steady on the ground. Leading her upstairs to the kitchen area, he assisted in setting out the coffee and pastries.

"Where's my wife's coffee?" boomed Mac, walking from his office into the kitchen. He reached Laurie and embraced her in a gentle hug. "And how's my favorite schoolteacher?"

She laughed. "I'm doing very well right now, Mac. Thank you for asking."

She started to leave, but Rob asked her to stay and eat with them. "Rob, this medicine makes me hungry all the time, so I have to watch it, or I'll gain a ton of weight."

"A little more weight on that luscious body will not

bother me at all." And with that, he gave her ass a discreet pat as they went to sit with the others.

A few minutes later, Rob's cell phone vibrated, and he looked down at the screen. Glancing sharply to the side at Laurie, he saw her smiling up at him. "Sorry, Laurie, need to take this call."

Rob, wanting privacy, walked out of the kitchen and down the hall towards the bunk rooms.

"MacDonald."

"Rob, it's Sid Gaskill." Sid was the private investigator he had hired.

"You got something for me."

Sid, used to Rob's abrupt behavior, knew that his client wanted to get down to business quickly. "Yes, sir. I found the military records for Brock Timothy Sinclair. He did a twenty-year career in the Army; retired about five years ago. Lives in the Richmond area. Regular military career, a purple heart, excellent commendations. Pays his bills. Pays his taxes. Never married. Never arrested. For all intents and purposes, a real stand-up guy."

"Got any contact info?"

"Yeah, I'll send it to your email."

"Got it. Thanks." Rob hung up, continuing to stand still. He realized that there were certain moments in life when a decision is made, and you hope like hell it is the correct decision but know that nothing else in life will ever be the same after it. He walked around the corner to look into the kitchen area where Laurie was still sitting. She threw her head back, laughing in delight at something one of the men said. He'd certainly been with beautiful women before, but she was different. She seemed to take life as it came. Never expecting more than what she could make from it. Her face, still alight with her smile, seemed to have a glow that spread out to those around her.

Watching her, he felt a tightness in his chest, and he rubbed it with his hand, trying to make it ease. It was then that he realized the tightness came from loving someone. Loving them so much that the thought of life without them was unbearable. Right then, she looked over at him from across the room. Her smile, aimed directly at him, only made his chest hurt more. She was the best of him. The best of what he could be. The best of what made life worth living.

He jumped when a large hand clapped him on his shoulder.

"Loving someone that much hurts, doesn't it, son?" Mac said gently.

Rob reached up and grabbed his dad's hand, still on his shoulder. "How do you ever know if you're doing the right thing, Dad?" he asked in an uncharacteristic moment of doubt.

Mac just squeezed his shoulder tighter. "You do the best you can each and every day and then turn the rest over to prayer, son." Mac patted him before walking away.

Laurie slid out of her seat and walked over to Rob. Looking back into his deep blue eyes, she smiled up at him. "Everything okay, honey?"

He wrapped his arms around her tiny body, pulling her in for comfort. Whether the comfort was for him or her, he wasn't sure. Kissing the top of her head, he whispered, "Everything's going to be fine, babe."

That night, Rob opened up his email. There was the email from the PI with the contact information for Brock. He decided that the only way to handle this was to be in person, and he thanked his lucky stars that the man was only three hours away instead of on the other side of the country. Each month, Mac had to drive to Richmond for a state fire chief meeting, and that meeting was in a couple of days. Rob decided to go along so that he could meet with Brock face to face.

If Mac wondered about Rob's motives for going with him on his next trip, he didn't ask. Once there, Rob dropped Mac off, and he punched Brock's address into his GPS. He passed the Army base on his way and knew that many military retirees ended up near the bases. Following the directions, he pulled up to a neat apartment complex. Sitting in the truck for a moment, he hesitated. Taking a deep breath, he hauled himself out of the vehicle and walked up to the brick building. The landscaping around the building was well tended, and the apartments faced a park across the street. Making his way to the second floor, he found the door. Lifting his hand to knock, he remembered what Mac had said. And he prayed. *Lord, make this right. Not for me but for Laurie.*

The door opened, and Rob stared into eyes as grey as an ocean storm. Laurie's eyes. Heart pounding, he continued to look at the tall, well-built man in his mid-forties. His hair was still dark with just a little grey at the temples. Dressed neatly in jeans and an Army T-shirt, he looked at Rob questioningly, and Rob wasn't sure what to say.

"Can I help you?" the man asked pleasantly.

Rob decided that the best way to play this was not to play it at all. Real. Just Real.

"I'm Rob MacDonald. I'm looking for Brock Sinclair."

"I'm Brock. What can I do for you?"

"Mr. Sinclair, I'm looking for a Brock Sinclair, who was in the Army on leave in July twenty-five years ago in the Richmond area."

At this, Brock's eyes narrowed in suspicion. "Well now, that is a very precise description of someone. I think perhaps I might need to know why you're looking for that person before we continue this conversation."

Rob nodded, "Fair enough, sir." Taking a big breath, Rob continued. "The man I'm looking for met a beautiful young woman and spent one night with her. I don't know what happened the next morning, but nine months later that young woman gave birth to an equally beautiful daughter. A daughter with grey eyes."

Brock's narrowed eyes opened wide at this point. He seemed to carefully consider Rob as though weighing his story. Stepping backward, he motioned for Rob. "I think perhaps you should come in."

Stepping into the apartment, Rob noticed right away that it was neat and clean. The walls, covered in pictures, depicted mostly photographs of young soldiers.

Brock looked at where Rob's attention lay. "Twenty years in the Army, I suppose these men I served with over the years are my family. Started out in Desert Storm, did tours in Iraq and Afghanistan, as well as trained many young soldiers right here at the base."

Offering Rob a seat, he stated, "But it seems you're not here to look at my war memorabilia."

"No sir, although I'm in awe of your service."

Brock just nodded as he sat across from Rob. "I take it you're here because you think that I'm the father of the girl you speak of."

"My friend was raised by her single mother who gave birth to her when she was only sixteen."

Brock's startled expression gave Rob the idea that the man had no idea how young Sarah had been at the time.

"It appears that she and a friend went out one night, and she met a young soldier named Brock. According to her, she fell in love that night and spent the night with him. Nine months later she gave birth to a daughter. She told her parents that she did not know the name of the young man. She and her daughter lived with her parents and sister. According to what I've been told by my girlfriend, they had a happy home, and she had a good childhood. Her grandfather died, and for a while it was just the four women in the home."

Rob had been staring at Brock during his tale, hoping for some facial recognition, but so far, Brock simply sat and listened quietly.

"When my friend was twelve years old, her mother and grandmother were killed in a car accident. She was raised by her aunt. They're very close, and again, she and her aunt were happy together. When she was eighteen, there was a gift that her mother had left boxed up for her to open when she became an adult. Inside, it contained an Army T-shirt, with the nametag inside saying Brock T. Sinclair. Her mother's letter said that she kept the shirt because she wanted a memory of the man she fell in love with, but that she knew she was only a one-night stand with him."

Brock stood suddenly. "What was the girl's name?" he asked shakily.

Rob pulled out the photograph that Laurie had placed on their end table. Turning it around to face Brock, he said quietly, "Sarah."

Brock sat heavily in the chair, his hand reaching out for the picture. "Sarah," he whispered.

Rob sat quietly letting Brock absorb the information that had avalanched onto him. Brock stared at the picture for a long time, his fingers slowly tracing the faces in front of him. Finally, he spoke. "We had a daughter. A daughter. I never knew." He looked up into Rob's face, seeing compassion.

Rob gently said, "Her name is Laurie. Laurie Dodd. She's a first-grade teacher in Fairfield." Smiling, he continued, "She's smart, funny, beautiful, hardworking, compassionate, everything that is good and loving."

Brock looked over at Rob with interest. "And you're in love with her, aren't you?"

Rob stared back, eye to eye, man to man and

responded, "Yes sir, I am. That's why I'm here. She has no idea I'm doing this. She always claimed that there was no need to find someone who considered her mother a fling. She said she didn't miss what she never had."

Brock hung his head at this. Looking back up at Rob, "I assure you that she was not a fling." He spent the next half hour telling Rob the story of meeting Sarah, falling in love with her in one night and then losing her the next morning.

Rob listened attentively, knowing that Laurie would want to know this. *Her dad loved her mom. This completely changes her life story. This could change her life.*

Finally, Brock asked, "Why now, Rob? Why did you decide to search me out now?"

Rob then shared about Laurie's illness. "She goes to the rheumatologist next week, and I know they want a family history. Maybe there isn't one thing you can tell us, but I had to try to find out." He hesitated again. "Mr. Sinclair, she will not be happy at all that I've found you. I went behind her back, but I would do anything to help her."

"Then you're a good man. And she'll recognize that even if she's upset at first." Grey eyes meeting blue ones, Brock said, "And call me Brock. It looks as though we're going to be getting to know quite a lot about each other. So, what now?"

"Well, if you just happen to make a visit down to Fairfield sometime, then I guess we'll figure out how you can meet. I just don't know how in the hell I'm going to bring this together."

Brock and Rob had exchanged phone numbers and email addresses before Rob headed back to pick up Mac. At the door, Brock shook his hand, thanking him.

"Brock, I know this information changes everything for you, but it can make all the difference to Laurie as well." With a final handshake, he headed back to his truck.

He drove back to where he was picking up his dad and sat in the truck waiting, alone with his thoughts. *No secrets. But what about secrets that keep someone from being hurt? What about secrets that can help?* His thoughts swirled around in his mind, coming to no conclusion. Knowing that Laurie would be furious when she found out, he tried to plan how to tell her and make the introduction to her father. But he came up empty. All he could see in his mind was the anger she was going to feel. His dad's words poured over him again. *You do the best you can each and every day and then turn the rest over to prayer.* Bowing his head, he prayed. *Lord, let her know how much I love her. Let her forgive me. Let her be all right.*

Just then Mac came out of the building, and they headed back to Fairfield. Back to what, Rob wasn't sure.

18

Over the next several days, Laurie focused on her classroom full of little first graders and tried desperately not to think about the appointment that was coming at the end of the week. The students were taking all of her attention, and she was glad when they headed down the hall to their music class.

Jean popped in to check on her. The two friends chatted for a while about several of the students, and then the topic rolled to Laurie. "How are you doing? Your limp is almost gone."

She laughed ruefully. "Yeah, the prednisone takes away the swelling, but now I want to eat all the time and I have to fight the urge to constantly snack. I don't think I can stay on it indefinitely, but it's good for now. When I go in on Friday, I'll learn about the other meds for lupus." Rolling her eyes, she added, "And I get to once again explain why I don't have a father's medical family history."

"You okay with all of that?"

"You know what's weird? My whole life, it was just Mom's family. I never really worried about what my father's family was like. It was as though they simply didn't exist. Not in reality and not in my imagination. Now, I find myself thinking about them. Or him. Or... oh, I don't know," Laurie said in frustration. Looking up, she said, "I find myself thinking about a grandmother that I never knew. What was her medical history? Did someone else have lupus? Or any other condition or disease? Were there aunts or uncles? All of the things that never meant anything to me, now I think about."

"Do you think that, as a child, you were given one story, then as a young woman you found out a different story so that it was just easier to pretend your father didn't exist? But now that you're an adult, you're starting to see things like an adult."

Laurie looked at her friend with a curious look, so Jean continued. "Look, here are the hard facts. No one knows exactly what happened but your mom and your dad. Your mom was a scared sixteen-year-old girl thrust into a situation that she wasn't prepared for. I think as young people we see the world as very black or white. Your mom may have done this. You did this. But as adults we realize that there are all shades of grey in between."

Reaching over to hold Laurie's hands, she finished, "I think that now you realize that it's okay to think about him, and you're not dishonoring your mother in any way. After all, she did tell you that she fell in love." Smiling, Jean stood up and left Laurie to ponder on her own.

That evening, Laurie noticed a difference in Rob. There was no caveman sex. As Laurie had discovered, Rob had different types of sex. There was the caveman sex, where he picked her up in a fireman's hold, carried her to the bedroom, and they fucked. Any position. Several positions. Lots of dirty talk. He always took care of her first, but still...caveman sex. Then there was dominant sex. He was in charge, told her what to do, where to touch him, where to touch herself, when to come, and ass reddening usually was incorporated. Then there was fun sex. Tickling. Playful. Adventurous. The kind where you wanted to yell "touchdown" when you had an orgasm.

But then there was also making love. Slow. Purposeful. Loving. Soft words. Gentle caresses. Sweet. Tender.

She liked all the different types of sex with Rob. But making love, well, what girl doesn't like this type best?

After dinner, he came up behind her as they were finishing in the kitchen. Wrapping his arms around her from behind, he pulled her back into his towering body. She felt instantly protected as though nothing in this world could ever harm her. He kissed the top of her head then began nuzzling a trail of kisses down her neck as he pushed her hair off her shoulder. She leaned back, moaning, angling her neck for better access to the whisper kisses. Slowly turning in his arms, she reached up to pull his face down to hers. What began as kisses along his stubbled jaw became bolder as she made her way to his mouth.

He picked her up in his arms, and she grasped his neck as he carried her into the bedroom, laying her down on the bed. Hair flowing behind her, eyes sparkling in the low lights of the room, he lay down next to her, gathering her in his arms once again. Rob kissed her, slipping his tongue between her moist lips. Her tongue danced with his as they both breathed each other in. While using his tongue to discover every crevice of her sweet mouth, he slowly slid his hand down her neck to the buttons of her blouse. Quickly unbuttoning her shirt, while never taking his lips from hers, he opened the blouse.

Pulling his mouth from hers, his lips followed the same path as his hand, over her jaw, around her neck, and down between the valley of her breasts. He leaned up just enough to unsnap the front of her lacy black bra and pulled it open to expose her luscious breasts. Full, natural, tipped with rosy nipples, hardened with desire. His mouth latched onto one breast, and he suckled and nipped until she felt as though her body was electrically charged. He gently lifted her just enough to slide her bra and blouse off her body, continuing his detailed worship of her breasts.

Her hands moved across his massive back from his neck down to his waist and back up again. She slipped her hands under his T-shirt, pulling it upwards until it slid over his head, and she could toss it aside.

Bare chest to bare chest. He rolled so that she was lying on top of him, feeling her breasts pressed into his chest. His arms wrapped around her, hands sliding down to her ass.

As he kneaded her globes, she focused on his mouth, first delving into his mouth then sliding down his chest to his nipples where she licked and nipped. His hips jerked upwards as he moaned in satisfaction.

She slid further down and began unzipping his jeans. Pulling them down his long legs, she couldn't help but notice the huge tenting in his boxers. They were straining with the force of his erect cock. She started to reach for the boxers, but he flipped her over onto her back. "No, babe, tonight is for you."

He slid her pants off her legs, kissing the exposed skin along the way. Once the slacks were off, he nuzzled her damp panties then grabbed them in his mouth. Dragging them down her legs by his teeth, stopping to nip at her skin as he went, he finally tossed them to the side as well.

He leaned back to peruse her nude form. Long hair splayed across the pillow, full breasts, pale in the moonlight, slim waist leading down to her mound. His hands moved gently over all of her curves as though he was discovering them for the first time.

She felt the fires burning brighter and brighter as his hands moved over her body. Cherished, adored. As his hands slid between her legs, she could feel the tingling that began deep in her belly spreading outward. Her hips started to move and press up against his leg, desperate to ease the ache.

He slid one finger into her wet sex, circling it around, hitting the spots that he had discovered that caused her to make the little sounds deep in her throat that went straight to his dick.

Building, building. She could feel the crescendo coming as he continued to play her like an instrument made just for him. He added a second finger, moving them masterfully in a synchronized motion, and that was all it took for her to fall over the edge. Digging her fingernails into his shoulders, screaming his name, Rob could feel her muscles contract around his fingers until she lay boneless beside him. Leaning down to capture her soft mouth once again, he realized how much he loved hearing his name on her lips as she came.

Laurie opened her eyes and looked deeply into his. What did she see there? *Love, concern, satisfaction.* She couldn't help but grin at that last thought.

"What's so funny?" he asked.

"You look very smug right now."

"Hell yeah. Any time a man can make a woman scream his name, he should be smug."

She wanted to pretend to be indignant, but his lips crashed back down on hers and she forgot everything except the feel of what his mouth was doing to hers. The feel of his lips melding with hers, tongues tangling, breaths mingling, was all she could think about.

He slid his boxers down releasing his straining cock.

She glanced down and giggled again.

"Woman," he said, pretending sternness. "Don't ever stare at a man's dick and then giggle."

"I just thought that he looked like he had somewhere he wanted to go," she said with a twinkle in her eye.

"Oh girl, you know it. He knows exactly where he needs to go and what to do when he gets there."

With that, he raised himself up over her and placed

his swollen cock at her wet entrance. Leaning down to barely touch his lips to hers, he whispered, "Love you, Laurie darlin'. With all my heart. Please don't forget that."

Before she could think about that last odd statement, he plunged inside of her, taking her mind off anything except the delightful sensations of fullness and friction. Gently thrusting in and out, over and over, he took her to a place she was sure she had never been before. Higher and higher she climbed. Searching for something that was just out of her reach. Rob began kissing her, thrusting his tongue in and out, mirroring the same movement of his dick. Overcome by the emotions of what he was feeling, he could tell that he was close to coming.

"Babe, come with me." He reached between them and gently rolled her swollen clit between his fingers as he continued to thrust his tongue into her mouth.

Finally reaching the peak, Laurie arched her back as she fell off the cliff, weightless, flying through the stars of the night. At the same moment that her inner walls began to convulse around him, he felt his dick straining one last time before exploding as he emptied himself into her waiting body.

Both panting, bodies slick with shared sweat, they lay together, silent for a few moments, letting the emotions and sensations flow all around. Slowly, he lifted off her, pushing the wet tendrils of her hair back away from her face. Kissing her swollen lips, he felt her breath go into his body.

Their eyes locked onto one another as they lay there,

mouths barely touching, breathing each other in. Laurie realized that she needed Rob's breath for her very being to live. Rob knew that Laurie's soul rested deep inside of him.

Two bodies, one spirit. Two bodies, one essence. Two bodies, one life.

19

Two days later, Laurie noticed the minivan outside of the playground again but was unable to see a license plate. Frustrated, she notified Ms. Darby once more, and this time, Jake and Tom actually came to see her. While her children were at lunch, she gave a detailed description of the van.

"I know that it simply could be one of the vans from the neighborhoods around here, but most minivans don't have darkened driver and passenger windows that are so dark you can't see anything in them at all."

Jake assured her that it was better to go with her gut feeling than to second guess herself and then put herself or any of the children at risk.

"We know that Cindy's parents don't want her to testify against the uncle, but even if it is not related to Cindy's case, you know pedophiles like to hang around school yards," Jake stated, grim-faced.

"I know," she acknowledged, shivering.

As they finished, Tom asked how she was feeling.

"I'm feeling much better although the fatigue is still a problem. At least, I'm not limping," she said grinning.

"I'm glad you're honest. Don't want you to sugar coat anything with us," Tom added.

"Oh no. Rob and I agree that 'no secrets' is the way to go."

Tom and Jake shared a glance so quickly that she was not quite sure she had actually seen it. But before she could question them, the children were returning from lunch, so Tom and Jake said goodbye.

Laurie headed home after work wanting to fix dinner for Rob since he had pulled a long shift. A warehouse on the edge of town had caught on fire, and she knew that he had been with the crew all day. Her phone beeped and she saw that she had a text from Emma.

Found some funny pictures to make your day brighter. Sent them in an email.

She had been in constant contact with Emma during the last few weeks, and she knew Emma was worried about her. Walking into the study, she started to open up her laptop when she saw Rob's already opened. Sitting down, she pulled his laptop over and opened up email. As his email program popped up, she was getting ready to minimize it to bring her own email up when she noticed an email from **Sinclair, Brock.**

She froze, not breathing, a sick feeling crawling in her gut. *Oh Jesus, Oh Jesus, Oh Jesus. How many Brock Sinclairs can there be?* The coil in her stomach slithered up, threatening to choke her. The pounding of her heart roared in her ears as she sat staring at the name on the screen. A name she had always known. A man she has never known.

No control. No choice. No turning back. Lifting a shaking finger over the keyboard, she clicked to open the email.

"Hey Rob, just wanted to let you know I'll be coming into town this afternoon. Staying at Fairfield Hotel in downtown. We can talk more tomorrow to see how we want to plan the meeting before the doc appt. Thanks for everything. See you again soon. Brock"

Talk more. They had talked before.

See you again. They had met before.

Laurie felt lightheaded as she realized she was holding her breath. She tried to breathe, but found the air would not go in. Gulping, she gasped for air over and over until she could finally feel her lungs expand.

Rob had looked for her father. He had found her father. He had talked to her father. He had kept it all a secret.

Laurie did not remember leaving the apartment. She did not remember getting into her car. She did not remember driving to the hotel. She did not remember going in and asking Helen which room Brock Sinclair was staying in.

She simply found herself standing outside of a hotel room, wind whipping around her, making her as cold on the outside as she felt on the inside.

Raising her hand, she hesitated. *What was on the other*

side of the door? Who would be there? The prince of her child-hood? The man who screwed then dumped her mother as a fling? Before her courage left her entirely, she knocked on the door. When it opened, she stared into grey eyes that mirrored her own.

"Sarah?"

She jerked out of her trance as the man standing in the doorway called her by her mother's name. Slowly shaking her head back and forth, her eyes never leaving his, she heard a whispered voice say, "I'm Laurie," before recognizing that the utterance came from her.

"Of course. I'm sorry. It's just...you look like...her. Do you want to come in?" he asked softly.

She looked around hesitantly. Usually cautious, she would never consider going into an unknown man's hotel room. Brock, noticing her hesitation but wanting to move her out of the cold, quickly said, "Or we could go somewhere public to talk."

With shaky determination, she walked into the hotel room. Heart pounding, stomach queasy, she made her way to the chair at the small table in the corner near the window. Deciding to sit down before her legs gave out from under her, she landed heavily on the chair.

Brock carefully sat on the bed, near the table, but not too close. He wanted to stare at her face but wasn't sure what he should do.

She looked at the man sitting in front of her. He looked...ordinary. *What was I expecting? Horns and a pitchfork? Smarmy playboy?* He was tall, slender but muscular. Dark hair with a little grey sprinkled in it. Nice face. Grey eyes. Grey eyes. *I have his eyes.*

Suddenly wanting to know what was going on between him and Rob, she bluntly asked, "Why are you here?"

Brock, taking a deep breath, sighed and raised his hands in supplication. "I never knew. I didn't know. I…"

She interrupted, "I want to know why you're here now. What brought you here today?"

Anger was beginning to burn slowly under the surface, and he was wise enough to see it starting to seep into her tone.

"Last week, a man named Rob MacDonald came to my apartment. I live outside of Richmond near the Army base. He told me about you and that you were ill. I explained the situation surrounding my meeting Sarah." Saying her name again, he looked away from Laurie's face, shaking his head. "Sarah," he whispered. "I never knew."

"Since I haven't been included in any of these conversations, perhaps you should enlighten me," Laurie said with barely concealed anger. Anger at whom she could not say. Anger at Brock, anger at her mom, and certainly anger at Rob. Her chest began to ache, as though her heart breaking over Rob's secrecy was an actual physical feeling.

"I can only imagine how upset and confused you are right now. I felt many of the same feelings last week," he admitted.

"I can imagine," she said truthfully, realizing that his world had been rocked as well. "Mr. Sinclair, I just need to know what happened. Don't leave anything out. Don't try to make it any different than what it was."

Nodding, he said, "I can do that. You deserve at least that. But may I ask first what your mother said about your father?"

Taking a deep breath, she agreed. She told him of the stories her mother would tell her every year on her birthday. "She always described you as a prince that she fell in love with but said that you had to go away. I used to imagine that one day you'd come back." She continued to explain her grandfather's death and then the death of her grandmother and mother. When her eighteen-year-old aunt and she became orphans, they lived together, creating the only life they could.

At that, he dropped his head into his hands and sat for a moment. Her chill towards him thawed just a bit. If nothing else, it did seem as though he hated to realize that she had been left parentless.

"When I was eighteen, I found out the prince my mom fell in love with only considered her to be a fling. She did keep your shirt; that's how I knew your last name."

His head jerked up at the word *fling*. "She was never a fling. Never," he spat out vehemently.

Brock and Laurie sat looking at each other in stony silence for a moment.

Sighing, he said, "Laurie, if you don't believe anything else, believe this, she was never a fling."

Laurie, looking as pale and forlorn as she felt, said, "Perhaps you could give me your side of the story."

He nodded in agreement and began his saga. "I was on leave and in Richmond with some buddies of mine. I was twenty years old. Thought I was a man of the world, but looking back I was just a young arrogant dick. I'd been with several women from the bars and was out prowling around for the night. Looked across the bar and saw an absolute princess walk in. Long brown hair, natural beauty...definitely not in the right place. I was drawn to her. And felt the most unusual protectiveness. I knew if I didn't get to her quickly, she would be taken advantage of, and I wasn't having that." He shuttered as he remembered that his buddy had wanted to go after her.

"We ended up talking for hours. She was smart as well as pretty, funny, had the most delightful laugh." Looking up into Laurie's eyes, he confessed, "I won't lie to you, Laurie. I was attracted to her like I had never been attracted to a woman before. I wanted her and I wanted to make her mine. I had no idea she was only sixteen. I had no idea she was a virgin."

At this, Laurie looked uncomfortable. Even after all these years, it was hard to imagine her mother being intimate with anyone.

"We went back to my hotel. Honest to God, I never meant to take advantage of her. I just wanted to spend more time with her, but that was us being naïve. It didn't take long for it to get out of hand and, well, we had sex. She did tell me about being a virgin, and I was so careful with her. I held her, and I swear that she had my heart from that instant on."

Brock stood up and went over to the mini refrigerator that was in the room. Opening the door, he pulled out a couple of water bottles. Offering one to Laurie, she agreed, and he brought it over, handing it to her.

Taking a long swig, he went on. "I planned on waking up with her the next morning and telling her that I had fallen in love with her. When I woke up, she was gone. I couldn't believe it. My princess was gone." He paused, taking another swig.

"Laurie, there are times in life when one act can change everything. And you can't go back. You can't change things. Oh, how I wished I could have gone back to that evening and told her then."

Laurie, entranced with the rendition of her parents' story coming from his perspective, asked, "What happened the next morning? Why did Mom think she was just a fling?"

Brock, looking past her shoulder, focused on a point beyond her as though he could see himself twenty-five years ago right there in the room. "My dumb-ass buddy came over to our room and sent Sarah on her way, saying shit about how I didn't ever want to wake up to one-night stands." He paused again as though not able to believe what he was remembering. "I was fast asleep in the room, and Sarah took off. I never knew her last name, and she never knew mine."

Looking back into the eyes that mirrored his own, he said, "I wanted to find her, but our leave was canceled, and we were called back. But I never forgot her. I *never* forgot her. And if you don't believe anything else, believe this. If I had known her last name, I would have come back for her. And if I had known about you, I would have come back for you."

The lump in her throat kept her from speaking, knowing that if she did the tears threatening to fall might not ever end. Her hand pressed up against the ache in her chest, and she squeezed her eyes tight, wanting to shut out the memory of her mother each year repeating the story of her father, knowing now that her mother never knew the whole story.

"Laurie, I've missed twenty-five years of your life. I have no idea if you have any place for me now or if you even want to go there. But Rob told me about your illness, and he was desperate for you to have all the pieces of your medical history. So, I came. I'll do anything to help."

Laurie continued to sit, not speaking for several minutes. Her mind whirling with thoughts, emotions, feelings.

"I don't actually know if there is anything you can help with. They have already tentatively diagnosed me with lupus. I think they wanted to see if anyone else in the family had it."

Brock dropped his eyes again staring at his hands for a long time. He spoke so softly that Laurie wasn't sure she heard him. "My sister had lupus."

His sister. My aunt. I had an aunt beside Emma. My aunt. Had. He said had. There is no cure for lupus, so "had" means....oh my God.

"What happened to her?" she whispered, her voice choking in her throat.

"She died about twenty years ago. There were no drugs then as there are now."

Laurie stood up quickly, hands gripping the edges of the table, her voice catching in her throat. "I've to get out of here. I can't breathe," she said, gasping. She took two steps and faltered, Brock jumping up to steady her. He held her by her upper arms momentarily then found himself pulling her towards his tall frame, circling his arms around her, cradling her head against his chest. Sob after sob ripped from her chest. Her world turned upside down once again.

She had a father, other relatives she never knew, a family history that had been hidden. She cried for her mother who had lived for almost thirteen years loving a man that she thought betrayed her.

Brock just held her. The daughter that he had never known about. Never held. Never comforted. How strange, he thought....it seemed so natural to have her in his arms. Rubbing her back, rocking her back and forth, murmuring soothing words.

Finally, the sobs subsided, and the tears ran their last tracks down her cheeks. Moving away on shaky legs, she looked up into his face.

"Thank you for everything you have told me. I...I...It is a lot to take in...for both of us. I need to go now, but I want you to know I, ... well, I'm glad you came."

"Laurie, I'm not going anywhere right now. I don't know what you need from me, but I'd like to stay a bit as we figure it all out."

She nodded in appreciation.

Saying goodbye, she retraced her steps from earlier. Back to her car, back to their apartment, into the bedroom where she packed all of her belongings. And walked out of the door.

Showing up at Jean's house, she walked in, collapsing into the arms of her friend.

20

Rob walked into a darkened apartment, Laurie nowhere to be found. Her clothes were gone from the closet. Her toiletries were gone from the bathroom. As he ran through the house, he saw the light of his laptop shining in the study. There was the open email. Heart pounding in his chest, he noticed a note on the desk.

Rob, we promised there would be no secrets. You have broken your promise and broken my heart. I have too much to handle right now to deal with your deceit. I'm going to Jean's house. Do not contact me now. I just can't take any more. Laurie

He grabbed his phone, calling Brock. Brock picked on the first ring, filling him in on their whole conversation.

"I don't have Jean's number, Brock, and she won't answer her phone. I've need to get ahold of her. I gotta make her understand."

"Son, right now, you need to back off tonight. She is over-stressed and must have gone to someone's house that she trusts. Let her have this evening. You can see her tomorrow."

Rob hung up, despair creeping over, threatening to choke him. Lying down on their bed, he could smell her scent on the pillows surrounding him with the thoughts of his body curling around hers. As he lay staring at the ceiling, he could feel moisture on his cheeks and realized that tears were falling. He couldn't remember the last time he cried. Afraid that in trying to keep her safe he may have pushed her away, he fell into a fitful sleep.

Laurie's cell phone vibrated in her pocket all day long. Refusing to look at it until the end of the day, she wasn't surprised to see that Rob had texted all day.

Please let me explain. Please call me. Please talk to me. Please let me know you're all right.

Shoving the offending object into her purse, she started out of her room when Jean appeared. "How are you holding up?" she asked with genuine concern on her face.

Placing her hand on her chest, she answered, "Oh, Jean, I feel…my heart actually hurts. Is that crazy?" Her chin quivering and tears threatening to fall once again, she took a shaky breath.

"It's not crazy, honey. You have suffered a shock and feel betrayed all at the same time. It's going to take time for your mind to process all that has been revealed and time," she said, hugging Laurie tightly, "for your body to heal as well."

Jean, slinging Laurie's bag over her own shoulder and wrapping her arm around Laurie's trembling form, led her outside and drove to her house.

That night lying in bed, tears rolling down her face, Laurie pulled out her cell phone, rereading the messages from Rob. *He betrayed my trust. He loves me, but my heart hurts so much.*

Barely making it through the next day, she tried to keep the children from seeing the heartache on her face. That afternoon Jean and Laurie walked slowly to Jean's car in the teachers' parking lot. As Laurie was about to get in, she looked up to see Rob standing by the hood. Hesitating when she saw him, she saw Jean walk straight to him. Sticking out her hand, she introduced herself.

"You must be Rob. I'm Jean, a friend of Laurie's."

Rob looked at her suspiciously, then seeing the kindness in her eyes, he recognized a possible ally. Jean, turning towards Laurie, said, "If you want to talk in a neutral place, come back to my house."

Rob could see Laurie's red-rimmed, swollen eyes and pale face. Her chin began to wobble, and tears threatened once again. She looked exhausted, and he remembered the words of the doctor several weeks ago. *You need to reduce the stress in your life.* Looking down at his feet, he felt his resolve stiffen. *Damn. I gotta make this right.* Stalking over to her, he wrapped his arms around her before she had a chance to pull away. Looking over Laurie's head to Jean, he nodded at her. Jean smiled at him and headed for her car.

Laurie tried feebly to push back. "I can't do this now,

Rob. I'm so tired. There's nothing left in me to deal with your deceit."

"Babe, you can't take care of yourself right now. I'm here. I'm doing this. We'll sort everything else out later." He picked her up and placed her in his truck. He wasn't kidding himself. Just because Laurie wasn't fighting him now did not mean he was forgiven. But her not fighting him also had him worried. That told him how weak she was right now.

Sending Brock a text, he followed Jean to her house. Rob carried Laurie in and following Jean, laid her gently down on the guest room bed. Feeling ill with no resistance left, Laurie didn't move as the tears continued to flow down her face. Jean brought a blanket and draped it over both of them.

Rob pushed Laurie's hair out of her face. "Babe, you need to calm down. You're making yourself sick. I know you're pissed at me. We can deal with that later. Right now, just breathe deep and slow."

Eyes closed, she felt herself drifting away. Blanketed by the warmth of the covers and his body, she gave way to the pull of sleep.

Consciousness creeping in slowly, Laurie began to awaken. Fighting the pull to drift away again, she sat up on the bed, realizing she was in Jean's guest room.

Angry voices could be heard coming from down the hall. She slid out of bed and walked over to the door. While not usually a proponent of eavesdropping, she felt no guilt about hearing what was going on in the living room of Jean's house. Hearing multiple voices, sorting them out in her mind, she listened.

"What on earth were you thinking, Rob?" Carol said in whispered anger."No offense, Mr. Sinclair, but meeting the father that you never knew existed after twenty-five years must have been a real shock to her system!"

"I did what I needed to do; can't you get that through your head?" she heard Rob retort. "I wanted to make sure the doctor had all the information and was going to make that happen."

"Don't take this out on Carol." Tom answered back. "She's just worried."

"Oh, come on, Tom. You thought it was a good idea until now!"

"Tom! You knew about this? I can't believe that you knew about this mess and didn't say anything to me!" Carol was no longer whispering as her voice crept higher.

"This is about my daughter. I don't care who is mad at who around here, but I want her safe and well."

"What the hell do you think I'm trying to do?" Rob answered back.

"Everyone calm the hell down." Laurie recognized Jake's voice. *Is everyone out there?*

Jean decided that a voice of reason was needed. "Stop! Jake is right; everyone here needs to take a deep breath and sit down." Laurie could hear shuffling as people were moving around.

Jean continued, "Here is what everyone needs to

focus on. We're all here because we love Laurie and want her safe. Right now is not the time for blaming or accusations. Right now is the time for calm reassurances.

"Carol, we cannot say that she never knew her father existed. She knew he was out there somewhere, but she never felt a reason to try to find him. Brock, in the past seven years that she knew your name, she never attempted to find you because she felt that you wouldn't have wanted to know about her, and she always said that she did not miss what she never had. But do not imagine that she did not think about you because she did. We talked about it. We talked about you."

She heard Jean continue and thought ruefully, *When Jean gets on a roll, she doesn't stop!*

"Rob, I understand why you searched for Brock. You love her and you're afraid for her. When those two things combine, love and fear, we often act in ways that we might not act otherwise. I honestly believe that Laurie will forgive you, but it may take time to earn her trust back. Tom, Jake – all I have to say to you two is how lucky Rob is to have friends that will support him no matter what. And once Laurie forgives Rob, she'll value that friendship as well."

Brock looked around the room, realizing that he was in the presence of people that loved Laurie and was awed that there was so much support. "I have to say I have no intentions of going anywhere," he said to the group. "I'll fit my life into whatever place Laurie wants to give me." He got up and walked over to Rob whose head was resting in his hands. "And son, while you may have messed up on the secret keeping, what you did for my daughter, well… you have my eternal thanks." At this Rob stood up, weary himself, and embraced Brock.

Laurie, with her ear pressed up against the door, couldn't hear a sound. *What are they doing now?* Suddenly bone-tired once again from the emotion of the day, she turned and crawled back into bed. Sleep overtook her as she dreamed fitfully.

Brock glanced at Jean, feeling a desire to stay in her presence for a while. She was not only beautiful, but she knew how to read people, read situations, calm anger, soothe wounded souls. She looked up at him as well, a smile playing on her lips.

The friends all left leaving just Brock and Rob with Jean. Having checked on Laurie, only to find her still sleeping, Rob rejoined the others in the kitchen.

"Jean, how do I make this right? I can't…I can't lose her." Rob's chest was hurting, and he rubbed it with his hand.

Jean watched the mannerism with a slight smile on her face. Eyes back up to Rob's, she observed, "Laurie does that too." Seeing his quizzical look, she explained, "When she speaks of you, she rubs her heart. It pains her to be away from you."

He grunted. "More 'n likely, it hurts her to think of me. Jesus, things are so messed up." Rob, in unchartered territory, realized he had no idea how to make things right. Ever since he saw Laurie in the grocery store, his world had been turned upside down. He wanted her. He wanted only her. He needed only her. He loved only her.

Sitting on the kitchen stool with his head in his hands, he felt Jean touch his shoulder.

"Rob, she loves you. That love will prevail. But allow her to go at her pace through this."

Nodding, he hugged Jean and shook Brock's hand, then headed out to his truck. Back to their home. Alone.

The trip to the rheumatologist several days later seemed almost anticlimactic after all of the drama from the previous days. Filling out the family history for the first time in her life, she did not have to list 'do not know' on the paternal medical section. *How strange to actually put down my father's information.* Brock had given Jean a list of family members and their health histories for Laurie to use.

She and Dr. Lawrence talked for a long time. He explained that there is no one test for lupus, but that all the indicators that they looked for were present in her case, so he was comfortable with the diagnosis. Determined not to fall apart, she mentioned that she just learned that she had an aunt that had died from lupus many years ago. He explained that medications were being created and new discoveries were being made every day, and he was confident that they could find the right combination for her symptoms.

Dr. Lawrence answered her questions, went over the

medications that she would be starting, and assured her that just because her aunt had died from complications from lupus there was no reason to expect Laurie not to live a full life.

Leaving the office, Laurie called Emma who was anxiously awaiting news of her visit. Filling her in first on the doctor's news, Laurie then began to talk about the rest of her life.

"Yeah, I'm still staying with Jean."

Emma, understanding Laurie's anger, also knew that her niece was heartbroken without Rob. "Sweetie, I know you're still mad as hell at Rob, but I want you to think carefully about what you're doing. Every relationship has its bumpy times. Are you willing to just walk away from him without at least trying to work things out?"

"I know. I'm just scared. What if he keeps other secrets? What if he starts lying to me? What if –"

Emma interrupted, "Laurie, you can 'what if' yourself until you go crazy with it. If you love him, you owe him the opportunity to explain why he did what he did."

"I know the why of it all. He wanted me to have a family history because he was scared about this disease."

Letting the silence float through the airwaves, Emma said nothing, waiting for Laurie to understand the meaning behind the words she had just spoken.

Sighing, Laurie admitted, "He loves me."

"Sweetie, love makes us do some crazy things, but it will especially make us do anything and everything we can to protect those we love. So…what are you going to do?"

Standing taller, head thrown back, Laurie announced, "I'm going to go talk to him. We need to work through this because not having him in my life is killing me."

Laughing, Emma agreed.

Tossing her cell phone back into her purse, Laurie walked over to her car. Looking down, lost in thought, she did not see Brock until she was standing at his truck parked next to her bug. She looked up surprised and yet glad to see him. Her gaze roamed his face which was already becoming familiar. The crinkles next to his storm-colored eyes, the greying hair at his temples, the lean strength of his frame. He pushed off his truck and walked the few feet over to her.

"Brock. What are you doing here?"

"I wanted to make sure you were okay." Jerking his head toward the medical building, he asked, "How'd it go today?"

Laurie looked up into her father's grey eyes, the same eyes that stared back at her each day in the mirror. Giving him a tentative smile she said, "It went...well. I gave him all of your information and he was very positive about things. I start some new medications this week, so we'll see how it goes."

The tentative smile on her face reached in and touched a part of Brock he never knew existed. Throwing caution to the wind, he stepped closer, looking down at his daughter's beautiful face and continued.

"Laurie, I don't know what place I have in your life or if you want me to have a place." Looking down at his rough, worn hands clutched tightly, he sighed. "I guess it sounds like I don't know much."

Tears welled in his eyes as he swallowed hard a few times to choke them back. Shaking his head as though to pull his thoughts from the past back to the future, he brushed a tear away and looked down at the face that reminded him so much of Sarah.

"No, that's not right. I do know something. I know I fell in love in one night with a beautiful girl that made me feel things I didn't know I could feel. I know I wanted to be with her and for twenty-five years I thought she was completely lost to me. I can't go back. I can't change what happened. Too many past mistakes in life for us to make ourselves crazy over. But I now know she isn't entirely lost to me. She lives on in you. I may have missed the first twenty-five years of your life, but I sure as hell don't want to miss any more.

"So, unless you tell me to leave, I'm not going anywhere, Laurie. I just hope you want to let me in at least part of your life," he said. Lips curling up in a small smile, he added, "I'm not too proud to beg."

Reaching over to capture his work-worn hand in her much smaller one, Laurie smiled up at him. Tears spilling over, heart aching with a need that she never knew existed, Laurie spoke a word that had never crossed her lips. "Dad."

His eyes looked into hers, and his brow furrowed in question.

"I have a dad. I knew that somewhere I had a father. I convinced myself that I didn't need a father. I had Mom, Grandma and Grandpa, and Emma. A father simply wasn't needed or missed. But now I have a dad. And I don't want to lose him."

Brock wrapped his hand around hers, holding it so tightly she could feel it right to her heart. Tears, falling freely and unashamedly, now coursed down his cheeks. "Well, all right then. You've got your dad. And I'm not going anywhere."

"And Laurie?" Jerking his head over to the other side of his truck where she noticed Rob standing, her dad said, "You need to go put that boy outta his misery."

21

Grey eyes latched onto blue ones. Heart pounding, Laurie glanced back into Brock's face, seeing him smile and nod. Kissing her cheek, he climbed up into his old truck and backed out of the parking lot leaving Rob and Laurie alone. She looked over at him, her heart pounding with both fear and love. Fear of what was going to happen to them and love for the man who risked everything to keep her safe.

He looked...ragged. His hair seemed as though he had run his hand through it continually. There were dark circles under his haunted eyes. Eyes that were staring back at her.

"Hey," she greeted softly.

"Hey back." Uncharacteristically anxious, Rob's eyes searched hers for some idea of what she was thinking. Wanting to pull her into his embrace, he faltered, not knowing what she would allow.

Looking around, she did not see his truck. Turning

her questioning gaze back to his face, she asked, "Did you come with Brock?"

Sheepishly, he admitted, "Yeah, I was hoping you'd take pity on a poor boy and give him a ride."

Arching one eyebrow, "Oh you did, did you?"

All semblance of joking gone, he stepped forward tentatively. "I just want to make sure you're okay, babe."

Taking a deep breath, she looked over his shoulder at the mountains in the background, momentary silence filling the air. Eyes moving back to his, she replied, "I'm fine. The doctor visit went really well, and I have some meds that he's putting me on. I've got some more information and have a better understanding of what I'm facing."

Nodding, he moved forward one more step closer. "I'd like to hear what all he said. Any chance we could go somewhere to talk?"

She leaned her head back as he advanced, keeping her eyes on his. Pulling her lips in, she nodded slowly, before agreeing. "I think that'd be a good thing."

He let out a breath he didn't know he was holding, feeling for the first time since he began the quest for her father that he might have a chance to repair the damage to their trust. "That's great, babe. Where do you want to go?"

Looking around in thought, she mused aloud. "Someplace private. Someplace quiet." As though a sudden thought came to her, she looked up and quickly said, "Your place. But only to talk. And I'm not staying."

"Laurie, I'll take whatever I can get."

As he was opening her passenger door to assist her into the bug, she looked over her shoulder. "You're driving my yellow bug?" she asked incredulously.

Smiling back into those gorgeous grey eyes, "I would drive you through the middle of town in this yellow crazy-ass bug just to have a chance to be with you again."

Settling onto the sofa, Laurie looked around. *Was it only a week ago that this was her home too?*

Rob, nervous, sat on the other end of the sofa as though afraid to crowd her. "Babe, I just need to start out by saying you've got no idea how sorry I am I kept all that shit from you. I wanted to help but was a wuss by not manning up from the beginning."

Looking over at this man that she loved more than life, she wanted to forgive him but needed answers if trust was to be rebuilt.

"I appreciate that, I really do. I just need more. I need to know what was going through your head knowing how all this was going to play out."

Rubbing his hand over his face, he nodded. Taking a few deep breaths, gathering his thoughts, he found his eyes searching hers again. Seeing her innocent questioning gaze, he understood that she wasn't fighting him. She wanted to know his thoughts, his reasons, his motives, his actions. *I can give her that. She deserves my honesty, not my charm. She deserves that...and much more.*

Twisting his body so that he was facing her, he began. "Honest to God, I never thought about your dad until you got sick. Then I was just worried all the time. What was wrong? What did you need? What could I do for you?" Looking embarrassed, he admitted, "I've never worried about any girl. Sex was just a physical way to get off, and a pretty girl was just arm candy for the night." Shaking his head as he looked down, he resisted the urge to look into her eyes, knowing he would see repulsion.

A small, pale hand slid across the distance, placing itself on his much larger tanned one. That innocent act gave him the courage to continue. Looking up, her eyes speared his with a look of...understanding, not rejection. Grasping her hand as a drowning man holds a life preserver, with the encouragement to continue, he said, "I never meant to lie to you or keep a secret. I simply thought that if I told you I was looking for him and didn't find him, it might disappoint you. And I just couldn't stand the thought of you being hurt.

"Once I located the person who may have been your father, I had to go see for myself or risk more hurt to you again. No lie, babe – I just did not want you hurt."

Watching his face carefully, she knew he was telling the truth. Emma's words flew through her mind. *Love makes us do some crazy things. But it will especially make us do anything and everything we can to protect those we love.*

Linking her fingers through his, she squeezed his hand tightly. *I love him. He loves me. Everything else can be figured out.*

"Laurie, am I forgiven? I'll never keep anything from you again as long as we live. From now on, we work everything out together."

Smiling softly, she replied, "Yes, you're forgiven."

Rob, looking down at their linked hands, felt the heavy weight sitting on his heart lift. Keeping his fingers tightly entwined with hers, he asked, "Babe, what all did the doctor say?"

Her gaze dropped to her lap then swept out across the room in an evasive move, not wanting to have this conversation now.

Tightening his grip, rubbing his fingers along her hand, he probed, "No secrets, Laurie. We tell the truth to each other, right?"

Grey eyes snapped back to his blue ones. Nodding slowly, she agreed. "I brought some literature home on lupus. I'll start some medications tomorrow and have to have monthly blood work." At this, her nose wrinkled in distaste.

He smiled, remembering her trip to the lab. "I'll go with you every time." He noticed she did not smile. "What else did he say?"

"The medications will make me very susceptible to infections, so I have to be very careful to try not to get sick." Shaking her head ruefully, "I have no idea how I can do that while working with six-year-olds." Sighing deeply, she continued, "Some days will be better than others. Some days I may not even notice anything; other days I may feel awful."

Rob, feeling that she was holding back, kept prompting. "What else? What is it that you think I don't want to hear?"

A tear slid unchecked down her cheek. "I may have difficulty getting pregnant. If I do get pregnant, I may have trouble carrying to full term." Afraid to look into his eyes and see the disappointment, she kept her gaze on their still linked hands.

Lifting her chin with his free hand, he forced her to look at him. "Laurie, I'm in love with you. I want a future with you. If that includes children, then fine. If not, that's fine too. I just want you, babe."

Leaning across the short distance separating them, he gently touched his lips to hers. This kiss was not about sex, not about passion, not about desire. No, this kiss was filled with promise, forgiveness, hope, and love.

As his lips moved over hers, Laurie knew this was the greatest kiss of all.

Rob was working long shifts for the rest of the week, so they decided to wait until the weekend to move Laurie back to his apartment. Not wanting her to be alone and since Jean gave so much emotional support to her, they thought it would be best if she stayed.

The medication was working so well that Laurie found herself feeling better than she had in months. More energetic, she would play with the children on the playground at recess. One day she had been assisting with the students playing on the monkey bars when one of the children shouted for her. "Miss Dodd, Miss, Dodd!" Turning to see what they were yelling about, she saw the minivan with darkened windows stopped along the fence of the playground. And playing near the fence was Cindy.

Heart pounding with fear, feet flying faster than she had run in months, she ran screaming for Cindy. Cindy looked over at her in confusion, and Laurie saw the van pull away quickly. Winded by the time she reached Cindy, she could barely speak but grabbed Cindy in a hug. Finally catching her breath, she walked her back over to the other children.

"Cindy, I need you to stay away from the fence during recess. There has been a van driving around that makes me nervous, and I want all my students safe, okay?"

Cindy agreed and ran off to play with the others. Clutching her chest as Jean came out with the principal to check on her, she reported what she saw. "My fear is that when the kids are all over the playground, I can't watch them all at the same time." The principal and Jean agreed on the risk and decided that when her students were outside, Jean would join them.

Heading back inside, Jean asked if she could talk to Laurie after school for a few minutes. Surprised that she even needed to ask, she readily agreed. That afternoon, Jean was uncharacteristically nervous.

"Jean, you always speak plainly and cut to the chase. What's going on?"

Looking down for a moment, Jean raised her bright blue eyes to Laurie's and said bluntly, "Brock asked me to dinner, and I said yes. I would really like to get to know him, but you're my friend, and I don't want any... awkwardness between us."

Laurie jumped up and pulled Jean into a hug, wrapping her arms around her friend. "Oh, Jean, I'm so happy for you! I don't mind at all. In fact, I think it's a really good idea! I think you two would be perfect together."

"It's just dinner, my dear, not an engagement!" Jean retorted.

"I know, but I think it just ... fits," Laurie said wistfully. "Let's call Carol and plan what you're going to wear!"

Laughing, they headed out of school.

That weekend, Laurie, Carol, and Jean were perched on the bar stools at Smokey's waiting on their men. Carol, always smartly dressed, was in a silky blue dress that showcased her slim figure and blonde hair. Makeup done to perfection, she looked as though she stepped off a designer runway instead of out of her nursing scrubs. Jean, finally out of the clothes she normally wore working at an elementary school, was in black slacks with a silky green top that draped in front, showing a little cleavage. Laurie, deciding to dress to kill, wore a red dress that came to a respectable length and gave plenty of coverage in the front. The killer part of the dress was the back. There wasn't one. Rob was going to flip. And Laurie was going to love it.

Several men were looking them over, making Smokey's owner, Bill, nervous. He knew when his friends' women were in the bar, he was expected to watch how much they drank, keep an eye on any man looking at them and be the bouncer if there were any problems.

Wendy looked over at her husband's glowering face and then back over to the women. "Girls, I hope your men get here soon 'cause my husband is not the most cheerful bartender under the best of circumstances, and when you're here alone, he gets downright surly!"

Bill glared at all four women. "I know how to take care of my woman. I work with her so I can keep my own eye on her. Your men don't get here soon, I'm locking up the joint."

Right then the door to Smokey's opened with a bang and in walked Tom, Rob, Jake, and Brock. Jake was alone, and Laurie thought once again how she would love to fix him up with her Aunt Emma. *Maybe, just maybe, if Emma moves here this summer...*

Walking over, Tom lifted Carol off the barstool admiring the way she looked. "Damn, Angel, you look gorgeous!"

Brock approached Jean, offering his hand to assist her off the stool, leaning over to privately complement the way she looked. Jean, blushing, took his hand, and Laurie noticed he didn't let it go as they walked to the table.

Rob approached the bar, never taking his eyes off his gorgeous woman. Fighting the urge to grab Laurie and carry her off, he decided to follow Brock's example and offer his hand to assist her down from the high barstool.

"Your dress is beautiful, just like the woman in it," he said gallantly.

Laurie's eyes lit up. "You really like it? I wore it just for you."

A mischievous twinkle in her eye had him wondering what she was up to. She moved to walk in front of him towards the table.

"What the hell?" Rob growled as he jerked her backward so that her back was pressed against his front. "Where the hell is the rest of your dress?"

Attempting without success to twist around in his arms to face him, Laurie sweetly said, "Why, darling, I thought you liked it."

Walking, with her back still covered by his front, over to the table where the others had gathered, Rob spoke. "Booth." The men stood, heading for a booth, taking Jean and Carol with them. Laurie could only imagine that was man-speak for "my woman is half dressed so we have to sit in a booth so no one else can see her naked back!"

"Babe, plant your ass in that booth."

Glaring up at him, Laurie couldn't help but ask, "Or what?"

Whispering in her ear, his breath barely grazing her skin, Rob answered, "Or you won't be able to sit for a week."

Eyes widening in shock, then narrowing in anger, she was about to retort when his large hand rested on her ass. More threatening than provocative, she still felt the flutter of desire. Her breathing hitched as her eyes widened in lust. He noticed and discretely adjusted his swollen dick in his jeans. She plopped down in the booth quickly, finding herself growing damp. Rob had insisted that she needed plenty of time to heal and rest after her ordeal. He had her move back into their apartment but had not attempted to have sex. After several days, she was ready to jump him, but he had been insistent on no sex. "I want you healed, both physically and mentally, when we come back together."

Squeezing her legs together, she spared a glance at Rob. He was staring at her, lust glowing in his blue eyes. Leaning forward ever so slightly, her lips grazed his. "I miss you," she said in a whisper.

He wrapped his arm around her, pulling her in tightly. "I miss you too, babe."

Knowing that tonight she was going to have him in *all* ways in her bed, she smiled and joined in the fun.

Laurie walked in front of Rob as they headed to their apartment. He insisted she walk in front – that gave him a chance to check out the non-existent back to her dress and how it curved around her ass. Walking became uncomfortable with his dick pressing in his jeans. The sex drought was finally going to end tonight.

She looked over her shoulder as she wiggled her ass, giggling as she made it to the door. A loud crack sounded as her ass was spanked, ending in a squeal. Once inside, she was determined to take care of him the way he often took care of her. Pushing his back up against the door, she unbuttoned his jeans, slowly sliding the zipper deliberately over his thick erection. Lowering his pants enough to allow his cock to spring forth, she grasped it with both hands, feeling the silky hardness as she stroked its length.

He started to take over, but she stopped him. "Oh no, honey. I've got something I want to try."

Raising an eyebrow, he looked down at her as she lowered herself to her knees, taking his length into her slick mouth. Grasping under her arms, he hauled her back to her feet. "No, babe."

Embarrassed, she tried to pull back. She knew she was inexperienced at blowjobs, but his rejection stung.

Rob, realizing her distress, spoke quickly. "You got me wrong. I'm not saying no to this. In fact, the thought of your sweet mouth around my dick is making me harder than I've ever been. What I'm saying no to is you being on your knees. My woman will never be in front of me on her knees. We do this, we do it where you can be comfortable."

With that, he scooped her up, carrying her to the bedroom. Stripping quickly, they lay on the bed together, Laurie sliding down to his impressive cock. Nervousness took over as she tried to remember all that she had read in her romance novels. Fondling his balls with one hand, she used the other hand to stroke firmly, feeling the length and thickness. Still amazed at how it fit inside of her, she momentarily wondered how she would fit it in her mouth.

Leaning forward, she swirled her tongue around the

tip, moving her lips further down as she became bolder. Continuing to stroke him, she took him as deeply as she could, sucking gently as she continued to use her tongue to tease. Ever so slightly she grazed her teeth over his shaft, drawing a hissing sound from his lips.

Rob fisted her hair, careful not to pull, but desiring to have his hands in her silky locks. All other women flew out of his mind as he realized this tiny woman with the power of her love chased his past away.

She continued her worship of his cock, moving faster and faster, taking him deeper. She barely felt him try to pull away saying he was coming. Refusing to stop, she felt his salty semen hit the back of her throat as she swallowed every drop. As he was spent, she raised up on her arms, smugly looking down at his astonished face. Licking her lips, she grinned, feeling as though she had won the lottery.

Rob, never having felt that satisfied from a blowjob, realized it was because of the emotion tied up in the act. Pride swelled in his chest looking at the pint-sized beauty lying beside him. *Mine. My woman. My love. My heart. My soul.*

The sex drought over, he worshiped her body that night. His tongue slid over her smooth skin from her shins up to her dripping sex. Licking her folds before pressing his tongue deep inside, he felt her hips rise, seeking more. With one hand fondling her breasts, he pulled her swollen clit into his mouth. Feeling her orgasm hit, he immediately forced two fingers into her sex, feeling her walls clench around his fingers, coating them with her slickness.

Laurie, sated, barely able to raise her head, looked at him. "Hey," she said softly.

Looking into her half-lidded gaze, he replied, "Hey back." Laughing, he slid up her body, covering it with his own. His chest pressed against her breasts, his cock rested between her legs, as he kissed her deeply, his tongue probing every corner of her mouth.

She tasted herself on his tongue. Wanting more, she pulled him down, kissing him fiercely, tongues tangling stroke for stroke.

Rob, needing no more encouragement, found her entrance with his cock and slowly pressed inside, giving her time to adjust to his size again. Once seated, he rocked back and forth, loving the friction caused by skin-on-skin contact. His pumps became more forceful as he pounded into her willing body.

Grabbing her and deftly rolling over, she landed on top. "Ride me, baby," he ordered, his hands on her full breasts.

She rocked, riding his cock, the friction tingling from her sex out to her womb. His hands, pinching her nipples, built the fire inside until she could feel her eruption close at hand. Head thrown back, she screamed his name as she exploded around his dick.

Rob, grabbing her hips, lifted her slightly while he continued to thrust until his own release poured into her. Neck straining, he pumped several more times until he was completely emptied.

She collapsed on top of his chest, panting as she attempted to catch her breath. Realizing she was dead weight on top of him, she tried to move to the side.

He stilled her. "No babe, stay right where you are." Wrapping his mighty arms around her body, he held her, heart to heart.

Exhausted, sated, complete. They fell asleep, Laurie still on top wrapped in his protective embrace.

22

Dead on her feet, Laurie was ecstatic that it was Friday. Knowing Rob was working tonight made it easier; she wouldn't have to deal with his phone calls and texts. *I know he loves me, but I'm feeling smothered. He is always checking up on me. How do I feel? Did I take my medicine this morning?*

Mind swirling, Laurie plopped down at her desk and put her head in her hands. *But I love him. When all is said and done, I love him. And what he did, he did out of love for me. Not to hurt me. But to help me. And now...now...I have a dad. And I have Rob to thank for that.*

She thought back to what Brock had said to her the other evening. He told her that Sarah had apparently fallen in love and so did he, but they never got their time. That was why she knew she wouldn't throw away her chance with Rob. Forgiving him gave her a sense of peace. Dealing with his constant concern was taking away her peace!

Grabbing her phone from her pocket, she quickly

called Rob's cell. It immediately went to voice mail. *Damn.* Not wanting to leave a voicemail, she hung up and decided to drive over to the fire station to talk to Rob in person.

"Ms. Dodd?" Ms. Darby called from the doorway. "I'm glad you're still here. We have a little problem." Cindy was standing next to the principal looking forlorn.

Laurie opened her arms, and Cindy ran to her, getting scooped into a huge hug. "What's wrong, sweetie?"

Looking over Cindy's head to Laurie, the principal told her that Mrs. Carlson had been delayed in a minor car accident and wasn't here to pick up Cindy yet.

Mouthing *"Is she okay?"* Ms. Darby nodded. "Yes, it seems that she was on her way here when she was side-swiped by a hit-and-run. She was wondering if you could drive Cindy over to Mr. Carlson at the middle school since Cindy is so comfortable with you."

"Sure, I'd be glad to." Looking down at the little girl in her arms, she gave her a squeeze. "Hey Cindy Loo, how'd you like to ride in my yellow bug car?"

Grinning her reply, the two got ready to leave. Cindy's grin got even bigger when she laid eyes on Laurie's VW bug.

"Ever ride in a yellow bug before?" Laurie asked, laughing. At Cindy's shake of her head, Laurie unlocked the passenger door and told her to hop in. Throwing Cindy's book bag in the back, she grabbed her cell phone before tossing her purse into the back seat as well. Leaning across to make sure Cindy was buckled safely, she started her car. She was just pulling out of her parking space when Ms. Darby came running out of the front door waving her hands frantically.

Leaving the car running, she opened the door, stepping out to hear her better. "What's up?" she yelled.

"The police just called. Mrs. Carlson was hit by a white minivan with darkened windows. They think it may have been purposeful. You need to..."

The squealing of tires had both women looking toward the area where the buses were normally parked. *Oh my God – the white van – it's headed this way!* She stood rooted to the pavement, stunned into disbelief as the van careened toward her bug as though in a movie's slow-motion scene.

Jolted by Cindy's scream, she jumped in, slammed the door, and stepped on the gas. The bug jumped into action, Laurie turning sharply to the right as the van barely missed them. Heart pounding, she floored it again, shooting out into the street.

In her rearview mirror, she could see the van turning around and pursuing them. Darting out into the street, her mind swirling, she heard her phone ring and glancing at the screen she saw the name "Tom." Turning sharply again, her only thoughts were to get away from the van as she clicked the phone on. "Tom! They're after us. I've got Cindy, and the van is after us. I don't know where to go. Cindy – hang on!" She ran a light that had just turned red, trying to do anything to put space between them and their pursuers. "Tom! What do I do?"

Tom, putting her on speaker and quickly translating the information to Jake, called the police chief over.

"Laurie, where are you? What road are you on? We'll get cars out to you."

"I don't know, I don't know. I'm in a part of town I don't know."

Tom, calmly speaking, "Laurie, look around. What do you see? What landmarks are around? Gas station, stores? Give me something, honey."

The chief began barking orders for an APB out on the white van and calling all cars to the neighborhoods around the school.

Jake walked away from Tom and called Rob.

"Yeah, man, what's up?"

"Rob, gotta situation. You need to hold onto your shit, man. It involves Laurie. Get over here."

Rob, yelling to Mac that there was an emergency with Laurie, ran out of the fire station and down the block to the police station, blasting through the doors and pounding down the hall.

"Talk," Rob ordered. Jake quickly told him what was happening while Mac followed on his son's heels.

"Dad, pick up Brock at the hotel. Fill him in."

Mac took off running, pulling out his cell phone as he went.

"Tom...Tom, where do I go? Oh, Jesus, they're back again! Tom!" Rob's heart almost stopped as he heard Laurie's voice coming through the cell phone speaker.

Tom, trying to calm her, was interrupted by Rob screaming at her. "Laurie! Laurie!"

"Rob? Rob! I don't know where I am! They're too close. We've got to get out of here. Cindy, get down!" she screamed again.

"Damnit!" Rob roared, feeling impotent.

Jake jerked him back away from Tom's phone. Rounding on his friend, Rob growled, "What the hell man?"

"Get it together. She has to stay focused on where she is, not distracted by your shit."

"Laurie," Tom said calmly, "Look at the next street sign and tell me what it is."

"Maple Court and ...," that was all she said before the screaming started.

Having to put both hands on the wheel, the cell phone went flying down into the floorboard. *Goddamn it!* Laurie's heart pounded as she drove wildly through the streets. She realized how much bigger the city was than she thought, especially the residential neighborhoods that were totally unknown to her. *We're going to get killed in this car. Either they're going to hit us, or we're going to crash.*

"Cindy, honey, I know you're scared. I'm going to try to get away from them and then we can stop and run and hide. Can you do that? I'm afraid we will get hurt if we keep driving like this." Careening around another corner, she drove one block and made another turn. *If I keep making turns, maybe I can lose them long enough to hide.* "Can you do that, honey?"

Stealing a glance to the passenger side, she saw Cindy, wide-eyed in terror, nod her head. Making another quick turn, she noticed that the van was no longer right behind them.

Yelling loudly, she called out to Tom. "I dropped the cell phone on the floorboard. If you can hear me, we're going to try to stop and run. Oh my God—Tom—there's a cemetery with a park next to it. We're running there."

Jerking the bug to a stop, Laurie snapped the buckle on her seat and Cindy's. Jumping out, she glanced in the floorboard to see if the cell phone was visible. *Damn! I don't have time to look for it.*

She ran around and threw open Cindy's door and pulled Cindy out of the car. There was a grove of trees close to the road, so Laurie and Cindy ran there.

Peaking around the trunk of a tree she saw the van coming down the street. "Cindy, we've got to run, baby!" Grabbing her hand again, they began to run through the trees growing along the side of the cemetery, then crossed into the cemetery when the tree line stopped.

Hearing sirens in the distance, they kept running. *Please get to us in time. Please get to us in time.*

"Cindy! Cindy!" came a voice from the road. "Come here, baby girl. It's Momma. Come to Momma, Cindy. That woman is trying to hurt you, baby. Come back to Momma where you belong," the woman's voice yelled through the trees.

"That little bitch has been enough trouble to us. Wait'll I get my hands on her," a man's voice followed.

Panting, not knowing how much farther she could force Cindy to run, Laurie looked down into her stricken eyes. *Jesus, help me. Give us strength.* She felt her resolve renewed. Picking Cindy up in her arms, she ran a little farther towards the high wall of the cemetery where some of the old family mausoleums were built.

Setting Cindy down, she squeezed into the tiny space between the wall and the back of the first mausoleum. There was only about a foot of space, but Cindy easily fit. Laurie pushed Cindy ahead of her. Whispering, she said, "Cindy, I'm going to help you climb up to the top of the wall, then I'll follow. We will get to the other side where they can't see us, okay?"

Cindy just nodded again, but her eyes were less panicked. Bending her knee to give Cindy something to climb on, Cindy scrambled up like she was on the jungle gym. Once she was standing on Laurie's shoulders, Laurie grabbed Cindy's feet and helped propel her upwards until Cindy could swing up on top of the old brick wall. The tall mausoleum hid her from the prying eyes of their pursuers.

Using the wall and the back of the brick mausoleum, Laurie began to shimmy and climb upwards. Fingernails tearing, knees and arms scraping, she inched up until she could grab the top of the wall with her hands. Continuing to inch her lower body up, she looked up in surprise when she felt small hands on hers pulling. Cindy and Laurie locked eyes for a second, smiling encouragement, each knowing that moment of shared trauma that binds people together.

The sirens grew closer, and she felt that surely the police must be nearby. *Please let Tom have heard my cry about the park and cemetery.* Not willing to take a chance on being found by Cindy's crazy-ass parents, she pulled herself the rest of the way on top of the eight-foot wall. Looking down on the other side, there was a gravel slope that ran down from the wall towards the rest of the park.

Deciding that she couldn't catch Cindy, she knew she would need to lower her down. Grabbing Cindy's wrists, she swung her gently over the edge of the wall and leaned down as far as she could go. *Damnit, that's not that far.*

"Cindy, where'd you go, girl? You hear them sirens? That there's the police. They're gonna come lock you up if you don't get over here to Momma."

Knowing there was no time to waste, Laurie whispered, "Sorry Cindy, I've got to drop you down." Cindy looked at her with such trust, instinctively knowing that Laurie would protect her. Letting go of Cindy's wrists, she watched as Cindy dropped about five feet onto the gravel, sliding down on her butt. *Oh, Jesus, she didn't even cry out! Thank you, Jesus.*

Swinging herself over the edge, hanging by her hands, Laurie dropped down near where Cindy fell. Her feet hit the gravel, but her weight made the gravel shift, and she went down hard on her knees and hands, hearing a cracking noise in her wrist at the same time her knee twisted at an awkward angle. *Shit! Shit! Shit!*

The pain was almost unbearable, but by sheer adrenaline, she stood up and grabbed Cindy's hand again. Making their way down the gravel slope, they entered another grove of trees. Weaving through the trees for several minutes, they found a safe hiding place. Laurie slid down in the bushes, pulling Cindy tightly into her body. *Surely, this is safe enough. Surely, they can't find us.*

Minutes ticked by, and Laurie heard nothing but the wind blowing through the treetops. Her knees were stinging from scrapes and beginning to swell from the fall. Looking at her damaged wrist, she felt lightheaded as she saw the swelling and bruising. Looking Cindy over, she couldn't see anything other than a few scrapes. *Thank God. Please, Rob, come for me.*

When Laurie last screamed was followed by silence, the crowd around Tom's phone did not move or make a sound, not knowing what was happening. Stomach churning, Rob dropped to his knees by the table. Having gone on many emergency calls to car wrecks, he kept imagining Laurie's mangled body.

A faint sound then came through, as though she was far away, saying that she had dropped the phone. Once they heard her yell out that she was near the cemetery, the police chief had the dispatcher radio for all available cars to go to the area. Rob, Tom, and Jake ran outside, jumping into Jake's truck as he put the portable siren on top. As Jake drove expertly at high speeds down the road, Rob sat in the back, hands shaking with fear and anger. *Jesus, be with her. Jesus, be with her.*

Within eight minutes, Jake saw Laurie's yellow bug and the white van surrounded by police officers. Rob was out of the car running towards the bug before Tom could stop him. Jake and Tom pounded up from behind, grabbing Rob's arms to hold him back.

"Report," Jake commanded to the police officer at the car.

"Both vehicles empty; cell phone in the floorboard of the victim's car."

"Victim?" Rob yelled as his heart stopped. *God, no!*

Just then Mac pulled up in the fire chief's car with Brock jumping out before the car was in park.

"What's the status of the search?" Jake growled at the rookie cop bringing his attention back to the case.

"Well, they're still looking for the girl and Ms. Dodd," he answered, looking from Jake to Tom, not knowing which detective he was more intimidated by.

"Why the hell did you call her a victim if you don't even know where she is?" Rob asked with deadly calm as he towered over the policeman.

"Rob, back off," Tom said as he pulled Rob back.

Just then, their radio announced that a male and female were in custody, and they were coming out of the cemetery. Hearing noises raised in anger near the trees, Rob took off running with Jake, Tom, Mac, and Brock right behind.

"Get your hands off my husband you dumb-ass fuckin' cop," the woman was screaming. Her hair was dirty and her clothes unkempt. She continued to scream obscenities as the police officers escorted her and her husband out of the woods. "Don't you touch me, you perv! Don't think I don't know what you're doing. I got rights. I know my rights!" she continued to scream.

Jake and Tom instantly realized she was not only

delusional, but she was also definitely under the influence of alcohol and possibly drugs. As far as Rob could tell she was just bat-shit crazy. But he didn't care. Stalking right up to her, towering over her and looking down, he roared, "Where are the girls?"

The woman's mouth stopped yapping and instantly snapped shut, staring straight up into his vengeful face. Her face immediately crumpled as huge tears began to fall. "She screwed it all up. She's messing up everything. She shoulda stayed with her momma and we wouldn't be in this mess." She continued to blubber as the cuffed man next to her finally spoke.

"Shut the hell up, woman. You're making it worse."

The police officers continued to haul the pair back to the patrol cars while the five men ran into the woods looking for Laurie and Cindy. They quickly came upon the other searchers and headed into the cemetery.

The men, along with the others on the search and rescue team, yelled for Laurie and Cindy.

"Where the hell did they go?" Rob bellowed rage and frustration.

"Over here," one of the officers called out from behind one of the mausoleums. The men raced over to see what was found. There was a piece of material wedged between some bricks of the building and a small amount of blood smeared on the bricks of the wall. Rob jumped up, grabbed the top of the wall, and with Tom's assistance, he pulled himself up on top.

"Laurie! Laurie!" he yelled as loud as he could. Looking down, he noticed the gravel had been disturbed. "It looks like they came over here."

Laurie's protective arms stayed curled around Cindy as they sat hidden in the trees. The calls from Cindy's parents had stopped, but she wasn't taking a chance by coming out of hiding too early. Rocking Cindy back and forth in her arms, rubbing her hands up and down her back, she offered comfort as best as she could. "You're so brave, Cindy," she whispered. "We're going to be fine, you know. Remember those sirens? They're going to come help."

With the memory of hearing Rob's voice on her cell phone earlier, she couldn't help but smile. *He'll come. I know he'll come.* Shifting on the hard ground, her knee screaming in pain as she tried to straighten it, Laurie felt weary. Looking back down at her arm, she knew her wrist must be broken. *Please come soon.*

Cindy sat up straight in Laurie's arms, her face alert, her body stiffening.

"What is it?" she asked the little girl. "Did you hear something?"

Nodding quietly, Cindy turned to look up at Laurie. "I heard a man call your name," she whispered.

"My name? Are you sure?" Laurie whispered back. Realizing that must mean their rescuers were near, she helped Cindy up and then attempted to pull herself up. The pain in her swollen knee was excruciating but determined to get to help, she forced herself up. Cindy reached over to help her. Warmth in her heart replaced the cold fear from earlier. Taking each other's hands, they moved through the trees slowly towards the wall they had crossed.

As she neared, she heard Rob's voice, calling out for her.

"Rob! Rob! We're over here!" she screamed.

Jake and Tom had just scaled the wall beside Rob and were pulling up Brock when they heard Laurie call back. Suddenly at the edge of the trees, Laurie limped out with Cindy holding her hand. The smile on Cindy's face was a sight the men would carry with them for a long time.

Rob lowered himself off the wall and ran toward Laurie. He gathered her and Cindy up in a bear hug as she cried and clung to him. Feeling Cindy stiffen, he forced his mind back to reality, remembering she was leery of men. He immediately set them down, but not willing to stop touching Laurie, he continued to keep his arm around her. Laurie leaned down to reassure Cindy but was greeted by a smile. She peaked around Laurie looking way up at Rob and grinned again.

"Cindy, this is Rob. You met him at the school one afternoon. He's my boyfriend and our hero, sweetie. He's a good guy, I promise." Turning to Rob, she added, "And Cindy has helped me so much in this adventure."

Rob, seeing Cindy's shy smile, squatted down to be at her level. Sticking out his huge hand, "Hello, Cindy. It is nice to see you again, little princess." Cindy's smile grew. "And it sounds like you helped save Ms. Dodd, is that right?"

"Well, little lady, that makes you an honorary policewoman. We will have to get you a badge," Tom stated softly as he and Jake approached the little girl. She looked up at them with a grin but slipped her hand back into Laurie's. Brock jogged over and wrapped his arms around his daughter, pulling her close.

"I..," he choked out, not able to finish his thought.

Laurie answered back with a hug. Sometimes that is all the words that are needed.

They turned back towards the wall walking over to where they crossed initially. The ambulances had pulled as close to the cemetery wall as they could. The firemen had ladders on either side of the wall ready for the rescue team. The men assisted Cindy and then Laurie back over the wall, Rob picking her up and carrying her as soon as he could scoop her up. Cindy allowed Tom to carry her as they made their way over to the ambulances. Jake and Tom radioed ahead to have the Carlsons meet them at the hospital. Rob insisted that Laurie go as well, and for once, she completely agreed.

23

The hospital waiting room was packed with friends and well-wishers. Carol was hurrying between the two ER rooms checking on both Cindy and Laurie. The Carlsons were in with Cindy who, other than a few scratches, had no injuries.

In the hard plastic chairs, Jean and Brock sat, fingers entwined. Jake had checked in with the police chief to see what the status was of Cindy's parents. Once the pair was interrogated, they turned on each other, then turned on the uncle accused of abusing Cindy. Tom had been in with Cindy and the Carlsons to see if Cindy could provide any more information to them.

Laurie was in her ER room, her scratches and abrasions having been treated, her broken wrist in a cast, waiting to see what the doctor wanted to do about her swollen knees. Rob sat on the bed, her good hand in his as though she were his lifeline. Fatigue showed in her face, but her smile was still bright. He was leaning in for a kiss when the doctor came back in.

"Ms. Dodd, I've conferred with your rheumatologist. We think that the medications you're currently on will be fine in the long run, but once your wrist is out of the cast, you will probably need physical therapy to maintain range of motion. For now, he agreed to steroid injections in your knees to reduce the swelling. I'm ordering them up now, and the nurse will be in to administer them." With that, he headed out of the room leaving Laurie beginning to panic.

"Rob, I can't, I can't, I can't..."

Realizing that she was panicking over the injections, he held her tightly, saying, "Babe, you can do this. I'll be right here with you." He looked down at her stricken face as she was shaking her head from side to side.

"Laurie, you just drove like a fuckin' race driver getting away from crazies; then you proceed to outrun those same crazy-ass people and get Cindy and yourself to safety. Baby, you can do this."

"What can she do?" Tom asked as he and Jake walked in, noticing Laurie's wide-eyed look of terror.

"Get a couple of steroid shots in her knees to take down the swelling. She and needles aren't friends," Rob answered, still holding her tightly.

"Shit, those hurt. Remember getting those when we played college football?" Tom asked.

Jake turned on his partner before Rob could tear him apart. "Not helping, Tom. You want to shut the hell up?"

Looking contrite, Tom mumbled, "Sorry, Laurie."

Jake spoke up facing Laurie and Rob. "Got some news about Cindy's parents. It seems the uncle was the one supplying the mom and dad with both drugs and their income. He paid their rent and expenses as long as he could use their place as a safe house to store his drugs. It was a win-win situation for them. Then when it came out that he was abusing Cindy and he was arrested, their money ran out. That was why they tried to deny that he did anything to her. They were desperate to keep her from testifying so they were attempting to kidnap her back."

Carol had come in by this time and was listening to the explanation. They all stood silent for a moment, realizing that if Laurie had not saved Cindy, she would have been back in the clutches of those vile people, possibly to never resurface again.

"Oh my God," Laurie whispered, tears sliding down her cheeks, slumping back into Rob as though the last of the adrenaline had completely left her body.

Jake, walking over to her bed, leaned down, and kissed the top of her head, saying, "You're a hero, darlin'."

"Sweetie, this won't be as bad as you think. The pain meds you're on will keep these injections from hurting so badly. You want to lie down?" Carol asked.

Rob assisted her as she lay down, and Carol injected her knees as quickly as possible.

"All done, honey. You just need to stay here about another hour for observation, and then you can go home." Carol turned just in time to see Tom slump down in a chair with his head down between his knees. "Oh, Tom honey, I forgot you hate needles!"

Laurie giggled and snuggled closer into Rob, lying

beside her on the bed. The room began to fill up with visitors. The Carlsons were taking Cindy home, and they wanted to come by to show their appreciation to Laurie. Cindy climbed up into Laurie's bed throwing her arms around her neck. Laurie hugged back, looked into Cindy's eyes and whispered, "Friends forever, right?" Cindy smiled and nodded, squeezing her little arms tighter.

Brock and Jean came in, and Laurie noticed his arm around Jean's shoulders. Carol, no longer on duty by that time, was back in the room with Tom and Jake.

Laurie looked around the room. New family. New friends. Real friends. Thinking back to what Emma had told her last summer...*I found it. I found my time.*

Rob parked in front of his apartment building. Walking around to her side, he picked her up and carried her up the stairs to his door. Leaning down to unlock the door, he pushed it open but paused before entering. He looked into the grey eyes that held his soul. "You with me, babe?"

Not able to hold back her smile, she looked into the face she loved more than life itself. Nodding gently, she replied, "Yeah, I'm with you. I found my time, Rob. Now it's our time."

They kissed. Long. Slow. Soft. Full of promise. Full of love.

24

(THREE YEARS LATER)

Rob, standing at the open door of the firehouse, deep in training of new recruits, continually looked over his shoulder and down the street for a familiar yellow SUV. Seeing it coming down the road, he trotted over to the parking lot, leaving the young firefighters smiling in his wake.

Laurie had continued to drive her yellow VW bug until last year when he finally insisted, she needed something safer to drive. Seeing her pull into the fire station lot put a smile on his face. Opening her door, he leaned over her large frame to unbuckle the seat belt. Holding carefully onto his wife, he gently assisted her to the ground.

Before he could finish hugging her, Mac came barreling out of the station. "How's the mother of my grandchild?" he boomed.

Laughing, she waddled over to Mac as he embraced her gently against his chest. Kissing her cheek, he placed one hand over her eight-and-a-half-month pregnant belly. Leaning down to her protruding stomach, Mac whispered, "Just a little bit longer, little fella, and I'll have you out here riding on the fire truck."

Rob came up behind Laurie, wrapping his mighty arms around her. One arm around her chest and the other across her stomach, he placed his hand where he knew he could feel his son kick.

Laurie, smiling over her shoulder, looked up into Rob's twinkling eyes. "We're almost there, sweetie. Just a few more weeks. I think we've made it."

Pulling her tighter to his chest, "Laurie, you're doing great."

"Yeah, well, I want to get my husband back," she pouted. For the last couple of weeks, Rob had declared that they weren't having sex anymore until after their son was born. With several miscarriage scares along the way in this pregnancy, he wasn't taking any chances.

She felt his chuckle rumble through his chest. Moving her hands around to her lower back, she tried to apply pressure to ease the ache. Rob, looking down in concern, brushed her hands away gently as he took over massaging her lower back.

"Are you in pain?"

"My back has been aching all day. Sometimes it comes around the side but mostly just in the back."

"Babe," Rob started, but she reached up and quickly placed her fingers over his mouth.

"Rob, I'm fi—aughhh." She bent suddenly as pain ripped through her abdomen. "Ohhh….."

Rob, momentarily stunned, jerked back quickly.

"Dad!" he shouted, then began yelling for the recruits to bring the rescue squad around.

Catching her breath, she protested. "Rob, I'm not going in an ambulance. We have our car right here."

"Babe," he started, as the others ran over.

"Rob. I. Want. To. Go. In. My. Car."

Knowing he couldn't deny her anything, he scooped her up in his arms, placing her in the back seat of their SUV.

Mac came barreling out of the fire station already on his cell phone calling Bernie. "I'll call Brock and follow you to the hospital," he yelled at Rob as he jumped into his own truck.

Laurie texted Emma and Carol in between contractions, knowing they would inform Jake and Tom. Emma had moved to Fairfield, and Laurie's plan to get Jake and Emma together worked perfectly. They had married a year ago and already had a little boy.

Rob careened around a corner, his foot pressing on the accelerator in time with her contractions; the more she moaned, the faster he drove. Finally reaching the hospital, he came to a stop, hopping out to carry her inside. Carol met them inside, ushering them to the elevator. Since she was pre-registered, they were able to head up to labor and delivery.

Laurie, walking into the bathroom to change into the hospital gown, turned to look at her husband. *Rob. Tall, strong, pure alpha with a heart of gold. Her man. Her love. Her life. Working every day to prove he was worthy of her when she knew he had always been more than worthy.*

Her grey eyes captured his blue ones as they stood

staring momentarily at each other in silence. The hustle and bustle of the hospital room was all around, yet they stood, just the two of them, no words, just emotion between them.

Rob, seeing her look at him from across the room, stared at his wife. *Laurie. Beautiful, caring, all woman, all his. His love. His life. The mother of his child. She had saved him from himself, making him worthy of her.* He remembered seeing Brock walk her down the aisle a year ago, thinking he could never be happier than he was at that moment. But now, with their child ready to make an appearance, he felt emotions he never knew existed.

Smiling at each other, they prepared to greet their son.

***

The maternity waiting room was filled with family and friends. Tom, Jake, and Emma were there. Mac, Bernie, and Suzy were waiting with them. Brock and Jean came in as soon as they received the call. Carol would come out every so often to update them on Laurie's progress.

Finally, the doors opened, and Rob came out, tired but smiling. Walking over, he spread his arms wide and announced, "You all want to come see my son?"

Everyone jumped up, congratulations flowing all around. They all went back to the room, quietly entering, seeing a tired but glowing Laurie sitting up in bed proudly holding her son. Rob walked over, sat on the bed next to her, and leaned over to kiss the tiny, wrapped baby. She leaned back against him, as he wrapped his strong arms around his new family. Everyone crowded around, cooing, smiling, and taking pictures.

Mac leaned in, speaking in an uncharacteristic soft tone, "Welcome to the clan, little MacDonald."

Emma, tears running down her face, asked, "Do you have a name picked out yet?"

Laurie, looking back at Rob, smiled. "Yes, we do." Rob and she shared an intimate smile before looking back at the group. "Say hello to Robert Brock MacDonald. We thought we would call him Bobby."

Brock gasped, looking at his daughter and grandson.

"You missed my early years Dad, but I don't want you to miss his," Laurie said, looking up at Brock. Tears fell down his cheeks as he walked over and kissed first the top of her head and then his grandson. Walking back over, he held fast to Jean as she smiled at Laurie.

The celebration went on for the next hour until little Bobby decided he had enough attention and Laurie was quickly tiring. Everyone filed out with best wishes and promises to help out as soon as she was discharged the next day.

Rob and Laurie watched their beloved friends and family leave then settled in together on the bed once more. He brushed the damp hair off her face. "You okay, babe?" His eyes searched hers. Seeing her smile, he relaxed. "You did good, Laurie. He's perfect."

She snuggled deeper into his embrace, feeling more content than she ever had in her life. "I love you, Rob. With all my heart and soul, I love you."

His arms tightened around her and Bobby once

again. "Laurie, you're my life. And this little boy here, he is my heart. You gave this to me, babe. I owe it all to you."

He leaned in, kissing her sweet lips with all the tenderness he felt. A kiss full of hope, joy, promise, love, forever.

She smiled. Emma had been right. Laurie did find her time here in Fairfield. And now, she had a family. The three of them snuggled in the bed knowing tomorrow would come with all its challenges. But for tonight, it was their time.

The Fairfield Series (small town detectives)
Emma's Home
Laurie's Time
Carol's Image
Fireworks Over Fairfield

Don't miss other Maryann Jordan books!

Baytown Boys (small town, military romantic suspense)

Coming Home

Just One More Chance

Clues of the Heart

Finding Peace

Picking Up the Pieces

Sunset Flames

Waiting for Sunrise

Hear My Heart

Guarding Your Heart

Sweet Rose

Our Time

Count On Me

Shielding You

To Love Someone

Sea Glass Hearts

Protecting Her Heart

Sunset Kiss

Baytown Heroes - A Baytown Boys subseries

A Hero's Chance

Finding a Hero

A Hero for Her

Needing A Hero

Hopeful Hero

Always a Hero

For all of Miss Ethel's boys:

Heroes at Heart (Military Romance)

Zander

Rafe

Cael

Jaxon

Jayden

Asher

Zeke

Cas

Lighthouse Security Investigations

Mace

Rank

Walker

Drew

Blake

Tate

Levi

Clay

Cobb

Bray

Josh

Knox

Lighthouse Security Investigations West Coast

Carson

Leo

Rick

Hop

Dolby

Bennett

Poole

Adam

Jeb

Chris's story: Home Port (an LSI West Coast crossover novel)

Ian's story: Thinking of Home (LSIWC crossover novel)

Oliver's story: Time for Home (LSIWC crossover novel)

Hope City (romantic suspense series co-developed

with Kris Michaels

Brock book 1

Sean book 2

Carter book 3

Brody book 4

Kyle book 5

Ryker book 6

Rory book 7

Killian book 8

Torin book 9

Blayze book 10

Griffin book 11

Long Road Home

Military Romantic Suspense

Home to Stay (a Lighthouse Security Investigation crossover novel)

Home Port (an LSI West Coast crossover novel)

Thinking of Home (LSIWC crossover novel)

Time for Home (LSIWC crossover novel)

Letters From Home (military romance)

Class of Love

Freedom of Love

Bond of Love

The Love's Series (detectives)

Love's Taming

Love's Tempting

Love's Trusting

The Fairfield Series (small town detectives)

Emma's Home

Laurie's Time

Carol's Image

Fireworks Over Fairfield

Please take the time to leave a review of this book. Feel free to contact me, especially if you enjoyed my book. I love to hear from readers!

Facebook

Email

Website

Information on Lupus
From the Lupus Foundation of America

"Lupus is a chronic, autoimmune disease that can damage any part of the body (skin, joints, and/or organs inside the body). In lupus, something goes wrong with the immune system, which is the part of the body that fights off viruses, bacteria, and germs. Autoimmune means that the immune system cannot tell the difference between those foreign invaders and the body's healthy tissues and creates autoantibodies that attack and destroy healthy tissue. This causes pain, inflammation, and damage to various parts of the body.

Lupus can range from mild to life-threatening and should always be treated by a doctor. With good medical care, most people with lupus can lead a full life.

Lupus strikes mostly women of childbearing age (15-44)."

Autoimmune diseases have struck both me and one of my daughters. For those of us with autoimmune diseases, please be aware that we strive for a normal, healthy life, living with the challenges it may bring. If you're interested in more information, please visit the Lupus Foundation of America website.

Maryann Jordan